NOTHING
BUT
GOOD

KESS MCKINLEY

NOTHING BUT GOOD

Kess McKinley

Nothing But Good
by Kess McKinley

Published by ONE BLOCK EMPIRE,
an imprint of Blind Eye Books
315 Prospect Street #5393
Bellingham WA 98225
blindeyebooks.com

Edited by Nicole Kimberling
Copyedit by Dianne Thies
Cover art by Dawn Kimberling
Ebook design by Michael DeLuca

This book is a work of fiction and as such all characters and situations are fictitious. Any resemblance to actual people, places or events is coincidental.

Print ISBN: 978-1-935560-81-4
Ebook ISBN: 978-1-935560-82-1

Printed in the United States of America

CHAPTER 1

The scene could have been on a postcard in one of the many souvenir shops in Faneuil Hall. Multi-million-dollar condos towered skyward, boasting views that stretched miles into Boston Harbor, from the distinctive twin hills of nearby Spectacle Island to rocky Hangman Island in the distance. Periodically, the beam of the far-off Graves Light swept in a flash across the water.

Near the harbor's center, two luxury yachts, each larger than Special Agent Jefferson Haines's one-bedroom apartment, were anchored side by side. One sported an infinity pool spanning the top level, the other had enough space on the deck to store a second, smaller boat on board for day trips. Dozens of sailboats rested about twenty yards off the shoreline, their masts standing dense as a forest with limp sails instead of leaves.

Overhead an enormous archway bridged the gap between two wings of a boutique hotel, creating the grand open plaza where Jefferson stood. Jefferson had been told that the pricey restaurants lining the ground level provided the perfect atmosphere in which to celebrate life's milestones like anniversaries and career-making promotions. But he wouldn't know, because he'd never had the occasion to go before now. It wasn't exactly the time to try the scallops at the Rowes Wharf Grille.

Early on a Tuesday morning, so much of the city still lay sleeping that Jefferson could hear the sound of every wave lapping against the Harborwalk where he stood. A steady breeze gave the already frigid air a bite. He hunched his shoulders as he walked closer to the barrier at the ocean's edge, the large concrete blocks connected by thick wrought-iron links, tugging his Bureau windbreaker closer to his chest. The official start of spring had come and gone, but in Boston the seasons rarely followed the calendar. Despite the rays of light glinting off droplets of morning dew on the cobblestones at his feet, warm weather wouldn't truly arrive until May. A little over a month prior, this part of the harbor froze solid and the pathway perpetually needed to be cleared of snow.

Contrasted against so much stately beauty, the body lying facedown, legs sprawled on one of the docks, head and shoulders submerged in water, looked especially lurid. Jefferson guessed the deceased might have been a man in his late twenties or early thirties—around his own age. The victim appeared to be 5'8 or 5'9, Caucasian with red hair. Strands of copper drifted aimlessly back and forth in the waves. It was hard to be sure about the victim's clothes at this distance, but Jefferson thought the gold bands shining brightly against the murky harbor water could be from a Bruins jersey.

A crime scene like this rarely became the business of the FBI. In a city with a large student population like Boston, young men drowned at higher rates than in the average American town. They got drunk and accidentally fell in bodies of water; they went on late night runs and slipped off cobblestone pathways; they intentionally took their own lives by jumping off bridges. Normally the Boston Police Department would pursue an investigation like this on their own.

But this hadn't been an accident. Although Jefferson couldn't see any signs of trauma from his vantage point, the signature painted on the wall behind the corpse told him that this had been murder: a crude black circle of paint several feet in diameter filled in with jagged yellow swaths of paint. Inside that, two thick black slashes for eyes and a single curled line for the mouth. Simple, yet effective. The twenty to thirty additional minutes the killer had taken to leave this calling card—putting them at a heightened risk of being discovered—revealed a lot about their personality. This killer did not feel remorse for their actions. They felt smug enough about what they'd done to effectively scream it for the world to hear. This killer was an even shittier person than the typical asshole Jefferson investigated.

Out on the water, a double-crested cormorant emerged briefly for air, craning its head to look curiously in Jefferson's direction, then dove deeply again.

"Special Agent Haines," someone called across the small crowd of agents, detectives, and officers gathered in clusters along the Harborwalk.

Jefferson turned, relaxing at the sight of the tall woman striding toward him, her black hair pulled back in a sleek ponytail.

"Special Agent Pelley," he said, matching the level of formality she'd adopted for the circumstance.

Side by side, they made an imposing pair: she stood only a few inches shorter than Jefferson's own 6'4" frame, with equally broad shoulders. Her dark skin complemented his own New England winter pallor. Caroline had been a Division I college swimmer at the University of Maryland. In the years since, she hadn't let her physical fitness slide. Every bit of her body was sculpted solid muscle, from her calves to her sinewy biceps. Once, a suspect told her she belonged on the cover of *Sports Illustrated*. It had been inappropriate under the circumstances and she'd probably cuffed him harder than she'd needed to, but Jefferson objectively found it hard to argue with the idiot.

"What are you wearing?" she asked once she'd gotten closer. She'd already dressed for a day at the office, in navy slacks and a fitted white dress shirt with her heavy FBI jacket zipped over top. "You still think you'll get in a work-out today?"

Jefferson huffed. "I wish." The call alerting him about the discovery of the body had come fifteen minutes before they usually met up to head to a sports club a block from their apartment each morning. Pressed for time, he'd only managed to grab his light jacket and clip his 9mm Glock Luger Pistol into a holster at his hip, not pull on sweatpants over his workout shorts.

"I brought you this," he said, offering the still-steaming Styrofoam Dunkin' Donuts cup in his left hand.

She took a sip with a pleased hum. "Mmm, thanks."

"Learned anything?" he asked.

Caroline brushed past him, stepping to the edge and looking down at the victim with a faint grimace.

"An early morning jogger happened to look down to-ward the water when she stopped to tie a shoe and caught sight of the . . . display," she explained. "After the 911 call was routed to them, BPD notified a wide range of agencies, including the Massachusetts State Police, the Coast Guard, and the FBI due to the location of the body and its . . . unique staging."

For the moment, an invisible fence surrounded the crime scene—none of the hovering first responders dared to approach it until jurisdiction was sorted out.

"The vic's name is Henry O'Brien," she continued. "Twenty-seven. Local boy, born and raised in South Bos-ton. He was at the Bruins game last night with his friends. Reportedly, they all walked out together but they lost him in the crowd outside the Garden. They figured he'd catch a different train and meet them back at their apartment."

Apparently Jefferson had been right about Henry wearing a Bruins jersey. He didn't need to guess if Henry had ever made it home, either. "Which he never did."

"No." Caroline's eyes flicked back to the water.

"We're a half-mile from the Garden," Jefferson said.

"So, either Henry got lost or someone moved him here."

"Had he been drinking?" Jefferson asked.

"It was a *Bruins* game," Caroline said pointedly.

So Henry'd had more than a few beers. Not that that made it his fault some sicko had decided to kill him. To abduct someone in a sea of twenty-thousand people—not to mention everyone else out at the bars on Causeway Street—you needed your prey to go relatively willingly, or at least be unlikely to cause a fuss.

"What do you think of that?" Jefferson asked, gesturing at the shock of black and yellow on the seawall. Parts of the graffiti tag were still trailing droplets of paint. It was fresh, only hours old.

"It means the case is ours," she said, meaning *FBI business*.

Jefferson shaded his eyes with one hand, looking toward to the distant horizon. Boats were starting to move through the channels in earnest now, fishermen headed back to the Seaport with their morning catches and ferries shuttling commuters to the city center. People were waking up and going about their day, oblivious to the fact that a monster lived among them.

Voice tight, he said, "It's about time."

By now they were all familiar with the methods of the rumored 'Smiley Face Killer'. Over the last ten years, the bodies of over a dozen men had been discovered along the Charles River and Boston Harbor in suspicious drowning cases. Although the victims had all been male, and between the ages of twenty and thirty-five, they had little else in common. They'd otherwise varied in race, socioeconomic status, and even sexuality. In several of the cases, a smiley face icon of some kind appeared within fifty feet of the scene.

In many of the cases where the death was ruled suicide, the family and friends of the victim insisted that the victim had no history of mental illness and no warning signs of suicidal thoughts. In multiple cases determined to be accidental drowning, toxicology screens found no alcohol in the victim's bloodstream at the time of death.

Gradually, as the victims' stories spread, a cult internet theory developed that a serial killer was hunting down young men in Boston and luring them to their deaths in nearby water bodies. Over time, the theory grew to a powerful urban legend. Every time a young man went missing, whether or not they were found alive, the whispers started—*The Smiley Face Killer is back.* Some variations of the myth depicted the Smiley Face Killer as a group of murderers acting together.

Yet for years, these similar cases had continued to be claimed by the Boston Police Department, instead of being directed to the FBI. Jefferson thought that could partially be explained by the misguided public emphasis on the smiley face as a potential signature. Until today, the smiley faces recorded were small, farther from the body, and more fragile—drawn in the sand or written in pen, easily washed away. Because the BPD didn't consistently find the signature, they could dismiss the common sign as unrelated to their investigations.

Maybe smiley faces had been intentionally left near the bodies all along, or maybe the killer had only now adopted the calling card to build on his growing public mystique. The more significant component to the cases, Jefferson believed, was the cause of death. Every single victim had drowned. From what little he could remember of the Intro to Literature course he'd mostly slept through in college, death by drowning was a deeply symbolic act. Studying that further could give them some insight into their killer's motivations.

"Is Deputy Director Strait here yet?" Jefferson asked. Their boss had been advocating for the FBI to take the lead on the Smiley Face Murders for years. Undoubtedly, Strait would be eager to hit the ground running with the investigation now. Better to be proactive and find him than to make him have to chase them down.

"He's over there," Caroline said, pointing behind Jefferson. "I wanted to brief you before we spoke with him."

Jefferson turned, immediately spotting the Deputy Director in conversation with a State Police officer. Strait looked even more stern than usual, his mouth set in a flat line to match his particularly square jaw.

"Thanks, Cee," he said, with feeling.

They were about ten feet away when Strait glanced up and noticed their approach, excusing himself to take several steps closer to them.

"Special Agent Pelley. Special Agent Haines," he greeted. He gave Jefferson's shorts a noticeable, disapproving once-over. His eyes said, *This isn't the first time you've been underdressed at a crime scene.*

Jefferson ignored the unspoken criticism. So what if he had a hard time finding his clothes at a surprise, early-morning callout? Wasn't it more important that he be quick to arrive to the scene?

They found a quieter stretch of iron railing to huddle. Deputy Director Strait held up a finger to his lips while he studied the body's staging. After a few moments, he met Jefferson's eye.

"Tell me what you think about this, then."

It felt a little like a test. Jefferson intended to show he could do his job no matter what he wore.

"I believe the discovery of this morning's smiley face—larger and closer to the body than with any victims before—was meant as a direct challenge to law enforcement," he said. "It's likely that our 'Mr. Smiley' is getting restless. For too long his work has gone unnoticed, written off in the Globe as just another suicide by a depressed college student."

Deputy Director Strait pulled a face at that, making it clear that he considered this a serious failure by the Boston Police Department and Boston's most respected newspaper.

"So, long-deprived of the attention and recognition he feels he deserves, the killer will likely continue to escalate their attacks," Caroline added. "They'll come more frequently and they'll come with other signatures that are impossible to ignore." She gestured at the smiley face still leering at them.

"I agree. I want you two to take point on this," Strait said.

Caroline stood straighter at attention, doing a good job of hiding her surprise. Jefferson followed suit. They'd known they'd be asked to help with the investigation, but there were agents with many more years of experience in the Boston office who would reasonably have been expected to take the lead on such a significant case.

"Do us proud," Strait told them, eyes hard. "Show the BPD exactly why they should have called us in years ago."

"Yes sir," Jefferson said. His partner echoed the words.

"I expect regular reports," Strait told them. Then he turned to leave, making his way toward Atlantic Avenue, where he presumably hoped to catch a car back to their office.

Once he'd disappeared from sight, Caroline turned to Jefferson. She looked pleased. It was a testament to their past success that the Deputy Director had chosen them.

"What's our plan?"

"First?" Jefferson asked, with a wave at his shorts. "Apparently I should run home to change."

She snorted a laugh. "Please do. I can't look at those pasty legs all day."

After checking to be sure none of their peers were looking in their direction, he flipped her off.

"Then interviews?" she asked, more seriously.

"Yes. Let's track down those friends Henry went to the game with."

CHAPTER 2

There were many things Jefferson liked about his job: feeling like he could make a difference in the world, putting the bad guys away, helping others, working with Caroline, the pressure to be in peak physical shape. Putting on a suit to conduct interviews of the friends and family of the recently deceased was nowhere near the top of the list.

Jefferson owned exactly three suits, one navy and two dark gray. He'd bought them off the rack five years ago during a *Buy two, get one half-off* sale at Jos. A. Bank. They were all the exact same size and all three fit wrong in different ways. The sleeves on one ended a quarter-inch too short, so the white cuffs of his dress shirts always showed. The pants in the ones he had on right now squeezed tight in the thighs. Whenever he sat, the fabric stretched to the point of being uncomfortable. For as long as they'd been partnered together, Caroline had been telling him to get his suits properly tailored. Jefferson kept meaning to, if only to make it easier to breathe while in interviews, but he hadn't gotten around to it yet.

The witness sitting across from them was a kid—no, not a kid. Peter McDonnell was twenty-six, but he *looked* like a kid: too thin, red eyes, arms wrapped around his body as if trying to hug himself, the frame of his body almost hidden by an oversized gray sweatshirt. Peter actively fought back tears at the thought that he would never see his friend again. He also clearly had a hangover; he kept wincing whenever he glanced toward the bright overhead light.

"Walk us through what happened that night," Jefferson said. He tried to sound approachable—sympathetic, even—but the instructions came out brusquer than he meant for them to. Neither half of their partner duo was a very touchy-feely kind of person. "Tell us everything you can remember. No matter how inconsequential a detail might seem, it may be important."

"The game ended," Peter said slowly. He closed his eyes, tipping his head back in what seemed to be an unconscious effort to remember more. "We'd been down 2-1 going into the third, but the B's had come back and won so everyone was excited. People were yelling, throwing their drinks. We were in the nosebleeds, so it took us a while to get down through the stairwell."

"How many of you were there?" Caroline asked. They already knew the answer to that question but sometimes it made a difference to hear how the witness answered it. If the number changed, or a member of their group stood out more than another, that could be key to unlocking a lead.

"Four," Peter said. "Me. Henry . . . " His face crumpled. "Our friend Bo and his girlfriend Julie. We all went to MIT together."

"Did you meet up with anyone else?" Jefferson asked. "Talk to anyone? Friends from school? Strangers?"

"No," Peter said. "We hadn't seen each other in a while so we just wanted to hang out. Bo and Julie, I mean. Henry is . . . was . . ." he made a broken, choked-off sound. "Henry was my roommate. My best friend. I saw him every day." He raised a fist to his face, scrubbing at his eyes.

Hundreds of people had cried to Jefferson over the years. Moms who'd lost sons. Children who'd lost parents. Husbands who'd lost wives. Most of the time, he didn't let it visibly affect him. It wasn't that he didn't feel for them—he *did*; he couldn't imagine what most of the people he interviewed went through. But if he couldn't turn his emotions off—if he always let himself be sucked in—he'd be overwhelmed by how fucked-up the world could be. He would drown in other people's hopelessness and loss.

Watching Peter wipe his eyes while his voice broke hit Jefferson hard—harder than any interview in a very long time, since maybe his first year on the job. He took too long to respond. Caroline gave him a sideways, curious look, then turned her full attention back to their witness.

"So you didn't speak to anyone else that night?" she asked.

"Not really," Peter said. "I mean we ordered drinks . . . we high-fived other people in the crowd when we scored . . . but no, we were just watching the game."

"Okay," Jefferson said, regaining control of himself. "Then what? What happened after the game ended?"

"It was really crowded," Peter said. "There were people everywhere. And everyone was in their jerseys, so everyone looked the same. We followed the crowd down the stairs and eventually ended up outside. It was freezing. We needed to take the T home, so we decided to cross Causeway Street and use the entrance there. With so many other people on the street, we couldn't get back inside North Station to get the train there."

"When did you realize Henry was missing?" Jefferson asked.

"A few minutes after we crossed the street. He was standing at the crosswalk with us," Peter explained. "He should've been right behind us when we got to the other side. But he wasn't. He was just gone."

"That was the last place you saw him?" Caroline prompted. "At the crosswalk by the Bobby Orr statue?"

Both Caroline and Jefferson lived very close to where Henry had last been seen and knew those streets better than anywhere else in Boston. Everything Peter described

Jefferson could picture vividly in his head without needing to walk the site in person. They still would, of course.

"Yeah," Peter said, with another hitch to his voice. "W— we waited a while on the corner thinking he'd somehow missed the light. We went back across to look for him. We tried calling him. He never picked up. Eventually, we decided to catch a train and go home. We were all tired. I said I'd keep an eye out for him back at the apartment."

"Did you suspect anything was wrong?" Caroline asked.

"No. I thought he was just being a drunk idiot," Peter said this with a healthy amount of self-disgust. "If I'd known—" he broke off.

Caroline tried a different approach. "You spent a lot of time with Henry. Had he started behaving differently lately? Disappearing for long periods of time? Taking more calls? Bringing new people over?"

"No," Peter said, looking bewildered. "He worked a lot so when he was home he just wanted to relax. We watched a lot of Netflix. Ordered delivery. He was taking a break from dating, so he wasn't using any of the apps."

"Had he pissed anyone off recently?" Jefferson asked.

Peter shook his head and said, "No."

Jefferson followed up on his previous question with: "Had either of you gotten any threatening messages, either online or in the mail?"

"I don't think so," Peter answered.

A brief silence ensued as both Jefferson and Caroline thought through any other questions they might like to ask. Peter filled the gap.

"I still can't believe it's true," he said. "Why would someone kill *Henry*?"

"We plan to figure that out," Caroline told him in her most authoritative voice, the one that declared *FBI Agent* to the world.

* * *

Henry's other friends from MIT—Bo and Julie—independently confirmed Peter's story. No, they hadn't spent much time with anyone else that night. No, there hadn't been any reason to worry when they first lost sight of Henry at the crosswalk. No, in the crowd they hadn't noticed anyone following them or getting too close. One minute, Henry stood behind them, and the next he'd vanished.

"Fans are always assholes at the Garden," Julie said, biting her lip and looking disappointed she couldn't be more helpful. "But no one particularly stood out. I would've noticed if someone was paying too much attention to us."

As much as Jefferson's gut told him this was the real thing—the Smiley Face Killer striking again— the legend of their Mr. Smiley had become too widespread in Boston. If someone wanted to kill Henry and had gotten creative about it, they could have intentionally staged the crime scene to throw suspicions off themselves. A little extra effort to hold Henry's head underwater and paint the seawall would have bought the killer time while law enforcement pursued a red herring. Before Jefferson and Caroline could determine if this was the work of a serial killer, they needed to investigate whether or not anyone in Henry's life might have wanted him dead.

Although Jefferson could admit to his bias in this particular instance, he believed it would be incredibly hard to fake the depths of despair he'd seen in Peter's eyes during their interview. Julie's boyfriend, Bo, had also come across as genuine in his grief. From what Jefferson could tell, Bo held the friend group together. Bo had been the one to plan the night at the Bruins game and now seemed guilt-ridden over having done so. Julie, though . . . .

Something didn't completely add up with her.

Jefferson studied Julie carefully across the table under the guise of giving her a moment to collect her thoughts. She wasn't sad in the same way her friends had been. Shocked, sure. But not necessarily sad. The red rimming her bright green eyes could just as easily be attributed to the night of binge drinking their little group had embarked on, as on tears.

Since she didn't seem inclined to start crying any time soon, Jefferson decided to shift his tact.

"I went to MIT too," he told her conversationally.

"Yeah?" Julie asked, tilting her head, looking hesitant to go along with the change in topic.

"Best four years of my life," Jefferson said, giving her a quick smile.

Caroline only glanced at him for a split second, but Jefferson could feel her rising curiosity. This hadn't been in the plan they'd outlined in advance of their meeting with Julie. Plus, Jefferson hardly ever got chatty like this in interviews.

"Is that where you first met Henry?" Jefferson asked.

"Yes," Julie said. "He took a programming class with Bo. They used to study together."

"Was that his major?" Jefferson asked. "Programming?"

Henry's major, Jefferson knew, had been Computer Science.

Julie's forehead scrunched. It looked like she was starting to get frustrated with these seemingly unrelated questions, although she tried to pass the emotion off as confusion. "I guess? It must have been something like that. He works with computers now."

"You've known Henry a long time," Jefferson observed. "How would you describe his personality?"

"I heard the Smiley Face Killer had done this to Henry," she said abruptly. "Why are you asking me all these questions?"

How the fuck had she heard that already? Nothing had broken yet in the news; not that Jefferson knew of. Her knowledge of the crime scene only compounded Jefferson's mounting suspicion of her.

Caroline, who had been leaning backwards with arms crossed over her chest while she let Jefferson take the reins in the interview, sat upright at that, placing her palms on the table.

"Because you're hiding something," she said, voicing Jefferson's thoughts exactly.

"I'm *not*," Julie protested. Her breath hitched, a clear giveaway that she was lying.

"Where were you last night between the hours of 10:00 p.m. and 5:00 a.m.?" Jefferson asked, speaking slowly and enunciating every word as he held Julie's gaze.

"With Bo. At his apartment," Julie answered, voice rising.

"Can anyone verify that besides Bo?" Jefferson challenged.

Julie's eyes went progressively wider with fear and surprise.

"No," she said, mouth twisting.

Jefferson made sure to trade a seemingly significant look with Caroline. They'd rehearsed that look for hours one night on Jefferson's sofa, wanting to find the perfect way to make their suspects sweat. By now they had it down pat.

"Wait, yes!" Julie said, as a flush of relief lit her pale cheeks. "The concierge can. We came in through the lobby. Bo said hello."

Jefferson made a scribble of that in his notebook, wanting to be sure not to forget: *Follow up w/ Bo concierge.* He circled it for good measure. The scratch of pen on paper came loud in the small room.

"What aren't you telling us, Julie?" Caroline asked.

Julie exhaled hard, staring at Caroline's hands. Then, in a jerky motion, she looked up to face the pair of them.

"I didn't like Henry, okay?" Julie burst out. "I thought he was an asshole. I hated that Bo was friends with him."

Now they were getting somewhere.

"Why?" Jefferson asked, watching her carefully.

"He was sleazy. Every time we all hung out, all he talked about was picking up girls," Julie told them. "And he was *handsy*. He was always touching my back or trying to put an arm around me. It made me uncomfortable."

For the first time in their interview, Julie looked and sounded genuinely honest. They often ran into that problem in their investigations: few people liked to speak ill of the dead.

"Was he like that with other women?" Jefferson asked, sensing another potential angle for Henry's death.

"Probably," Julie said. Then she immediately looked guilty. "I'm not sure," she amended. "I didn't really see him with other girls."

"Did you ever want to kill Henry over it?" he asked bluntly.

"No!" Julie said, with audible horror. "I just wanted to stop going to bars with him."

This time, Jefferson shared a real look with Caroline, double-checking that they were still on the same page. She shook her head just once.

Jefferson leaned forward, feeling the edge of the table digging into his stomach as he said, "One last question: what makes you think that Henry was killed by the Smiley Face Killer?"

Julie's expression shifted. She seemed stubbornly determined to answer this question well, clearly hoping to detract from the suspicion on her. "It wasn't me. Or Bo, or Peter. I was with them. We didn't tell anyone else when we were leaving or what exit we'd take. So, it had to be someone we didn't know. It's a lot less terrifying to believe it was the Smiley Face Killer than that there's a second person out there killing people in Boston."

Jefferson wasn't ready to rule out the idea that someone might have seen Henry at the game and recognized him, then followed him out. And he definitely planned to verify Julie's whereabouts from the night before. Nonetheless, she'd made an interesting point— *was* it easier to believe they were hunting the same serial killer who'd been targeting men in Boston for ten years now? That Henry might've simply had the bad luck to be in the right place at the wrong time? Or, did this fit the pattern of most murders—had Henry been killed by someone close to him? The idea that they might be looking for *two* killers—the copycat and the original— made Jefferson's skin grow clammy. The air from the vents overhead blew cold against the back of his neck.

CHAPTER 3

Shortly after he'd been partnered with Caroline, Jefferson's apartment building in Somerville had been purchased by a new owner, and he'd been evicted so that the units could be converted into condominiums. There'd been a move-in special in Caroline's building, located in the heart of the city, close to T.D. Garden and the North End, and right off 93, which they needed to get to the FBI offices in Chelsea.

"We work all the same hours," she'd pointed out. "Might as well save on gas."

They'd lived five floors apart from each other ever since. By now, they'd settled into a post-work routine. It was his week to drive, so Caroline followed him down to the parking lot and slid into the passenger seat of his Nissan Rogue, waiting for him to start the engine.

Traffic always clogged the highway approaching Boston. Even this late, Jefferson could see a steady line of red taillights heading away from the city. For their reverse commute, the roads were as clear as they would ever get, which meant they only had to slam on the brakes for an unexpected slowdown a few times. After about ten minutes, they passed under the bright lights of the Zakim Bridge and pulled into the garage at their high-rise.

Jefferson parked the car in his designated spot, then sat without moving, thinking about what he had in his fridge for dinner. He had one meal kit remaining from his weekly delivery, so in theory he could make something. That would take a half-hour to prepare, though. Right now, he really didn't have the energy to do any cooking.

"Should we hit up Harp for dinner?" he asked hopefully as Caroline unbuckled her seatbelt. It didn't get much more convenient than the sports bar across the street from their building's lobby.

Caroline laughed, her brown eyes lighting up with it.

"I thought we were trying to eat out less?" she asked.

"We can start tomorrow," Jefferson said, with a one-shouldered shrug. That garnered another snort of amusement

"I'm not going to Harp if it's a game night," she said, caving easily. Caroline hated cooking too. Most of the nights they ate out were thanks to her bad influence, not his. "You know it'll be a madhouse."

"The Bruins played yesterday, as we know all too well." Jefferson made a quick search on his phone. "Celtics play tomorrow."

They headed over. Harp typically either had a forty-minute wait or ran mostly empty, depending on the schedule at T.D. Garden. Since the arena sat empty for the night, they were seated right away. The arrival of a cold glass of beer, a cheeseburger, and a plate of fries went a long way toward getting rid of the pain in Jefferson's head. He'd been hungrier than he realized. The smell of grilled meat and fried food set his mouth to watering. In three bites, he'd downed half the burger.

"Never gets old," he told Caroline, still chewing.

"You're disgusting," she said, raising a perfectly manicured eyebrow in his direction.

"I have a good metabolism," Jefferson informed her. He eyed her plate of chili-loaded nachos pointedly. "Besides. Pot, kettle."

"I promise I don't get any complaints about my body," she said, with a leer.

"No, you don't." Jefferson laughed as he raised his glass to toast.

He had a hard time keeping up with Caroline's never-ending stream of guys-of-the-month, but there was always someone kicking around.

He usually met each one of the poor saps at least once. Inevitably, one morning the guy would get into the elevator, trailing behind Caroline, looking desperately in need of several more hours of sleep before work. Those days, Jefferson would offer Caroline a grin and say "Hi," the elevator would descend in quiet to the lobby where the guy would exit to the street, and Caroline and Jefferson would continue to the parking garage en route to their morning workout.

"You still seeing that doctor?" he asked, washing down a bite of burger with a swig of beer.

"Nurse," Caroline corrected, around her own mouthful of chips. "And yes. For the time being."

Jefferson whistled. "Five weeks. That's practically a record."

She shot him a wink in return as she said, "He's very good with his tong—"

"We're not *that* good of friends," Jefferson interrupted, dropping a fry so he could pretend to put his hands over his ears. "I don't want to hear it."

"Would you rather I tell you about his penis?" Caroline asked, faux-innocently. "It's been what? A year-and-a-half since you last saw one, right?"

"You're a bitch," he told her, with far too much amusement. The suspects always liked to call her that. For some reason, it had taken on its own life as an affectionate nickname. He waved to the waitress for another beer for both of them. "Stone cold, Caroline."

"What happened to that guy who gave you his number at the Trillium taproom? You ever go out with him?"

"Nope." Jefferson shrugged. "Wasn't feeling it."

"You're never *feeling* anyone," Caroline told him. She threw a stray jalapeno at him. "You're the biggest waste of a six-pack I've ever met."

"I have high standards."

"You have impossible standards. If it weren't for Provincetown, I'd think you were studying to be a priest."

"We are *not* talking about Provincetown," Jefferson insisted, feeling his face heat.

"Oh my god," she said delightedly. He watched her expression as she actively relived the night.

A couple of years ago, Caroline's old University of Maryland Swimming teammates had decided they needed to have a reunion. They'd rented a house on the beach at the very tip of Cape Cod. Most of them had brought their boyfriends or girlfriends, but Caroline had invited Jefferson instead of her current slam-piece who'd been away on a business trip. Or so she'd claimed.

Jefferson's first partner at the Bureau had taken the news he was gay so badly that Jefferson had waited for the one-year mark in their partnership, once he was pretty sure he could trust Caroline, to tell her. In the weeks following, she'd alternated between seeming hurt he hadn't told her sooner and hyper-focused on proving to Jefferson she didn't care about his sexuality. It had been awkward as fuck, nothing like their usual easy friendship. Although she denied it to this day, Jefferson still suspected she'd invited him along on the Providence trip so they could bond again, or some other sappy crap like that.

After a day filled with drinking, their group had somehow ended up at one of Provincetown's many gay nightclubs. It hadn't been Jefferson's idea. At the club, Caroline had been on a crusade to find Jefferson a hookup, plying him with shots and making him rate the men around them by their "sexiness". There'd been one guy they both found hot—Max, as he'd later introduced himself. Max was as tall as Jefferson and ripped from four years of playing college football.

Caroline had dragged Jefferson over by the arm to strike up a conversation.

Max's attention had been undeniably flattering. After a long time without, Jefferson had enjoyed the feeling of Max's hand resting low on his back and Max's lips brushing Jefferson's ear whenever Max leaned in close to be heard. But after several more shots, any desire Jefferson might have felt mostly became subsumed by a mounting irritation with the night on the whole. When push came to shove, he only asked Max back to the vacation house to force Caroline to put her money where her mouth was.

Like an asshole, he'd picked her bed. And he'd done his damnedest to make sure Max had a good time. Which Max had. Loudly.

In a lot of ways, Jefferson's stunt had worked perfectly. After that, he'd known Caroline was chill. Their friendship had quickly gone back to normal, particularly after she let off trying to wingman for him at bars. He just hadn't appreciated that he'd be giving her mocking fodder to use against him for the rest of his *life*.

"I thought we agreed to never speak of this again."

"Never," she said. Then a wicked gleam came into her eye. "It was your finest moment."

"I'm going to request a new partner," he told her.

"Sure," she said with a snort. "Enjoy being partnered with Gilbert again."

Jefferson grimaced. Special Agent Gilbert weighed in just shy of the FBI limit, with a pronounced beer gut. After three divorces, he seemed to have stopped trying for a fourth. He was also the homophobic prick who'd almost soured Jefferson on FBI partnerships altogether.

"Caroline, you have enough sex for the both of us," Jefferson told her.

"No, now I've actually thought about this a lot," she continued, once again ignoring him. "I'm so curious who could possibly satisfy the mighty Jefferson Haines's standards."

Caroline wasn't *wrong*; Jefferson could admit that. He wouldn't mind getting laid, either. His last boyfriend had been . . . Jesus, months before they were partnered together. However well they knew each other, he'd never quite figured out how to explain to her how hard he found it—with the exception of a few nights where he'd had so much to drink things were a little hazy the next day—to want to have sex with someone unless he really liked them. And he didn't like a lot of people.

"You probably want someone taller than you, which is basically impossible," she mused. "And you like muscles, right? That guy in P-town was jacked. I wonder if anyone on the Patriots is gay. We could probably pull some strings and figure it out."

"It's already been a long day, Cee," Jefferson said, groaning.

"There'll be a lot of long ones ahead." Caroline relented, reaching across the table to pat him on the arm. She didn't say *Buck up, buddy,* but it was implied.

"Until we get this sick bastard," Jefferson said, determinedly returning his focus to the case.

"Cheers to that," Caroline said. They clinked glasses.

Jefferson took a long pull of his beer, then set it down. He wiped the lingering foam off his upper lip with the back of his hand.

"A day in, what's your take on this case?"

"Let's see," Caroline said thoughtfully. "Did someone get tired of Henry's wandering hands or is Smiley back at it? I'm still curious who else Henry might've made uncomfortable."

Julie's alibi had held. When Jefferson called shortly before leaving the office for the day, Bo's concierge had verified seeing Bo and Julie enter the lobby shortly before 23:00. The concierge hadn't seen them leave after, either through the lobby, or on any of the building's ancillary security cameras.

"You think he was that way with other women too? Not just Julie?" Jefferson asked.

"Yes. If he didn't respect boundaries with her, he likely didn't respect them with most women," Caroline said, briefly letting her own exhaustion with the day show through as she raised a hand to massage the place where her neck met her left shoulder. "It's believable that some woman could've gotten fed up with Henry's advances. Or that some woman's boyfriend decided to put a stop to them."

"Peter didn't think Henry was seeing any women," Jefferson pointed out.

"I'd still like to get Bo's take. See if he noticed how Henry was with Julie or anyone else."

"He's coming in again first thing tomorrow," Jefferson said. "We should reach out to some of Henry's coworkers, too. Maybe there was someone at work he hadn't mentioned to Peter."

"I want to figure out what dating apps he was on," Caroline said. "Request the records. See if any messages stand out to us."

"Peter should be able to tell us," Jefferson agreed.

"But you don't think this is about unwanted affection, do you?" Caroline asked shrewdly.

"My gut says it isn't," Jefferson admitted. "It'd be a hell of a coincidence, someone finding Henry outside the arena." Based on the sheer size of the crowd at the Bruins game, and the many possible exits someone could take from the Garden, he considered it unlikely that someone would've been waiting outside for Henry specifically to leave. "Unless they were at the game too," he added. "And so far, all three of our witnesses don't remember seeing Henry talking to anyone."

"He couldn't have been with them the entire time," Caroline pointed out. "He must have gone to the bathroom. Gotten a beer alone."

"Yeah," Jefferson agreed. "We'll see what comes out of our second interviews tomorrow. I just don't want to miss our window if this is actually the work of the Smiley Face Killer."

"Deputy Director Strait is eager to move on that theory," Caroline said.

"I don't blame him. He's been waiting for the FBI to have this moment for almost ten years."

The waitress came by to clear their plates. They both paused until she was out of earshot.

"Tomorrow I want to send photos of the graffiti tag to the Bureau's handwriting analyst," Jefferson decided. "See if it matches any of the previous markings. At least get the ball moving."

"Sounds good," Caroline said. She paused to take a sip from her beer. "If that comes up a match, it raises a lot of other questions for us. Like why is Mr. Smiley escalating from his previous murders now?"

"And what will he do next?" Jefferson added.

That thought kept them mostly silent as they finished the rest of their drinks and paid the bill.

※※※

The next morning found Jefferson and Caroline in a community workspace at an apartment building near Kendall Square, opposite the friendly Bo. Bo had been perfectly cooperative during the first interview, but they hoped that by meeting him at a more comfortable location, he might be more open to the difficult questions they needed to ask him.

He wasn't. Bo looked mortified to be asked to speak critically of his late friend.

"I'm not sure," he said for the fifth time, in response to a question about whether he'd ever noticed if women seemed uncomfortable around Henry.

"How was he around Julie?" Caroline asked, voice soft in the way it only ever got in certain kinds of interviews, when an individual got emotional and she wanted to de-escalate. For now, Jefferson let her lead the questioning, hoping she might be able to develop an affinity with Bo.

"He was friendly!" Bo said. His face had turned a blotchy red. "They've known each other a long time."

"Did you ever feel like he crossed a line with her?" Caroline asked.

There were dark shadows under Bo's eyes. Lines had deepened on either side of his mouth. He couldn't have gotten more than a couple of hours of sleep the night before. When he spoke, he pursed his lips as if they were forcing him to chew on something sour. "Maybe a few times when he'd had too much to drink, he touched Julie a bit too much. He didn't mean anything by it. He was our *friend.*"

"Did he act that way with other women?" Caroline asked.

"I don't remember," Bo said, sticking out his chin. His jaw trembled like he was struggling not to cry.

"You never noticed him talking to women at bars?" Caroline persisted.

"*Talking,*" Bo agreed. "But Henry was a good guy. You're making him out to be some kind of *creep.*"

He'd grown too defensive. Jefferson smoothly took over. "Let's go back to the Bruins game," he said. "Can you think really carefully for us—did you notice Henry speaking with anyone besides the three of you at the game?"

Bo crossed his arms over his chest, slouching further in his chair as he said, "No. He was hanging out with us."

"How were you sitting in the stands?" Jefferson asked. "Was he at the end of your group?"

"No. I was. It was me, then Julie, then Henry. . . . " Bo's mouth twisted further when he made the admission.

"Did he interact with anyone around you? No detail you can remember is too small to share," Jefferson urged.

Bo looked down to the table. Then he closed his eyes. For several seconds he remained quiet, mouth parted.

"There was a girl a section over from us," he said eventually, gaining momentum as the memory returned to him. "Henry stood up to wave to her a little into the first period. He'd been on his phone before that, scrolling through Instagram."

"Did you catch her name?" Jefferson asked, with little hope.

Bo shook his head.

Jefferson tried a different angle, asking, "Can you describe her for us?"

The description he got didn't help much: she'd been white, with either dark blonde hair or light brown hair. She'd been wearing her hair down. Maybe it had been curly but maybe it had been straight.

Once they'd escorted Bo back to the elevator bay, Jefferson turned to Caroline.

"It's time to look at the security tapes," he said. "I want to know if someone followed Henry out."

CHAPTER 4

Few tasks absorbed time like examining security footage. A single recorded minute of raw tape could take ten
minutes to get through by the time Jefferson finished slow-
ing the scene down, zooming in and out, and changing the
angles. Multiply that by the thirty to forty-five minute window of time in which the crime could've occurred and the
eight different cameras in the immediate vicinity around the
intersection where Henry had last been spotted, and that
amounted to a lot of time sitting and staring at his monitor.

Jefferson turned up the music blasting through his
headphones and adjusted his position to lean closer to
the screen. This review could've been delegated to another
member of their case team, but neither Caroline nor Jefferson was good at giving up control, at least not on the
important things, and right now this seemed to be their
most promising lead. In fact, Jefferson had volunteered to
watch all of the footage, taking a good chunk of what could
have been Caroline's responsibility. He secretly enjoyed
watching tape in the same way he enjoyed lifting weights:
all the stress of the job faded to the background and his
mind went blissfully quiet as he focused on the repetitive
task at hand.

Video clips were not like life: they could be paused, re-
wound, fast-forwarded. You could go back if you made a
mistake and what you found stayed the same. They comforted him. For hours he sat exactly like that, watching
cycle after cycle of pedestrians step up to the traffic light

by Beverly Street, wait, and then cross over at the blinking white signal.

The footage showed that the immediate aftermath of the game had been a complete shit show. For a while after the final horn, pedestrians had spilled into the streets, blocking traffic while they walked in whatever direction they wanted across Causeway Street. That helped Jefferson start to narrow down the timeframe he should be searching because according to Peter's account, his group of friends hadn't made it out of the arena until after traffic cops managed to get the crowds under control and restore normal patterns. Only watching clips that showed cars flowing through the street whittled Jefferson's search from at least a thousand to a few hundred. For each clip remaining, he focused on freeze-frames of groups of dozens of people, all dressed almost identically in team colors, in the dark, searching for one or two familiar faces, one of which he'd only seen in person once, and the other he'd only ever seen in photos. It wasn't an easy task.

He relaxed into it, going frame by frame, stopping countless times to look more closely at some white kid in his twenties who slightly resembled Peter, until his eyes started to burn with the strain. His lunch sat half-touched by his elbow. He'd had to piss for over an hour but kept putting it off, not wanting to break the flow of his focus.

Then finally all of his efforts paid off. Abruptly he sat up straighter, unconsciously reaching out to touch the screen. *There.* To the far right of the group, waiting at the curb at timestamp *22:11*, he could unquestionably make out Peter.

Bo and Julie were a step behind him, each half-hidden by his body, and then another step behind them stood someone of the right height and weight to be Henry. Henry wore a bright green baseball cap, which made him stand out in the sea of black and gold.

To the naked eye, it was exactly as Peter and his friends had described it: they'd started across the street expecting Henry to follow, but Henry never stepped off the sidewalk. Jefferson's eyes kept focusing on movement—the people flooding toward the entrance of the underground train station. It took a conscious effort to focus on inactivity; to keep his gaze where Henry remained. Only then did he catch the moment where Henry turned away from the street, attention snared by something happening at his back.

A few rows over from Jefferson's cubicle, two agents abruptly burst into laughter. The sound broke the near-trance Jefferson had fallen into. He swore, slamming his mouse down hard. Afterwards, he had to work to find that pure state of concentration again.

Jefferson slowed the footage of Henry down, zooming in as far as he could before it became too pixelated. No matter what adjustments he made, he couldn't get the angle he needed. He could only see that someone—or something—behind Henry distracted him enough that he looked away from his friends, keeping his attention long enough for him to miss the light. *Then what?* That was the million dollar question. Whatever happened next, it was hidden by another wave of people leaving the arena and stepping up to the crosswalk. All those new bodies swallowed Henry up.

There would be many more cameras to check—every possible one between T.D. Garden and the Boston Harbor Hotel—but Jefferson was certain that this was the best view for the final moments before Henry's abduction. It had the closest, most direct line of sight from any building on that street, and it still came up short.

He turned to footage from the hotel security cameras facing the stretch of Harborwalk where Henry's body had been found. The timestamp on the video that began playing on his screen said *04:35*. Not much happened for the first few seconds. Jefferson stared at twinkling lights set against a dark backdrop.

Then Jefferson noticed a hint of motion against the night. At once he could see pulses of light in the darkness, there and gone, like the blur of a hummingbird darting up to a feeder. He leaned even closer to the screen, jostling his monitor without meaning to. As that distant beam of light grew closer, he figured out its source: a headlamp bobbing in gentle waves.

Jefferson called for Caroline immediately. Her cube adjoined his, so it only took her a second to step around the divider and join him.

"Look at this," he said.

"You think our perp came by *boat?*" she asked, bracing an elbow on his shoulder as she leaned over him to study the footage.

Jefferson nodded. Despite himself, he felt a little impressed. It was no easy feat to navigate Boston Harbor, even by day, with so many moored boats and jutting wharves. To move so confidently, with limited visibility . . . .

"If that's true then they must be local," Caroline said as if reading his mind. "Very familiar with this part of the city. If they're an experienced sailor, they could be registered with one of the local boathouses or yacht clubs. That may help us generate some names."

On screen, the small sailboat came under the glow of the lamps lining the Harborwalk, about ten feet from the walkway where they'd been standing yesterday, studying the scene around Henry's body. The outline of what appeared to be a man became visible, carefully steering in the direction of the dock.

"Male. Five foot ten?" Jefferson hazarded. "A hundred and sixty to sixty-five pounds?"

"I'd say so," Caroline agreed. "Caucasian?"

"Or Latinx, maybe," Jefferson added. "Thirty to fifty years old I'd guess."

A large mass lay in the boat behind the man. If it weren't for the stripes of gold illuminated in the light, the lump would've blended in with the shadows. The small boat pulled in close to the seawall, presumably docking, and disappeared out of sight of the hotel's security cameras, hidden by the drop from ground level to the water.

"Is there a camera at sea level?" Caroline asked.

"Yes," Jefferson said, pulling a face. "This time of night, with no additional lighting, all it picks up is a few flashes of light."

She sighed. "Amateur hour."

"Seriously."

On the keyboard, Jefferson typed a command to accelerate the footage. At 04:53, he resumed normal speed. They watched in silence as darkness consumed the little boat with its tiny bobbling light, conspicuously absent its original cargo.

"You did good, Haines," Caroline told Jefferson as the footage returned to the cheerful view of warm lights bathing a quiet pathway. "We have the start of a physical profile. That's something."

"It is," Jefferson agreed. He kept staring at the screen, mouth pursed in thought. "We need to see if any of Mr. Smiley's past drop sites might have been accessed by boat. *That's* a detail a copycat wouldn't have known and would prove that Henry is one of his victims."

"I'm not sure whether to hope for that or not," Caroline said. "It would be easier if we could've found a jealous boyfriend."

Jefferson nodded. On the one hand, if Henry was the most recent victim of the Smiley Face Killer then they at least had a larger pool of resources to work from—the details of other murders. But it also meant that just like that, the odometer had been reset to zero because if anyone had any leads on those murders, the killer would have been brought to justice by now.

Privately he hoped that a past investigator might have missed some clue buried in the sheer volume of files from past cases; something that would tell them where to start looking. That was unlikely, though. Until he and Caroline could find a new angle to approach their search, the killer would remain at large, able to strike again. Jefferson resolved to make sure no one else lost their life on his watch. The weight of that potential consequence pressed heavily upon him during what already promised to be the most challenging case of his career.

Except they *did* have something the previous investigators hadn't, he realized, feeling a flicker of excitement—they had an image of the suspect. Maybe that clue could break this whole thing wide open.

"I think maybe your gut feeling was right. It's time to have a real look at Smiley's career," Caroline told him.

It wasn't the kind of victory to feel proud of.

"Yes," Jefferson agreed. "Let's see if we find any good comparisons."

Caroline spent the next several hours developing a digital map marking where the other possible victims were first taken and their bodies dumped. After the FBI took over the investigation of Henry's murder, on their request the Boston Police Department had delivered a portable hard drive containing material from all past deaths by drowning in the Charles River and Boston Harbor. The agents assigned to support them in this case had already done a first pass to consolidate the material, flagging the cases that had the potential to be the Smiley Face Killer's work.

Jefferson brought his laptop to her cube so he could reference those case files as she added detail to her location pins. The drive held a massive volume of reference information, including ten folders, dated by year, ranging all the way back to 2010. Each folder had dozens of documents and sub-folders inside. As he clicked through the file explorer, he thought aloud.

"If Smiley started at eighteen—which would be young – he would have to be in his late twenties by now."

She added a new marker, then briefly looked over her shoulder at him. "It's more likely he started killing around thirty."

Although there were exceptions on either end of the age spectrum, most serial killers got their start at twenty-eight.

"So, we're looking at what? Thirty to fifty? Fifty-five?" Jefferson asked. "Which would match what we saw in the video still."

"Right. And the kills are never more than a year apart. If he's ever left, Smiley hasn't stayed away from Boston for long."

The majority of the bodies had been found in the upper Charles River Basin, particularly concentrated along the stretch of land near the State House, where some of Boston's wealthiest residents lived, and along Boston Harbor, close to the North End, known for its high density of Italian restaurants, and the booming Financial District, where many young professionals in the city worked.

By toggling the pins on and off by year he and Caroline tried to better understand how the Smiley Face Killer's movements might have shifted over time. The maps were particularly useful to see the obvious clusters where the bodies had been discovered and to visualize the distances between where the victims were taken and where they were discovered. In some cases, that difference spanned upwards of a mile-and-a-half apart.

"I think he also has access to a car," Jefferson observed.

"I agree," Caroline said. "If he does, that could tell us something about his finances."

It cost three hundred and fifty bucks a month, at least, to keep a car in a dedicated spot in downtown Boston. To have parking and regular access to a sailboat, their suspect likely needed to be affluent.

Jefferson stared at the list of names, locations, dates, and times beside each pin. Something nagged at him. He had to take a few seconds to formulate his theory.

"I think he's holding the victims somewhere," he finally realized. "There are a lot of gaps here . . . like on that security footage. Henry was last seen at *22:11*, but the Boston Harbor Hotel cameras didn't catch the dump until *04:35*."

A wrinkle cut into Caroline's brow. She took a second look at the screen. "Holding their bodies? Or holding them?"

"Is he killing them right off or keeping them around to chat, you mean?" Jefferson asked, stomach twisting. He had no idea what the better answer would be. "I don't know."

While Jefferson knew he would be referencing that map constantly in the weeks to come, over the years he'd spent with the Bureau, he'd learned that looking at something on a screen didn't substitute for seeing it in person. In order to analyze the movements of their killer, he wanted to *re*visit the scene of each murder, allowing himself to better understand the setting the killer had chosen to work with, especially the potential entry and exit points. To enter the mind of the killer, he first had to see the sets where the drama had played out.

Whenever they ran an investigation on another agency's property, custom dictated that they should notify the agency and meet with an appropriate representative who could brief them and provide any context that might be helpful as they worked. Figuring out who to contact involved unraveling a confusing mess of bureaucracy. The murders along the harbor had taken place on City of Boston property, managed by the DUP, Boston Department of Urban Planning. Each of the murders along the Charles River, meanwhile, although technically within the boundaries of Boston, had taken place on state land, owned by DPM, the Massachusetts Department of Parks Management.

He wondered if the killer was connected with either agency somehow, considering their familiarity with so many of these difficult-to-navigate areas. Maybe their Mr. Smiley worked in local government? Or for a contracted utility?

Jefferson and Caroline requested meetings with the heads of both agencies to ask for ongoing cooperation with the investigation. They scheduled a meeting with Commissioner Heather Hardiman of the DPM first, for 08:30 the next morning, obviously wedged in before the start of the workday due to the last-minute nature of the request. Commissioner Hardiman had been in her job for a little under two years. Caroline and Jefferson had met her once before, during a multi-agency security briefing for the Fourth of July fireworks show. Although she was a political appointee, and had a background in public works, not recreation, she seemed like a good fit for the Department, as she'd grown up hunting, fishing, and canoeing in Western Massachusetts.

The DPM was located on Causeway Street, no more than a block from where Henry had last been seen alive and not even a five minute walk from Jefferson and Caroline's apartment building. An older, unassuming red brick building with bands of tan over the windows and a giant concrete cornice housed the offices. Compared to the sea of new construction around it, the building sat low on the skyline at only nine stories tall. After showing their IDs to the security guard in the lobby, they were directed to take the elevator to the top floor. Upon arriving on the ninth floor, a receptionist promptly directed them to the seventh floor, where the Commissioner actually worked.

Jefferson exhaled heavily, waiting for the elevator to slowly creak back down two floors. "It's not that hard to tell us the right floor."

Caroline laughed at his displeasure. "It's not," she agreed as the elevator doors opened.

Despite the early meeting time, a woman in her mid-fifties sat behind the reception desk. She wore a pastel green button-down with severe collars. Makeup caked her face, cheeks a bright pink and a light blue shadow covering most of her eyelids.

"Hello," she said tightly, as if she wanted nothing less than to be sitting behind a desk greeting them.

"Good morning," Jefferson said, pasting on his most charming smile.

The receptionist didn't soften. The phone on the woman's desk started ringing in a shrill tone, and although she ignored it to watch Jefferson warily, like he might make a break for some off-limits area of the office if she looked away from him for a single second, her expression became even more pinched at the sound.

Seeing her, Jefferson wondered if they hadn't intentionally been given the wrong floor for this meeting.

He let the call ring through before he continued, "Agents Caroline Pelley and Jefferson Haines here for Commissioner Hardiman."

The phone started ringing again and the woman grimaced. She lifted the phone to her ear.

"Department of Parks Management," she said into the receiver. She paused, listening. "Good morning, Reginald." She pulled the phone slightly away from her mouth. "Have a seat, Agent Haines."

The conversation went on for a while. From what little Jefferson could make of it, the person on the other end of the line was furious about something and refused to get off the line until directed higher up in the department.

"She's not here," the receptionist kept saying. "I'll *take* a message."

To kill time until they were escorted to their meeting, Jefferson pulled out his personal cell and opened the Audubon app. A few weeks ago, he'd spent a mild Saturday hiking at Belle Isle Marsh in East Boston, one of his favorite spots, a sea of grass and meandering streams juxtaposed against the city skyline in the distance. He'd spent fifteen minutes watching a striking and unusual-looking duck float through one of the channels and had been wondering since what species it might have been. With the virtual bird guide and these few spare minutes, he could figure it out. He typed in as much as he could remember: black wings, head, and tail; green plumes at the neck; a very distinctly-shaped orange beak. Several birds came up in his search, but he quickly found the one he remembered. It had been a common eider, a large sea duck.

"Oh wow. The FBI is already here?" a new voice asked. Although the guy kept his pitch low as he asked the question, that didn't hide his surprise to see them. Apparently the receptionist hadn't let him know they'd arrived.

Even distracted by a gallery of photos of eiders, something about that soft voice tugged at Jefferson.

"The Commissioner sends her regrets," the man said, addressing Jefferson and Caroline now. "She's been held up on an urgent matter and won't be able to join you today."

An electric frisson of recognition went down Jefferson's spine. His head jerked up and he almost dropped his phone as he stared, gaping in disbelief at the person who had spoken to them. Ten seconds ago, he'd been more or less relaxed but now his heart pounded. He didn't need the lights going off on the fitness tracker on his wrist to tell him how much his pulse had just accelerated.

The man was shorter than average and very lean. He extended his hand to Caroline, who rose to her feet to greet him.

"I'll be meeting with you in her stead," he said. "I'm—"

"Finny," Jefferson interrupted, in a voice that didn't sound like him at all.

The world tilted on its axis. Because inexplicably his college roommate Finny stood here, in the middle of a random government agency in Boston, struggling to hide the look of shock spreading across his own face. Their eyes locked across the drab waiting room. Jefferson's breath caught. Everything else in the room went fuzzy, faded to a distance as Jefferson's focus narrowed solely to the person he'd thought he'd never get to see again.

Then Finny seemed to shake his surprise, expression shifting to something more strained.

"Fred," he corrected. "Fred Ashley. Chief of Staff to Commissioner Hardiman."

"Special Agent Caroline Pelley," Caroline returned. She looked equally curious and amused, although she tried to keep both from Finny. "You can call me Caroline. Did Jefferson forget your name?"

"Old college nickname," Finny said. He nodded in Jefferson's direction, no longer making any eye contact with him. "Agent Haines. I didn't realize you'd be in this meeting."

"I thought you lived in Philly," Jefferson said, then immediately wanted to kick himself. He hadn't meant to sound like he'd been keeping tabs. With great effort, he managed to stop himself from asking, *Why didn't you tell me you moved back?*

He knew why. They both did.

"Not anymore," Finny said shortly. "If you two could follow me, I have a conference room reserved for this meeting." He turned, putting his back to them, and started walking down a long hallway.

For a moment Jefferson froze in place, watching as Finny retreated. He worked his jaw, trying to loosen the sudden constriction of his throat. What had started as a dull ache in his chest gradually worsened in its intensity.

Agent Haines.

That coolly polite tone hurt worse than a punch would've.

Eight years hadn't been long enough for Jefferson to forget how Finny used to talk to him: bright and affectionate, like hanging out with Jefferson was the best part of his day. Or how he used to drag out all the syllables of Jefferson's name (*Jeff*-er-*son*), laughing, instead of biting out his formal title the way he had in the reception area.

As much as he had missed Finny all this time, he'd never felt the sense of loss as acutely as in this instant, watching Finny walk away from him again, feeling the unforgiving and unwelcoming way Finny had been looking at him seared into his skin like a brand. He might have stood there forever, knees locked, had Caroline not pushed past him, intentionally knocking her shoulder into his.

"You coming?" she asked. She didn't wait for an answer, heels clicking with her long strides when she trailed Finny.

Caroline only ever wore high-heeled shoes when they had official, external meetings such as this one. The rest of the time she donned black sneakers. The sound of her heels, along with the stiff weight of his own suit jacket, served as a pointed reminder that Jefferson had come here because he had a job to do, not to wallow in self-recrimination and regret. He shuffled his feet until he was taking full steps, trailing Caroline as she turned left at the end of the hallway toward a large open work area shared by dozens of cubicles, then made another left into a small, windowless conference room where Finny stood by the door waiting for them.

When Jefferson stepped through the doorway their eyes locked again, from a much closer distance this time, close enough that time seemed to freeze as Jefferson saw the sepia shade of Finny's eyes as vibrantly as if it were paint splashed across a South End gallery wall. There was a depth to that brief gaze—an unreadable emotion that Jefferson knew for certain wasn't fondness, but didn't seem entirely negative, either. Could it be something like reminiscence of the years before they'd fallen out? A long time ago, Jefferson had been the best friend Finny had. They had plenty of good memories together, shared over four years, to balance the final day of their friendship. There had to be *something* about him Finny remembered warmly.

Or maybe he'd deluded the hell out of himself.

Since he couldn't stare wordlessly at Finny forever, Jefferson continued into the room, taking the seat next to Caroline, closer to the door. Although it was farther inside, Finny took the seat across from her—making sure, Jefferson thought, that he could avoid looking at Jefferson more easily.

Time had changed Finny very little from the guy who'd so thoroughly captured, then held, Jefferson's attention in college. Except, he'd aged into his looks. The baby fat that had stubbornly clung to his cheeks for so long had finally melted away, leaving him more handsome than youthful; but he still looked achingly familiar, the same person Jefferson had seen every day sophomore through senior year once they'd become roommates. Finny was nearly a foot shorter than Jefferson, with a wiry runner's build, every muscle streamlined for speed. The sun perpetually tinged his cheeks pink, even now, coming off another brutal Boston winter, and when the light hit just right, it burned golden streaks in his short brown hair. Even several feet of snow had never stopped Finny from putting in the miles outside.

The biggest difference was in how he dressed. Their clothes told the story best: two men in suits faced each other as working adults instead of friends in basketball shorts playing a game of shirts vs skins at the MIT gym. Today,

Finny had dressed sharply in a slim-fit blue dress shirt, skinny pink tie, and fitted slacks held neatly at his waist with a brown belt. His loafers were obviously high quality, trimmed around the edges with a gold bar across the toes. He looked...professional, exactly like someone twenty-nine years old with a respectable job should. As much as Jefferson usually hated wearing his suit, he felt suddenly grateful to have it on today. Only, he desperately wished he'd taken Caroline's repeated advice to make the time to get it tailored. The extra fabric at his shoulders kept bunching up, making it look like he'd added in padding.

They'd been apart longer than they'd known each other. There had been plenty of time for Jefferson to get over Fred "Finny" Ashley. At some point, he'd even managed to convince himself he'd moved on. He'd made new friends. One really good one. He'd dated other men. This encounter had shown him that he'd done a really good job of kidding himself.

"Thank you for taking this meeting on such short notice," Caroline opened, once they were all seated.

"It's no trouble," Finny said. He pulled a yellow legal pad out of his messenger bag and placed it on the table, resting his forearms on either side. In a seemingly unconscious motion, he started twirling a cheap pen between the thumb and index finger of his left hand. His fingers were long, nails neatly trimmed. Jefferson got distracted studying the coarse hair below his knuckles. "As I mentioned, Commissioner Hardiman regrets that she couldn't join us. She's asked me to let you know that you'll have the full cooperation of the department during the investigation."

"We appreciate that," Caroline said. She turned her head, looking expectantly at Jefferson. It took him a second too long to return her gaze.

Caroline gave him exactly that one second, if not less, and then she discreetly rolled her eyes at him.

Oh. Well, shit. On the walk over from their apartment, Caroline and Jefferson had decided that Jefferson would kick-off the meeting, introduce the two of them, and provide background on the case. Jefferson had dropped the ball on this one.

"Special Agent Pelley and I are leading the investigation of a recent murder that may be tied to a series of murders in Boston over the last twelve years." Jefferson began to feel more at ease as he recited the familiar facts of the case. "The so-called 'Smiley Face Killer' exclusively targets men between the ages of twenty and thirty-five, drowns them, and stages the bodies along local waterways."

"I did some reading on the case last night when the meeting request came through," Finny said. "I wasn't able to find much. Most of what's online seems to be unsubstantiated rumors."

Knowing him, or the way he used to be, at least, that probably meant he'd stayed up half the night committing any information he could to memory. If Jefferson studied him without the rose-colored lenses of an unexpected but much-hoped-for reunion, he could see that Finny looked tired. There were faint lines at the corners of his eyes and the barest hint of shading under them, skin like a freshly-dropped peach set to bruise later.

"As you might imagine, some details of the murders have been withheld from the public," Caroline explained.

"I see," Finny said. The skin on his nose crinkled as he thought, a hopelessly charming tic Jefferson had seen him do a hundred times over. "I'd like for our department to be helpful but I'm not sure how. We have no oversight for safety in the park."

"As Special Agent Pelley mentioned, the bodies have been staged primarily in two places: the harbor, where the most recent one was discovered two days ago, and along the Charles River. Over half have been found on properties managed by your agency," Jefferson explained.

"Yes, I'm aware of that," Finny said, with dry humor. "We do notice when people get killed in our parks."

Jefferson continued as if Finny hadn't spoken, mostly to cover his own discomfort.

"We are requesting your assistance in viewing the sites along the shoreline where bodies were discovered—by water," he explained. "We'd also like you to facilitate interviews with the members of your staff who made the discoveries."

"Okay," Finny said. He'd been avoiding looking directly at Jefferson as the meeting began, but his eyes suddenly skittered toward him as if curiosity had gotten the better of him. His lashes looked particularly long when he did that, splayed across his cheeks. "By water?" he asked.

"We have reason to believe he's an experienced sailor," Caroline said. "Or at least comfortable on the water."

"Interesting," Finny said. His mouth opened as he started to say something else, but after another furtive look at Jefferson, he clamped his lips together and a muscle ticked in his jaw.

"Do you sail?" Caroline asked with her usual canny perception.

"I've been learning," Finny said, still visibly distracted by something. "It's weird to think . . . . " He didn't finish the sentence.

Jefferson filled in the blank. "That a serial killer could be sharing the same boathouse with you?"

The thought apparently hadn't been real for Finny until Jefferson voiced it aloud. The blood drained from Finny's face as his lips parted on an uneven breath. Jefferson immediately felt like an asshole.

Finny was always prone to over-worrying about things, however unlikely they were to happen. From now on, whenever he went to his sailing lessons, he would be jumping at shadows, wondering who could be lurking around every corner. The urge to say something reassuring almost overwhelmed Jefferson.

"Don't worry," Jefferson told him. "We're here to get the bad guys wherever they are."

Instead of being comforting, the words sounded unbelievably pompous. Caroline dug her heel into the top of his foot.

Finny gave him an incredulous look that Jefferson could read all too well, one that said, *You sound like a bad actor in a bad cop movie.*

It was embarrassing, but at least Finny didn't look quite so scared anymore.

"Do you have a map of the Charles River locations?" Finny asked. "I could probably sail you there myself depending on where they are."

"We do," Jefferson said, at the same time Caroline said, "Yes." He twisted, reaching into his bag for the roll of ledger papers he'd printed before this meeting, and undid the rubber band so he could pass them around.

"I hope you understand that all of this is strictly need-to-know," Caroline told Finny. "The information has been withheld from the public for a reason. So, whoever guides us must be able to keep this confidential."

"Of course." Finny pulled his copy closer, glanced at it briefly, then leaned down to dig in his bag again. He emerged with a pair of square-frame glasses in hand and slid them on. Those were new and very distracting.

"Each spot represents a location where a body was discovered," Caroline explained. "We're most interested in the yellow stars. Those are more recent—within the last five years."

She kept going, expanding on each of those locations and what they would be looking for on a tour: Why might the killer have chosen those particular drop sites? Were there any sites that he could only have approached from the water? Could the escalation in scale of his calling card have begun before the most recent murder?

It was instinctual for Jefferson to follow along on his own copy, which he appreciated because it kept him from staring at Finny in those damn glasses. They were a physical manifestation of the quiet, studious kid Jefferson had first met on a hot fall day outside of a MIT fraternity house; the one he'd dedicated so much of his time to push, prod, and goad into having a little *fun* from time to time. The same kid who'd pushed Jefferson to take his humanities classes as seriously as he took statistics. Having those strong grades across subject areas had paid off later for Jefferson when he applied to the Bureau.

As Caroline pointed out each of the three yellow stars, the memory of a file flashed up in Jefferson's mind:

Randall Allen, 35, Mixed-race, Stay-at-home father

Omar Halim, 27, Middle Eastern, Researcher at Biogen, a major pharmaceutical company in Cambridge

Gregory Jackson, 21, Caucasian, Student at Boston University

Three men with dramatically different backgrounds, all taken from streets that would've been teeming with people, even after dark, when Gregory and Omar went missing. Randall had been taken at twilight on what should've been one of the safest running routes in Boston. The murders were confoundingly random and terrifyingly competent.

"I'll go through our incident reports from the field," Finny said. "I can share contact information for the employees who reported the bodies. And I . . .Oh, I think you're missing a marker on this map."

"What? *Where*?" Caroline asked.

Finny reached for the sheet in front of her. "Can I see your copy?"

Once she'd slid it across the table to him, he drew an *X* and circled it.

"Here," Finny said. "Off the shoreline near the cherry tree grove."

Jefferson leaned toward Caroline, trying to get a closer look at Finny's mark.

"We'd have known if there was another murder." He said it as a matter-of-fact—they would have been notified if a body was discovered. Finny, of course, took it as a challenge, eyes flashing.

"Five months ago, an attempted murder was reported at this location," Finny told them.

A moment of stunned silence followed. Finny had managed to surprise him and Caroline both, which rarely happened in interviews.

"What happened?" Jefferson asked, intentionally making his voice softer.

"Last November, one of the park rangers found a man—his name was Reginald Shapiro—struggling to climb out of the Charles River," Finny explained. "Reginald reported that a masked man had overpowered him and tried to *drown* him. Wouldn't you say that's related?"

Jefferson briefly pressed his leg against Caroline's under the table. That could be a huge lead. They'd never heard of one of Mr. Smiley's attacks failing before. And according to the timeline Finny had shared, it would be the most recent incident before Henry's death. God, Finny was still so fucking smart.

"Quite possibly," Caroline said. "Any information you could share on that would also be helpful."

"Yes, I can—" Finny began.

"Reginald," Jefferson remembered, inadvertently interrupting. "The receptionist got a call from him as we were on our way in."

Finny blinked. "Ah, yes. He calls often. He lives nearby and is very concerned about safety in the park. I don't think you'll have trouble getting an interview with him."

"Good," Caroline said. She added, "You know . . . if you wouldn't feel comfortable sailing us yourself, let us know. We can enlist the cooperation of Sailing for All."

Sailing for All was a local boathouse open to the public for instruction where Finny likely took his lessons. They'd need to enlist SFA's cooperation anyway, along with all the other local boathouses, in order to get a full list of registered sailors and students in the area.

"It should be fine," Finny said. His gaze flicked briefly to Jefferson, a glancing look so quick Jefferson might have missed it if he blinked. "And we know our property better than anyone you could find there."

"Thank you, Finny," Jefferson said.

"Fred," Finny corrected, eyes narrowing.

"Sure," Jefferson said.

"I'm happy to provide anything you need for the investigation," Finny said. Reaching into his back pocket, he pulled out a business card, pointedly only handing one to Caroline. "Here's my contact information for any follow-up."

Humiliation sparked in Jefferson's stomach, the burn of it spreading rapidly, traveling up the back of his throat.

"We appreciate your help, Fred," Caroline told him. "We'll be in touch soon to confirm next steps."

Finny looked far more relieved the meeting had ended than Jefferson thought warranted. Some of the tension across his shoulders visibly eased.

"You know the way out?" Finny checked.

"Yes," Caroline said, while Jefferson stood there like an idiot, grinding his teeth against all the things he wanted to say to Finny that definitely weren't appropriate for the time and place. She dug her elbow into Jefferson's side, urging him to move back toward the sea of cubicles and the hall to the elevator bay.

CHAPTER 5

As the elevator car creaked down floors toward the lobby, Jefferson shifted from side to side, remaining silent in the face of an expectant, oppressive wait. Neither of them said a word until they'd crossed Causeway Street and entered their apartment lobby where they had to take another elevator down to the garage.

Jefferson felt uncharacteristically depressed, already weary with the day even though the clock had barely struck 09:00.

"You're driving," he told Caroline, even though it was his week on.

"Fine," she said sounding admirably restrained.

The elevator door opened, spitting them out to the below-ground level where their cars sat about thirty spaces apart. As soon as they could see her gleaming white Jeep Cherokee, the dams burst.

"Was that your ex-boyfriend?" she asked in an unfairly scandalized tone for someone he knew for a fact had once been required to interview a guy she'd banged.

"No," he answered tersely. "If only."

"I think he was," she pressed. "I've never seen you that uncomfortable in a meeting before, *Agent Haines*."

He stifled the urge to flinch. "He wasn't."

"You just fucked him then?"

Jefferson did cringe then. "Christ, Caroline. No. He was just my roommate. In college."

They approached Caroline's car and at the flashing taillights that signaled she'd unlocked it, he slid into the passenger seat.

"And you had a thing for him?" she theorized as she slid behind the wheel.

"I don't want to talk about it," he told her in a tight voice.

Except he kind of did. In eight years, he hadn't told anyone the full extent of how he felt about Finny; how much their fight had gutted him. The old mutual friends he met for a quick beer when they passed through town weren't the kind he'd spill his guts to. On those occasions he'd focused on playing it cool, looking for whatever scraps of information he could get. Over the years as they all gained more responsibilities, those meetups had become few and far between until he almost never talked to anyone from school anymore, which meant he hadn't learned Finny had returned to Boston until he saw it with his own eyes.

A part of him desperately wanted to talk about it. What that part really wanted was to go home, change into his sweats, have a few beers, and then tell Caroline about it.

"You absolutely did have a thing for him," she said with supreme confidence. "Is that seriously your type, Jefferson? Nerd chic? Skinny boys? Wow, I had that wrong. I was really banking on a stud quarterback type."

Jefferson didn't dignify that with a response.

"So, what—you told him and he wasn't into it?" she continued anyway.

"You're a fucking bloodhound," he told her, fidgeting in his seat. He stared fixedly out the window even though they were still underground with nothing to look at except concrete pillars and dozens of parked cars. "And no—I don't know if he knew. I never told him." His fist clamped tightly in his lap. He forced himself to relax. "I know he wasn't into me."

As the first beams of sunlight told him they were approaching the exit to the garage, Caroline briefly turned to him.

"Well he was *pissed*. You must've been a really shitty roommate back then."

That was her cutting him a favor and dropping the subject. For now, at least. It would come back up eventually, though. Caroline excelled at interrogation for a reason. She knew that more lay behind his story and probably even sensed that he wanted to get it off his chest. But it was still only nine in the morning. They had a whole day to get through before any danger of having some kind of heart-to-heart loomed.

"Guess so," Jefferson said, playing along. He crossed his arms over his chest, leaned his head back against the rest, closed his eyes, and resisted the urge to sigh.

"I can't wait for that sailing trip," she said. "You better not make an ass of yourself."

"Don't let me then," Jefferson said. Judging by how today had gone, odds were high that he would make an *enormous* ass of himself. Every time he tried to think about how to make their next meeting go better, he came up blank. He wanted to fix things with Finny so much it choked him, overriding all rational thought. He didn't trust that he could talk like a normal person if they were in the same room together. "That's what partners are for."

"Okay, Jay," she said indulgently. The first light they stopped at, she reached over and patted him briefly on the knee, a fleeting motion as comforting as Caroline ever got. "The good news is that my gut's telling me Fred's not involved."

Jefferson turned away from the crowds of morning commuters moving on the sidewalk outside the window to gape at her. "Of course he's not involved."

She raised an eyebrow, giving him a quick, unimpressed look. "Just because you want to believe it doesn't mean it can't be true. He has the right access and knowledge to be.

And he so helpfully pointed us in the direction of a new crime scene."

"No—he—" Jefferson had to cut himself off twice so he wouldn't argue with her. To this day, he still felt fiercely protective of Finny and it manifested itself as anger Caroline didn't deserve. He ground his teeth to hold back the instinctual protests on his tongue.

Caroline huffed a laugh. "Look at you, your face is all red."

"I just don't think it's a good use of our time to look into him right now," Jefferson explained.

"Oh, Jefferson. Who'd have thought you'd lose your head over a pretty boy?"

"I have *not*," Jefferson protested.

"I'm going to remember that time you went stupid on me in an interview forever."

Jefferson had wished Caroline would drop the Provincetown weekend story. He hadn't meant to give her something new to rag on him for.

"Ugh," he said, with feeling.

Lacking any further witnesses to question, they returned to their office. About six hundred agents worked in the Boston Division of the FBI, dispersed between the main Chelsea office and ten additional resident agencies in New England. The Chelsea office had been reconstructed early in Jefferson's tenure with the Bureau. Where they'd once reported to a dark, old, heavily concrete building, they now had a gleaming white eight-story building filled with natural light.

Depending on the case, Caroline and Jefferson teamed up with a wide range of the agents stationed in Chelsea and beyond. For Henry's murder, they were supported by Special Agent David Valdés and Special Agent Kenneth Gilbert—Jefferson's former partner, with whom he had a strained relationship, to say the least. During their brief check-ins, Jefferson felt grateful to have Valdés as a go-be-tween. Although Valdés tended to be soft-spoken, he could be firm when he needed to, and he generally kept his partner in check.

So far, Valdés and Gilbert had spent most of their time interviewing T.D. Garden's security staff and Henry's colleagues at the cyber-security start-up he'd worked for. They hadn't turned up any new leads yet.

Eager to lose himself in the case, Jefferson retreated to his desk immediately. He spent most of his morning contacting the local boathouses that rented or stored sailboats, of which there were many—Boston University Sailing Pavilion, MIT Sailing Pavilion, Harvard Sailing Center, Union Boat Club, and Sailing for All, just on the two-mile stretch of the river where they had initially focused their search—requesting a complete copy of each of their membership databases as well as lists of members of staff and volunteers.

As the materials came in, he spent hours sorting and cleaning the largely inconsistent data. Even filtering by gender, age, and previous criminal convictions left them with a daunting list of potential suspects to investigate. And the possibility their killer wasn't officially registered anywhere lingered in the back of his mind.

The incompleteness of the records irritated him, breaking the flow of his concentration. Whenever that happened, he couldn't keep his mind from turning to Finny.

His body's response to the other man betrayed him. Time and distance should have done something to take the edge off Jefferson's attraction to Finny. Instead, Jefferson found Finny exactly as gorgeous as before, only now he couldn't blame it on being young, or a small dating pool, or a buzz, or lack of sleep, or any of the other excuses he'd used to comfort himself that his thing for his former best friend wasn't as bad as it seemed.

Around noon, Caroline emailed Finny to thank him for their morning meeting and copied Jefferson. He'd been able to feel her glee as she typed the note even through the divider wall separating their desks. She was simultaneously teasing him for finally showing an interest in someone, flaunting that she got to be the one to contact Finny and he didn't, and taking what seemed to be a genuine interest in trying to help him, practically winking at him with every keystroke.

In response, Finny shared the incident report from the attempted assault and contact information for the two maintenance workers who'd reported finding bodies on DPM land. Jefferson reached out to both of them to schedule interviews while Caroline kept emailing Finny, coordinating a water-based tour of the river. Within a couple of hours, they'd locked in a date and time: Thursday at 13:00. Two days away. Afterwards, Jefferson lost a good hour of his day trying—and failing—not to think about what could happen on that sailing trip.

For lunch, he grabbed a tasteless pre-made sandwich from the cafeteria and then kept his head down for the rest of the afternoon.

At 18:30, Caroline came to claim him, getting his attention by reaching around him and shutting off his computer monitor.

"Come on, fat ass. We missed our workout this morning to go chat with your boyfriend."

"I should report you," Jefferson told her, blinking away the crust of too much time staring at a computer screen. "All you do is harass me."

"Do it, you big baby," she said, physically pulling his chair backwards until he couldn't reach his keyboard.

Considering how exhausted he felt, the last thing Jefferson wanted to do was go to the boxing studio with her. In place of those beers he'd been craving earlier, he increasingly wanted a shot of something *strong*.

He flipped her off with both hands and she took advantage of his preoccupation to snatch the bag resting next to his desk and stride off down the corridor with it.

"You're such a witch," he called after her.

"I think you mean bitch," she told him, sounding pleased with herself.

Reluctantly, he hopped out of his chair to follow. Jefferson would never tell her this, because she might actually kick his ass like she always threatened, but a good twenty percent of his motivation for going to the gym was making sure no one could argue that his female partner was stronger than him. Equal, maybe, but not stronger.

When he caught up to her and snatched his bag back using a loose strap, she looked thoughtful in a way that didn't bode well. Caroline didn't usually overthink anything. She tended to go with her instincts.

"I guess it wouldn't be a fair fight if you're too busy drooling over a suspect," she said, almost sweetly, loud enough to be heard by anyone still working on their floor.

Despite his better judgement, Jefferson let himself be baited. "I wasn't drooling," he argued.

Her smile turned brilliant, the pale purple lipstick she'd been wearing all day still perfectly intact. "So, you're coming to the gym?"

❋❋❋

They stopped by their apartment building to change and lock up their weapons. Only once they'd gotten several minutes into a boxing session did the rest of what Caroline had said back in the office sink in.

"I'm telling you we don't have to waste time investigating Finny," Jefferson stated, throwing a brutal right hook that she weathered with a firm stance.

She held the pads for him while he threw punches. When he got tired, they'd switch, and he'd block for her.

"Well I already looked him up," she told him. He lobbed two more right hooks and then a left. Since punching with his left arm—his weaker arm—didn't make the satisfying *thwack* he liked, Jefferson kept up that rhythm for a while: *right, right, right, left, right, right, right, left.* She gave him an annoyed look when one of his punches finally had enough force to knock her back a step. Then she squared her feet again, bent her knees slightly, and looked determined. "Do you want to know what I found out?"

"No," Jefferson said, unsure whether or not he'd lied. He desperately wanted to know more about what Finny had been up to in the years they'd been apart, but he also didn't want to have to consider Finny being under suspicion. Sweat beaded at his temple now. A drop of it that clung to a strand of his hair fell, landed on his cheek, and then curled under his jaw. He could feel the spots where his damp shirt clung to his lower back. "Because he couldn't hurt anyone. He doesn't have it in him."

She tossed her long ponytail. "Maybe he's changed. Maybe you don't know him as well as you think you do."

Jefferson gestured for her to adjust the angle of the pad, so it was parallel to the ground and then switched to a series of uppercuts. It was no coincidence that the uppercut was his hardest strike.

"Fine," he said, giving in to the urge to learn more. "Wow me. What has Finny been up to for the last few years?"

"Fred moved from Boston to Philadelphia in 2013. Which you already knew."

Jefferson didn't respond to that dig. He didn't particularly like to think about 2013.

Caroline relentlessly continued. She timed each of her discoveries to match the cadence of Jefferson's sets. "He got a job at a non-profit. Quit after less than a year. Started working at an insurance company. Quit after *three* months.

Then started law school and dropped out after a semester. *Hmmm,* couldn't seem to make something stick, could he?"

That wasn't like the Finny Jefferson knew at all. Finny had been one of the most reliable people he'd ever met. In any other case he'd say Caroline absolutely should bring that up—an inability to maintain commitments frequently came up as a red flag when they looked for suspects. Nonetheless, hearing it, Jefferson couldn't help but think that Finny'd had a rough couple of years in Philadelphia. He wished badly that he could have been there for him.

"Be that as it may he hasn't been living in Boston. He doesn't fit the pattern," he countered, finding an entirely new pool of strength to tap. His next uppercut pushed the pads several inches up.

"He lived here when you were in college," she pointed out. "During one of the peaks for the murders. You know the killings slowed over the last few years before this recent escalation. Maybe he was flying back in between."

"I don't buy it," Jefferson said. He lifted his elbow at an awkward angle so he could wipe his forehead on the sleeve of his shirt. The thick red glove on his hand had started to feel like it weighted down his arm.

She only shrugged. "*Someone* should be considering it, since we're going on a boat with him. We should at least alibi him for Henry's murder."

"Fine," Jefferson repeated shortly. "What else do you have?"

"I read over the incident report for the attempted drowning your boy flagged. I've already reached out to the victim—this Reginald—to request a meeting. The report also had contact information for the EMT who was first to arrive on site. We'll be meeting with her as well."

"Sounds like we have a busy day tomorrow," Jefferson said.

"What about you?"

Jefferson let out a breath of annoyance. "I spent most of the day wrangling the different lists from the boathouses. We now have a fairly comprehensive list of local sailors. It's searchable as names come up. I pulled out all of the individuals who had a prior criminal record. There are several hundred. We should talk to Deputy Director Strait about pulling in some additional agents to help us go through them."

"Ten-four," Caroline said. "Enough work talk. Can it be my turn now?"

"Yeah, I'm wiped," Jefferson said. He took two steps back and dropped his arms, vigorously shaking them out.

"So, what happened with you and Finny, anyway?" Caroline asked. Her tone sounded perfectly innocent. She was seemingly focused on undoing the Velcro on her padding.

Jefferson still felt irritated with her, regardless of how rational the feeling. He couldn't resist pushing back. "Is this Caroline asking or *Agent Pelley*?"

"I said work talk was over," she protested, pouting at him. Under the guise of leaning over to catch his breath from the workout, Jefferson took a moment to consider. He'd never described any of what happened between him and Finny out loud to anyone. Even Caroline wouldn't get the full story. But after an entire day of thinking about it, he'd crack if he didn't tell her something.

Straightening, he slowly began, "He was my best friend at MIT. We shared a room for three years, so we spent a lot of time together."

"I gathered that," she said with a wave of the hand. "Fast forward, please."

"And then. . . . " Jefferson shook his head, feeling nauseous. "And then one night I blew up at him over something stupid. He never spoke to me again after."

He mostly expected Caroline to make fun of him, if only to try to lighten the mood. He was shocked, instead, to see the horror he felt at himself mirrored on her own face.

"You didn't *hit* him, did you?" she hissed, voice dropping.

Jefferson recoiled. "Fuck. *No.*" He felt briefly offended that she could think something like that of him after knowing him for three years, before he realized why her mind had gone there; what they were in the midst of doing. "Just. I yelled. I was a shithead. It wasn't the kind of drunk argument you laugh off the next day."

Now that he had started speaking, he couldn't stop the rest of what had been sitting with him all day from spilling out. Bitterly stripping out of his gloves, he admitted, "I always thought that if I could just see him again—if I could apologize— then we could go back to how we used to be." He looked down at the floor. "Clearly not."

He wished she could tell him that it wasn't his fault—that he hadn't massively overreacted. But Caroline would never lie to him just to spare his feelings.

She pressed the stack of pads against his chest. The feel of them was strangely comforting. Her big brown eyes had gone a little soft. "Forgiveness takes time, Jay."

"I know," he said. He didn't feel much hope. If almost a decade hadn't dulled the force of Finny's anger, what would?

Blocking for her took up most of Jefferson's attention for the remainder of the workout.

✳✳✳

Although he wouldn't have admitted it out loud, because he didn't want to validate her underhanded techniques to get him to spar with her, he did feel marginally better by the time he showered and made it home to his apartment. The high of the workout gave him a second wave of energy. Afterwards, he felt up to tackling one of his neglected meal kits:

pan-seared scallops in butter with sides of orzo and brussels sprouts. While he cooked, he downed that beer he'd wanted for so much of the day.

Making a meal from a kit had neither the easy convenience of dining out, where you only had to sit and someone would bring you everything you needed and then do the dishes after, nor the satisfaction of making something fully from scratch. It did the trick for Jefferson, though, when he wanted the semblance of something home-cooked, particularly since he rarely had time to go to the grocery store. He appreciated that he didn't need to research any recipes—he only had to choose between a few different options provided for him.

The finished meal turned out fine, if a little bland. After he cleared his plate, he still felt unsatisfied. As he opened another beer, he wished he'd been eating with someone else. With Finny. Even in college, when everyone else lived off ramen and the dining hall, Finny had enjoyed cooking. A few nights a week, Finny had taken over the kitchen in their fraternity house to make dinner, and Jefferson had almost always benefited from the fruits of his labor.

How had he not known Finny had moved back to Boston? Despite everything, Jefferson still found it hard to believe Finny hadn't reached out upon his return. They used to be inseparable. There had been a time, years and years ago, when it would've been impossible to believe they'd ever be this estranged. When Finny had been weighing job opportunities their last year of college, he'd initially chosen to stay in *Boston instead of exploring a new city,* in part because it meant they'd be closer together when Jefferson returned to the area from his FBI training. Hundreds, if not thousands, of his happiest memories revolved around Finny. Like . . .

. . . Finny twisting at the waist from the pitcher's mound, using his non-gloved hand to shoot Jefferson a quick thumbs-up during a game of intramural softball.

Those uniforms had been ridiculously flattering on Finny's lean body—tight pants and knee-high socks highlighting the taut muscles of his thighs and quads. Every game, Jefferson worried he might drop a fly ball, his eye on Finny's ass instead of the ball.

. . . Finny absolutely plastered after a day of tailgating, leaning against Jefferson while they waited to get into Steinbrenner Stadium. Finny's obsession with running always counted against him on days like those. He could never pack on any mass, which made him a major lightweight. Two beers in, Finny started stumbling, cheeks dimpling. Whenever Finny got drunk it usually meant Jefferson *didn't*, because he wound up devoting most of his attention to making sure Finny didn't pass out in a dark corner somewhere. What a change: he'd gone from protecting Finny from having dicks drawn on his face to protecting strangers from being murdered on the streets.

He realized he was smiling, staring absently into the amber liquid in his glass. They'd had fun, him and Finny. The rest of the fraternity house had known they were a package deal. You wanted one of them to skip class or plan a party, you had to get the other onboard. It had been the two of them against the world, like it was now with Caroline in a lot of ways. God, she lived five floors down from him, Jefferson never had to be alone if he didn't want to be. But still, he missed Finny. All the time. Even today, sitting three feet across a table from him.

How had it gotten so screwed up, so fast? That memory returned five times as vivid as the good ones: Finny's whole body went mottled red when he got angry. There had been blotches of color on his cheeks, his neck, and chest when he'd been yelling at Jefferson. *I thought you were different! I thought you were better than the rest of them!*

That night, Finny had been so angry his voice changed, dipped several notes lower to something rough, like the scraping sounds old trucks made passing by on the road out front of the house.

Over the course of one night—a drop in the bucket in the amount of time they'd known each other—he'd lost his best friend, lost him for good. Their relationship had gone to radio silence on Finny's end; not a single call, text, or email to fill the sudden vacancy in his life. Jefferson wondered if that was why he empathized so much with Peter McDonnell, the witness to Henry O'Brien's disappearance: he knew how it felt to gradually have to come to terms with the knowledge that you were never going to see someone you cared about again.

Of course, based on what Jefferson had learned so far, Finny had very little in common with Handsy Henry. Casanova tendencies aside, Henry had worked in Computer Security and Finny was a Political Science major. Granted, according to Agents Valdés and Gilbert, Henry had been well-regarded at his job, considered a hard worker, and Finny seemed equally dedicated to his role at the DPM.

What a ridiculous line of thought. Why was Jefferson comparing Finny to a murdered man? What he should be doing, he realized with a start, was comparing Henry to Mr. Smiley's *other victims.*

Jefferson hadn't brought home his laptop, but he had his work phone with him in case of emergencies. He decided to take the three most recent victims before Henry and spend thirty minutes on each of them, combing through what he could find about them online to try to build a fuller picture than the impersonal biographies in their case files.

An hour and a half later, he didn't have any more answers than he'd started with. On Randall Allen's memorial Facebook page, his love for his daughters shone through. Most of his posts celebrated their various milestones in life. Gregory Jackson could only be found via a locked Instagram page, but creative googling told Jefferson that Gregory had played high school baseball and that he'd rushed Kappa Sigma at BU. Omar Halim had been active on both Twitter and LinkedIn, a thoughtful writer about developments in neuroscience.

They appeared to be men wholly different in occupations, interests, hobbies, looks, and even preferred social media channels. Why had Smiley chosen them?

CHAPTER 6

Since they'd arranged to hold three interviews in different areas of Boston throughout the day, Caroline and Jefferson didn't make the commute to Chelsea the next morning. Their first took place less than a ten-minute walk from their apartment, in the Government Center area, home to a majority of City of Boston functions.

Few buildings in Boston were as polarizing as City Hall's enormous concrete cube structure. Even the two of them disagreed—Caroline considered it a hideous eyesore, while Jefferson liked how the brutalist style contrasted against everything else downtown. The building sat on a vast brick plaza that was largely empty most of the time outside of rush hour and large events. As they crossed the plaza, they saw ten or so people spread in eyeshot— a group of homeless men sleeping in the shadow of the Government Center train station, a few stragglers dressed for a day in the office, walking at a brisk pace, and tourists meandering over to the nearby Freedom Trail—as well as several clusters of pigeons.

A woman wearing a Pittsburgh Steelers hat crossed their path.

"Go Steelers," Jefferson told her. She smiled at him, looking pleased to have found a fellow ally in the midst of a city that could be vicious toward opposing teams' fans.

They had to go through metal detectors to get inside the lobby. When they arrived at the Department of Urban Planning offices on the fifth floor, an empty desk where a receptionist would usually sit greeted them. Jefferson checked his watch. Two minutes before their scheduled meeting time someone should have been expecting them.

There were no other workspaces in immediate view, just a dimly-lit hallway. The waiting area only held a couple of plastic chairs that Jefferson wasn't confident enough he would fit in to test.

Right when Jefferson began to grow restless, wondering if he should go in search of someone who could help, a man emerged from farther down the corridor. Jefferson recognized him from his headshot on the DUP website. Director Dylan Jacobs was a handsome man who appeared to be in his mid-to-late forties. Caucasian. Around five foot ten. He had jet black hair neatly slicked to one side, piercing blue eyes, and a smile that dimpled both sides of his mouth. He wore a navy bespoke suit with white pinstripes, showing a well-proportioned form. A maroon silk pocket square added a flash of color, matching his tie.

"Good morning," the director called, giving them a wave. He came to a stop beside the empty desk. "Sorry if you had a wait. My assistant is out sick today."

Caroline reached out her hand. "Special Agent Caroline Pelley. Thank you for meeting with us."

"Dylan," Director Jacobs said. He turned to Jefferson, who offered his own hand. "Special Agent Jefferson Haines," Jefferson told him.

Dylan took his hand with a firm grip. He held on for a fraction longer than Jefferson expected—the span of an inhale— briefly tightening his grip before letting go. It was somehow, despite the simplicity of the action, the most blatantly a man had ever come on to Jefferson at work. What should have been a routine introduction flustered him, making his skin feel hot and itchy.

They followed Dylan to his office, which appeared to be the only part of the suite that had a window. Stacks of paper cluttered the room. Blueprints and maps rested on every surface with extra space, including a few spots on the floor. Several coffee mugs were clustered to the left of the screen beside the mouse.

"How can I be of help in your investigation?" Dylan turned on that megawatt smile.

Amidst the chaos of the desk, Jefferson noticed a single personal item: a silver-framed photo of a family kneeling together on a beach, all wearing matching white tops and khaki pants. Pictured were Dylan, a beautiful blonde woman, and two kids who looked to be in their pre-teens. Looking at that photo, palm still warm, Jefferson felt an instinctive distrust for the man sitting across from them ignite.

"As I mentioned in our emails, three days ago Henry O'Brien's body was found off the Harborwalk near the Boston Harbor Hotel," Jefferson opened.

Dylan nodded, expression sobering. "A tragedy. My heart goes out to the young man's family."

"Special Agent Pelley and I believe Henry's murder may be tied to a series of deaths in Boston over the last twelve years," Jefferson continued. "We're requesting your assistance to help us navigate the wharves surrounding the Boston Harbor Hotel to reach the dock where Henry's body had been staged. We're interested in approaching the area by sea."

"I can put you in touch with my contact at the Coast Guard," Dylan offered.

"Not a sailor?" Jefferson asked, keeping the question friendly. He found himself studying Dylan closely as he waited for a reply.

Dylan shrugged ruefully.

"You might be surprised to hear this considering where I work," he gestured at the spectacular view of Boston Harbor outside his window. "But I have a somewhat debilitating fear of being on water."

The answer seemed genuine. Then again, so did Dylan's smile in his family portrait. Jefferson couldn't think of anything to say in response. He thought of Finny, so casually offering to take them out on the river himself.

Dylan rose to his feet. "Is there anything else I can do for you two?"

"That's all for now," Jefferson said.

Back in the lobby, Dylan fished in his pocket, retrieving two business cards and handing one to both Caroline and Jefferson.

"Please circle back to share your availability in the coming week and I'll connect you with the Coast Guard." As he spoke, Dylan stared into Jefferson's eyes, his intent gaze offering an additional meaning to the words *Please circle back*. Just as quickly, he turned to Caroline. "If you think of anything else I can do, let me know."

"Thank you," Caroline told him, tucking the card into her purse.

Dylan was smooth, Jefferson had to give him that. Caroline didn't seem to have noticed the tiny signals Dylan had given Jefferson. From what he could tell, Caroline liked Dylan.

"That was helpful," Caroline said, once they were in the elevator.

"Sure," Jefferson agreed.

Her tone went teasing. "A little less dramatic than the last one of these."

"Shove it," Jefferson told her good-naturedly.

He became distracted, though; going quiet as they left City Hall Plaza. His mind raced, thoughts moving in a direction that left him feeling unsettled. Their perp only killed men. Of that, they were fairly confident. Was Mr. Smiley gay? Could this be a case like John Wayne Gacy, a "homosexual homophobe," perhaps punishing the men he found attractive by murdering them? Or was he a closeted married man who occasionally escaped a life he found constraining for the thrill of the kill?

That was the last direction Jefferson wanted this investigation to take. When they arrested Smiley, every detail of the man's life would become public knowledge. Jefferson didn't want to give a platform to another person who hated queer people.

"What's that face?" Caroline's voice jolted Jefferson back to awareness, standing at a crosswalk on Tremont Street.

"Oh, nothing." Jefferson shook his head. He refused to give voice to this theory until he had more reason to accept it as legitimate.

Before anything else, he wanted to do some reading on Dylan Jacobs. The director's role with the DUP included oversight of Boston Harbor, so he had the knowledge and access to have staged many of the murders. Had he flirted with Jefferson as a distraction? Had he made up that fear of water to throw them off his tracks?

"Thinking about tomorrow?" she asked knowingly.

"Huh?" At the same time, Jefferson realized what she meant. Shit, he would see Finny again tomorrow afternoon. "No. I just spaced for a minute."

She didn't look convinced. "Speaking of. . . I have an update for you."

That moment of hesitation made Jefferson go wary. "What's that?"

"This morning I checked to see if Fred had an alibi for the night of Henry's death. He says he was home alone. There are no cameras at his residence to verify."

Jefferson's most immediate and strongest reaction, which he hated himself a little for, was to feel relieved. Relieved that Finny had been alone, because that likely meant some serious boyfriend hadn't followed him from Philadelphia to Boston. How selfish did that make him, if he would rather Finny remain under suspicion than be dating someone?

"And?" he asked. "Because that would be my alibi for that night, too."

"No *and*," she told him, voice going harder, turning into

the tone she used on uncooperative suspects—not fun to be on the receiving end of. "I just want you to remember that until proven otherwise, he's still a person of interest. You need to be alert around him, especially when we're sailing with him."

Jefferson felt suitably chastened. He made a low sound of acknowledgment. No matter what, if they were confined to a small boat together he would be attuned to every little thing Finny did.

During the fifteen minute walk to their next interview, Jefferson made himself seriously consider the idea of Finny as a suspect. They believed that Mr. Smiley had committed his first four murders while Jefferson and Finny studied at MIT. Only one had received enough public attention for Jefferson to have been aware of it at the time. The other three had initially been ruled suicides. Even if Jefferson had the dates of each murder in front of him right now there was no way he'd be able to remember, eight years later, if he'd been with Finny on any of those nights. The odds weren't necessarily in Finny's favor, either. Their senior year Finny had slept somewhere other than their room almost as often as he'd been home.

Jefferson made an honest attempt to compare what he knew of Finny to the profile they'd started building. A couple of Finny's personality traits could fit the mark: the obsessive focus on running, plus the overwhelming need to excel in school, which could both be considered a form of exerting control. Although with the advantage of age and experience, Jefferson thought his Finny—MIT Finny— might have been suffering from an undiagnosed anxiety disorder, whereas it was more likely for a serial killer to have a personality disorder. Mr. Smiley's search for attention—the recent flashy signature—also didn't match with the Finny Jefferson knew, who had never enjoyed being the center of attention.

This exercise made him feel sick, hollow inside. The idea that Finny might have been flying back to Boston for years, not to see his family or Jefferson, but to *kill* people, cut painfully deep.

His voice sounded tight when he finally spoke again. "I know you think that I don't have the balls to arrest a former friend if he turns out to be a murderer, but I guarantee I do."

Caroline gave him a sideways look, searching his face.

"Okay," she said, seeming content to drop it for the moment.

Jefferson couldn't tell if she actually believed him.

Their next interviewee, Reginald Shapiro, lived in the Back Bay neighborhood. Entering the Back Bay was like visiting another country. Beautiful brownstone homes formed neat rows, each with a small, meticulously landscaped garden out front. Cyclists rode through the streets, which were only lightly-trafficked by cars. As they walked, the air felt five degrees cooler than it had by their apartment thanks to the density of trees overhead. Jefferson heard the trill of a cedar waxwing, and then a little later, the insistent chirping of a sparrow.

"This is some Stepford shit," Caroline observed, making Jefferson give a grudging laugh.

They found the address they needed a few blocks down Marlborough Street, a townhome with huge bay windows that looked into an open kitchen. A rich shade of red adorned the front door and the shutters on the second and third floors matched. The window boxes were in full bloom despite the late arrival of spring this year. To get to the entrance, they had to climb a flight of steps lined on either side by a black iron railing.

As they got closer, it became clear that the red door led to a small annex, with several letters and packages stacked along the wall. Inside that, they found a call box containing three buzzers and a camera. The name Shapiro was written next to the third buzzer, which Caroline pushed. After a short pause, an audible *click* signaled that the inner door had been unlocked.

They stepped into the foyer of what could have been a small museum, with marble floors and the kind of silence so loud that it immediately became noticeable. A twelve-foot gilt mirror hung above a walnut entry table holding a vase of fresh cut flowers. A large painting on the wall showed the Longfellow Bridge with the Charles River and Boston city skyline behind it. To their right, Jefferson saw Unit #1. In front of them, a carpeted staircase curved upstairs. It was hard to believe anyone actually lived here.

"Should we move here?" Jefferson joked in a low voice.

"I don't think they'd let me in," Caroline whispered back.

More art hung on the second and third floors, all scenes of historic Charles River bridges, presumably chosen to emphasize the building's prime location two streets over from the water. An older man wearing an oversized hunter green cable knit sweater and corduroy pants opened Reginald's door. Streaks of white peppered his hair. He had sharp cheekbones that made his face look almost gaunt.

"Come in," the man said. "You must be Agents Pelley and Haines."

The doorway was set lower than Jefferson was expecting. Both he and Caroline had to duck to step inside.

"Shoes off, please," Reginald requested— a first for Jefferson in an interview.

The sense of being inside a museum further intensified as Reginald led them to a sitting room containing a fireplace and floor-to-ceiling built-in shelves housing books and photos. Honest-to-god sculptures were displayed on the largest shelf, framing an elaborate two-foot-tall floral display at the center that included what looked like real pheasant feathers, rising tall and thin between the blossoms. Art of all styles, from landscape to contemporary, brightened the room. A five-foot by four-foot plane of blue paint, gradually darkening in hue decorated the wall next to what appeared to be a dining room. Jefferson was certain he'd seen something like it before on a trip to the Smithsonian Museums with his mom several years ago.

The room was warmer than Jefferson preferred. The heat seemed to be on, even though today's seventy-degree temperature invited keeping the windows open. Reginald gestured for them to take a seat on a pristine, all-white sofa. Jefferson sat carefully. If he had a white sofa in his own apartment, he would stain it within a week.

Reginald eased himself into a nearby chair with a cushion that looked like it might be hand-embroidered.

"I want to thank you both," he said. "It's good to see the attack on me finally being taken seriously. Back Bay is a historic treasure. Every resident here contributes essential property taxes that fund services for the rest of Boston. This *cannot* be an area where people are afraid to leave their homes at night." Reginald coughed. "Excuse me. I've been saying this for ten years to no avail."

A crystal glass rested on a coaster on the small table beside his chair. When Reginald lifted it, his hand shook, and water splashed onto his wrist. Jefferson wondered if age or fear from relived memories caused the tremor.

"How long have you lived here?" Caroline asked, as they both gave him the courtesy of pretending not to have noticed.

"Twenty-five years now," Reginald said. He took another sip then returned the glass to its spot.

That was enough small talk, Jefferson thought. "About the night you were attacked," he said. "Can you tell us as much as you can remember about it?"

Reginald pulled his arms further into that large sweater, as if instinctually trying to get warmer. "It's a tough night for me to talk about."

"We understand that," Jefferson said. "We appreciate you doing so for us."

"As many nights as I can, I like to go for a stroll by the water," Reginald began. "I look at the sunset, admire the gardens. It clears my head."

"And did you walk there that night?" Jefferson asked.

"Yes," Reginald answered. "It was cold, but I'd been inside all day. I wanted to stretch my legs. There was a heron standing in the shallows along the shoreline and I stopped to take a closer look at it."

Great blue herons were occasionally spotted in the area. Jefferson could picture the scene perfectly. The birds averaged about four feet tall, with long legs and an even longer wingspan. The silhouette of one against the sunset would have been an incredible sight to see.

"Then out of nowhere I was shoved from behind, into the river," Reginald continued. "I fell on my hands and knees. Then I was pushed again, toward deeper water. A hand took hold of the back of my neck and started to press my head under. I was lucky a passing jogger shouted and scared him off or I would certainly have died."

"Can you tell us anything about the man who attacked you?" Caroline asked. "Any little detail could be useful."

Reginald stared at his suede slippers, frowning in concentration. "He was wearing a mask so I couldn't see his face. I think he was a few inches taller than me, though. And very strong. As quickly as he'd come, he was gone."

"How long do you think the attack lasted?" Caroline asked.

"I'm not sure," Reginald said. "The park ranger found me after I'd been in the water about five minutes. I had trouble climbing out of the slippery banks and my phone was ruined so I couldn't call anyone."

"And what about the jogger?" Jefferson asked.

"After she screamed, she kept running," Reginald explained, frowning.

One day maybe Jefferson would stop being shocked by how selfish people could be. "She didn't try to help you or return to see if you were all right?"

"No," Reginald said. "I . . .I guess she was afraid."

"Do you remember what she looked like?" Caroline asked.

Reginald shook his head. "It was so dark and I was focused on the man attacking me."

After a few more questions, Caroline and Jefferson gave their thanks and reclaimed their shoes from the front door.

"Catch this man," Reginald urged them before they said goodbye. "The people of this neighborhood deserve to live here in peace."

Halfway through the mile walk to Massachusetts General Hospital, the tracker at Jefferson's wrist buzzed, alerting him that he'd already hit 10,000 steps for the day. MGH was close enough to their apartment to mostly complete their tour of Boston.

"I didn't know it was possible to be that rich," Jefferson observed as they made their way in that direction.

Reginald's penthouse had screamed *upper class.* Every detail casually flaunted a level of wealth Caroline and Jefferson could never dream of obtaining in their lifetimes. When people talked about the modern-day Boston Brahmins—the elites who could trace their ancestry back to the original settlers of Massachusetts; for whom museum galleries and hospital wings got named— they meant men and women like Reginald.

Caroline shook her head, looking as awed as Jefferson felt. Still, she joked, "That isn't what your grandfather's house looked like?"

"Definitely not," Jefferson said. "He lived in coal country. From what my dad told me, he grew up in a two-bedroom shack."

"I didn't know my grandfather on my dad's side, but my Grandpop grew up four miles from here, in an apartment in Roxbury."

The thirty-building Mass General Hospital campus now dominated the West End, a historically working-class, largely immigrant neighborhood in Boston. Unlike Reginald's neighborhood, the air reverberated with cars honking, sirens blaring, and the sound of an argument being held at full volume in a small park nearby. The streets nearby looked dirtier too, with litter strewn on several sidewalks. Yet, there were signs of increasing change—on one side of the complex sat a former jail converted into a five-star hotel. On the other, a perennially busy luxury supermarket.

The EMT who'd been first on scene the night of Reginald's attack was named Priya. She was short, close to Finny's height and had long black hair pulled into a braid that trailed midway down her back. She met them in the lobby of the main entrance off Fruit street and escorted them to an empty doctor's office where they could speak in private.

"Yes, I remember that call well," she said. "It was an unusually cold evening for early November. I was surprised anyone was outside."

Jefferson felt a rush of excitement at the possibility. "The individual who assaulted Reginald Shapiro is possibly connected to a string of murders in Boston," he told her. "Anything you can tell us about that night would be helpful—if you noticed anyone else in the park as you were coming or going. Or if there was anything else interesting you remember observing."

Priya had been listening thoughtfully as they gave their standard introduction, but as Jefferson spoke a kind of awkwardness took over her expression and body language. "I was worried you were hoping for something like that."

"Pardon?" Caroline asked.

"I'm guessing that this didn't make it into the report you saw," Priya said, sounding regretful. "I noted to DPM staff later that week that I didn't believe there was ever an assailant."

"What do you mean?" Jefferson asked.

"The patient was sixty years old. The temperature with wind chill that night felt like eighteen degrees. I believed the patient had become disoriented in the cold," Priya explained.

Caroline's expression turned openly skeptical. She crossed her arms over her chest. "Enough to imagine an assault?"

Priya spoke patiently. "What he thought was a hand could have been a tree branch. A push, the wind. The mind plays incredible tricks."

"What about the jogger who helped him?" Jefferson asked. "Did you see them?"

"There are always runners out on that stretch of path. I must have seen a dozen while I was there," Priya said. "No one was close by when I arrived."

During their interview, Reginald hadn't seemed confused. He'd described his memories of the encounter with crystalline clarity. Then again, Jefferson remembered how passionately Reginald had spoken about the park being dangerous; Finny saying that Reginald called the agency frequently about that same topic. Could the incident have been a stunt designed to spur more investments in public safety along the river?

"Was there any chance he could've been making it up?" Jefferson asked.

"I don't think so," Priya said, eyes widening with surprise at the question. "We held him overnight to treat mild hypothermia. He's lucky he didn't get frostbite."

Jefferson blew out a breath. He felt his hand clench, not in frustration at Priya, but at the loss of a promising lead. "Okay then. We appreciate your candor."

He waited until they made it outside the hospital to curse vehemently, startling a Herring gull off the basket of a metal trashcan. Caroline added a few choice words herself.

"What a waste of time," Jefferson vented. "How did that not end up in the incident report?"

"Maybe everyone was trying to spare an old man's feelings. I don't even think Priya told Reginald her theory."

"I think they didn't want to make someone so rich angry," Jefferson said. He ran his fingers through his hair. "Although you'd think they'd prefer him being mad about being called senile than believing the danger is worse than it is."

"I'm not entirely surprised it was a false lead," Caroline said. "He didn't fit the typical victim age profile."

"True. And it would explain the missing jogger."

They both fell quiet for a minute. Jefferson reflected back on both conversations, trying to determine if they'd learned anything of use.

"Then again, what if Fred intentionally sent us on a wild goose chase?" Caroline asked.

Jefferson felt his heart sink. That sick feeling in his stomach returned. Only one thought gave him any kind of hope. "Finny started the job two months after that. He might not have known."

"But he might have," Caroline said.

Jefferson didn't have a good response to that.

CHAPTER 7

The following afternoon, Caroline parked in a garage on Charles Street, a charming thoroughfare lined with local shops and restaurants. From there they took an elegant pedestrian footbridge across a four-lane highway to the boathouse where Finny had rented a sailboat for their tour of the Charles River.

The weather had finally started to thaw. With a forecast of sixty and sunny, it was the first time they'd had two days in a row over fifty degrees in about six months. The bridge descended gradually, showcasing views of trees—the earliest, most delicate buds of spring starting to emerge from their branches—glittering water, and dozens of sailboats, looking like tiny white triangles in the distance. A laughing gull flew overhead, casting a fleeting shadow across their path.

Sailing for All was a quaint two-story structure painted robin's egg blue. A light breeze stirred the row of American flags which had been hung across the front of the building. An iron fence separated the riverfront park, filled with a steady stream of people even in the middle of the workday, from the docks housing the boats. At the front entrance, a full-sized model boat welcomed visitors.

Finny stood beside it, hands deep in the pockets of his slacks. He wore a slick green jacket with his agency logo embroidered on the breast pocket. As he scanned the pathway in front of the boathouse, Finny kept rocking from foot to foot then reaching into his pocket to check the time. They weren't late; a few minutes early, actually. Apparently

Finny had driven himself to restlessness during whatever time he'd been waiting for them.

"Good afternoon," Caroline called out.

Finny's head whipped up.

"Hello, Agent Pelley," he said. He gave Caroline a smile that looked almost believable, except his dimples didn't show and his eyes didn't light up with it. Jefferson remembered the impact of a real smile from Finny. Those smiles used to stop him in his tracks, rendering everything else going on in the world insignificant.

"Hi, Finny," Jefferson said pointedly.

That got Finny to look properly at him, at least.

"*Fred*," he corrected, sounding exasperated. His eyes flickered from Jefferson's face to his shoes and back up in quick succession. He crossed his arms. "You're going to freeze on the water."

In light of the beautiful day and the fact that they would be spending several hours outside, Jefferson had opted to wear his khaki shorts and an FBI polo. Before they drove back to work, they would run home and change into something more professional for the office, but for now he enjoyed the feel of the sun on his face, arms, and legs. Standing directly in a beam, he felt so content he thought he could lay on a bench and take a nap. Caroline, who sported black leggings, her FBI windbreaker, and a little black backpack, did not receive the same lecture.

"I'll be fine," Jefferson said.

Years ago, they would've gone back and forth on it. When they were friends, Finny would've persisted in fretting at him until Jefferson went back to get another layer. He'd always been like that: *The sun's going to go down in the third quarter and then think of how cold you'll be!* he'd insist as they stepped out of the house to go to a tailgate. Most of the time it had been easier to carry around a sweatshirt than to push back, even if Jefferson did tend to run hot. Besides, he'd always liked the small, pleased smile Finny gave him when he got his way.

As things currently stood between them, Finny bit back some remark, his Adam's apple bobbing. He twisted on his heel, leading the way into the boathouse. Caroline and Jefferson followed Finny past the front desk, through a double set of doors, and down a ramp onto the docks where the water sparkled like mad in the bright sunlight.

"Wait here while I check in," Finny ordered, abandoning them near a row of idle boats, masts stripped bare, waiting on sails so that they could take to the wind.

To their left, the Hancock Tower loomed high over the city, its signature blue windows reflecting puffy white clouds. To their right, trains went rattling by between the salt-and-pepper-shaker towers of the Longfellow Bridge. Jefferson admired those views so he wouldn't watch Finny walk off.

Caroline stepped closer. "You've got to stop pissing him off first thing each time we see him," she hissed, voice low.

"I'm not!" Jefferson protested.

"Call him by his name," she told him. "It's not that hard."

"That *is* his name," Jefferson snapped. He shoved his hands in his pockets.

She'd been teasing him as much as genuinely chastising him, and it wasn't like he didn't yank her chain just as much, but it surprised him how much that hit a nerve. He couldn't shake the uneasy feeling that if he gave in and called Finny "Fred," it would be as if they'd never known each other at all; that doing so would erase all the history they shared.

"I called him that for four years. He didn't have a problem with it then."

She put a hand on his shoulder, gently shaking him before letting the weight of the touch rest there. The gesture was supportive while still conveying her overall point of: *Get over yourself, Haines.*

"Maybe he's grown up," she said.

The sound of Finny's voice interrupted him mid-response, mouth half-open. It startled him enough that he jerked slightly, making Caroline's hand slip. Somehow, despite his near-constant awareness of Finny, he'd failed to notice Finny approaching.

"It'll take me a few minutes to rig the boat," Finny said, brushing past them to climb into the nearest sailboat.

The boat was fifteen-feet long, painted white with a dark gray trim. It had a flat back end with a mounted wooden rod that looked like it might be used for steering, while the front came to a sharp point. An open area in the back half of the boat barely looked large enough to fit three people.

In the time they'd been apart, Finny had acquired a sail that he held tucked under his arm and three life preservers.

"In the meantime, put these on," Finny said. He tossed them each one of the vests.

Caroline shot Jefferson a pointed look while she zipped hers up. Admittedly, Finny did sound pissed, although Jefferson didn't understand how he could be the sole cause. So far today, he'd only said five words to Finny. Considering that two of those words had been deliberately annoying, he could admit he might have played a part.

During their last meeting, Finny had told them he was still learning to sail. Watching him rig the boat, Jefferson thought he hadn't given himself enough credit. Finny's hands moved quickly and with complete assurance: pulling rope, tying complex knots, and unfurling fabric. The quiet confidence to his actions spoke of hours of practice.

Soon after, Finny turned back to them, carefully stepping so one foot rested on the gently rocking boat and the other remained on the dock, using his weight to stabilize the vessel.

"We're ready to go," he said. Performing the rote activity seemed to have soothed his brief spell of irritation. He sounded perfectly congenial until he ruined it a moment later, adding, "Agent Haines, I'll have you step in first."

"Sure," Jefferson said, trying to be agreeable. He took two steps closer, stopping just shy of getting into the boat, in arm's length of Finny, while he waited for further instruction.

"Climb in slowly," Finny said. "It'll rock with your weight so pay attention. Take a spot on that bench there once you're in." He pointed at a ten-inch strip of painted wood hammered in to form a seat on the far side of the boat, a little closer to the front than the back.

Jefferson did as instructed. Finny waited until he'd fully settled to turn his attention back to the docks.

"Sit across from him," Finny told Caroline. Unlike with Jefferson, when she stepped close to the boat he offered his hand to help her climb over the hull.

Caroline accepted the hand and the help—two things she would normally outright refuse from a man—with a smug, sideways look at Jefferson. Jefferson had to remind himself that he couldn't push Caroline into the Charles River, no matter how much she goaded him. He also tried to tell himself that it was stupid to be jealous of the few seconds when their hands had been interlocked. Why would Finny have offered a hand to him? Jefferson had gotten in the damn boat all by himself.

They were both so tall that they had to stagger their legs so Caroline could sit across from him without their knees jamming painfully together. As soon as they'd completed that puzzle, Jefferson lightly knocked his leg against hers, feeling a wave of excitement, and she flashed him a bright smile. Unless he'd forgotten some time he'd gone with his dad as a kid, he was pretty sure this was his first time sailing. He looked forward to seeing what it was like being out on the Charles. Would the views be different by water than from land?

Finny unhooked the rope tethering them to the dock and took the spot at the back of the boat to steer. He looked as comfortable there as he had with the rigging, sitting in a mostly relaxed position, legs splayed, one hand on the tiller and another braced on the bench underneath him. Being outside suited Finny, had always particularly flattered him. The sun gave his hair a luster it sometimes lacked in dim light, glinting off streaks of blonde. The fresh air invigorated him, putting color in his cheeks. Whenever he got to be outdoors he looked young and happy and so very handsome. Maybe that was why he'd gone to work for a Parks Department—to get to spend as much time out of the office as he could get away with.

"Push us off?" Finny asked Caroline.

She twisted and leaned over to do so, powerful arms capably sending them several feet away from the dock. The boat moved slowly, heading out of the little inlet that contained Sailing for All.

"Are we starting at the Boston University Bridge or the Longfellow?" Finny asked while the boat drifted toward the main channel of the river where they'd be less sheltered from the wind and current and thus better able to catch momentum.

"BU," Caroline answered. The question seemed to remind her about her backpack. Carefully shrugging it off one shoulder, she shifted it to the front of her chest. From it, she handed Jefferson a folder of laminated sheets—crime scene photos, maps, and anything else they might need for the day—took a copy for herself, and then secured the bag over her back again.

"The boom is going to swing whenever I go to turn us," Finny said, pointing at the heavy metal pole jutting out from the mast. "Whenever I tell you to get down, I need you to duck. You could be knocked out of the boat or knocked unconscious."

"All right," Jefferson said. He considered Caroline. If they both went forward at the same time, they were going to smash their heads together. "You go to your right, I go to mine?"

"Got it," she said.

They headed for the chain of tiny rocky islands that formed a barrier to shelter the cove and then to where the water opened to the full majesty of the Charles River.

As soon as they crossed that line of islands, the wind hit them, astoundingly cold after the pleasant warmth on shore. Around them the water grew suddenly choppy, tiny waves crested in white spreading in all directions. Goose bumps sprang up along his forearms and Jefferson rubbed at them, startled by the abrupt change in temperature.

"It feels wider out here than I expected it to be from land," Jefferson shouted.

Behind him, he thought he heard Finny chuckle.

"Down," Finny barked abruptly a moment later, an edge to his voice like a gust of wind had caught him by surprise.

Jefferson immediately obeyed. Hardly a second passed before the boom swung in a violent arc, crossing the full span of the boat. It locked in place at a ninety-degree angle on Caroline's side with a loud *crack*. Finny sucked in a sharp breath.

"Sorry," he said. "Good job there, agents."

Caroline sat up, not a hair out of place in the enormous bun she'd made the switch to after their workout yesterday. She looked like she belonged on a boat—like she was ready to open a bottle of champagne and turn up the music, not to investigate a series of murders.

They went silent as they shook off the disconcerting sense of how badly that could've gone. Then, Caroline reminded him exactly why he loved her so much. As they glided upriver, she nudged Jefferson's leg then asked Finny, "How long have you worked for the DPM?"

That was one of the questions Jefferson had been dying to ask. He wanted to know everything about Finny: where else he had been; what he'd been doing; why he'd chosen to come back to Boston; and so much more.

Finny hesitated, then said, "Four months."

It could have been much worse, Jefferson told himself, but it still stung. Four months ran well past the initial period of time where Finny would've been busy getting unpacked and getting used to a new job. Jefferson hadn't looked at Finny while he answered and he was glad he hadn't when his jaw clenched in response and he could better hide it from view.

"What were you doing before that?" Caroline asked.

"I was in school at Penn," Finny said. "I got my Masters in Public Administration."

Caroline hadn't mentioned that when she told him about Finny dropping out of law school. Jefferson thought about all of those nights he'd watched Finny studying politics and history at the kitchen table.

"That's great, Finny!" Jefferson told him.

"Fred," Finny corrected. Bit by bit, that got easier to ignore. It came so frequently it was starting to sound like white noise. Grudgingly, Finny added, "Thanks."

"Honestly just ignore him," Caroline said, waving a hand at Jefferson. "It's what I always do." Finny huffed a surprised laugh. She asked, "What brought you back to Boston?"

"The job," Finny said. "And I have family close by."

The ride might've been more awkward without Caroline around. But like many meetings where Jefferson was off his game or couldn't easily build a connection with a suspect, she stepped up to fill the silence. Jefferson drank in every tidbit of information Finny gave away, hoarding it all for later when he could obsess over it as much as he wanted. Gradually they made their way in the direction of Fenway Park, crossing under the Mass Ave Bridge. The longer they sailed, the more Finny seemed to lower his guard.

"Do you live near here?" she asked.

"In South Boston," Finny said. For the first time, he asked a question in return. "You?"

"We both live in the Avalon Tower," she said. "Close to your office."

"Oh," Finny said. His face did something funny. "Yeah. I know the building."

Jefferson thought about what Caroline had said and how it could be construed and hurried to add, "She lives five floors below me."

"Right." Finny glanced out across the water then back to Jefferson, face neutral. It was so much harder to read him now than it used to be. "We're getting close to the BU Bridge," he said. "Where exactly do you want me to pull in?"

Jefferson raised his map in the air and tilted it, lining everything up to get his bearings: the tiny Boston University boathouse; the boardwalk jutting into the water; the steel and stone BU Bridge, busy with cars, cyclists, and pedestrians; and under it, the rusty railroad bridge covered by graffiti.

"There." He pointed to a cluster of reeds to the left of a row of five boats reserved primarily for BU student use. "Pull in as close as you can."

Everyone at the Bureau had a victim type that hit them harder than most. Kids were a common one. Pregnant women, too. Caroline's was young Black men. And for Jefferson, fathers. After losing his own, even though it was to leukemia, not an attack, fathers always hit too close to home. Like this victim: Randall Allen had been in the prime of his life, age thirty-five with two young children. Those girls would live the rest of their lives without their dad.

"Walk through this with me," Caroline prompted. She'd turned fully to business now. "Randall Allen went out for a run last November around 16:00. It was after Daylight Savings, so it was getting dark early. He said he was going to run laps around Boston Common. When did his wife report him missing?"

"Four hours later," Jefferson answered. "Around 18:00 she started to worry but thought he might've stepped into a coffee shop to warm up. She became certain something was wrong when he missed dinner."

"He lived off Washington Street, right?" Caroline asked.

"Yeah, in the South End." Jefferson said.

"And he was found *here*. Almost three miles away," she said.

"Yeah, well he obviously didn't get lost and fall in the water," Jefferson said, with scorn. That had been the initial verdict on the police report: that disorientation from the cold had led him to wander into the Charles—two and a half miles from where he'd started his run—and drown. "Gilbert and Valdés flagged this case because the autopsy recorded bruising on his shoulders."

"Consistent with being held underwater?" Caroline guessed.

"Likely," Jefferson said. "Although the body was deteriorated from being in the river."

Caroline asked, "How much later was he found?"

"Two days," Jefferson said.

"Time of death?" She asked.

"Only a range," Jefferson said. "Anywhere from 23:00 the day he went missing to 05:00 the next morning."

"Another gap," Caroline observed.

"A weird one," Jefferson said. "The Common would have been packed on a Saturday. Mr. Smiley couldn't have assaulted Randall without witnesses. So, what, he . . . are we thinking the assailant lured Randall somewhere, overpowered him, then dumped him in a car without anyone noticing? Where did Smiley take him then? He couldn't have been dead at that time because forensics showed that Randall drowned in the Charles River."

"How could they know that for sure?" This question came from an unexpected source: Finny.

Jefferson and Caroline both swung to face him in what had to be equal astonishment. A wave of water splashing against the side of the boat sounded especially loud in the silence that came after. For a few seconds Jefferson had honestly forgotten Finny was there. Outside of the occasional case team check-in, they weren't used to anyone else participating in their brainstorming sessions.

"Microbial composition of the water was consistent with the Charles River," Caroline explained.

"But that just means he drowned in water that originated in the Charles River," Finny said. "Not that it's where he was when he drowned."

"What are you saying, *Ashley*?" Jefferson took some pleasure in giving Finny a taste of his own medicine and calling him by his last name. "That someone dragged a bucket of river water to the Common and drowned Randall in it to confuse law enforcement? Then dumped the body back in the river for the same reason? Seems like a lot of extra steps to take to kill a guy."

They'd often debated like this in college, Finny coming up with ideas to puncture one of Jefferson's assumptions and Jefferson shooting down the especially wild ones until they came to a mutual agreement.

"Sorry," Finny said, flushing instead of arguing back. "I'm sure you didn't want me—"

"No," Caroline interrupted. "Go on. It would be helpful to hear your perspective."

"Well," Finny said, clearly thinking out loud. "That does sound ridiculous when you say it like that but also, unless I didn't understand you correctly, the wife said that Randall went to the Common to jog but you don't actually know if he got there, do you? Maybe Randall was never there. So, he wouldn't need to be moved."

"We do have some proof that Randall was on the Common," Jefferson said. "He sent his wife a photo of the Frog Pond."

"Okay then. If I was going to kill someone—which I would never do," Finny added a beat later, seeming to remember who he spoke to. "I would want to go somewhere I was sure no one else would be . . . sorry," Finny repeated. "This is probably really obnoxious. Somewhere quiet."

Jefferson remembered Caroline's idea that Finny could be a suspect and internally cringed, hoping Caroline didn't read into that.

"Not at all," Jefferson said. He felt a flash of pride for Finny, who no matter the subject had always been a quick study, logical and smart. The suggestion was so obvious they hadn't taken enough time yet to walk through it, examine what it might mean.

"I like the way you're thinking so let's keep going," Caroline said. "What kind of place would you consider quiet enough to kill someone?"

"I'm not sure," Finny said. The skin on his nose scrunched as he thought. "Not a house—somewhere else. A warehouse? An abandoned building? Somewhere you could park a car inside, isn't it? But also access by boat? Because that's how you're thinking that Randall got from the Common to here, right? First by car then by boat?"

"Honorary Special Agent Ashley," Jefferson announced, slapping a hand on his own thigh. He turned to Caroline, mind whirling. "My gut tells me it would be close. Within a mile or two? Five at the most. Farther and there would be too much opportunity for something to go wrong."

"I agree," Caroline said. "We should access city records. Get a sense for how many vacant buildings there are in that radius."

"Sounds like we have a lot of work to do," Jefferson said, finding himself grinning. He remembered worrying they might have to wait for Mr. Smiley to strike again to get more information about him. It invigorated him to have another line of inquiry to pursue. "Good thinking. Both of you."

They headed east again, hugging the same shoreline they'd taken upriver. Heading that direction, the breeze hit him right in the face, magnifying the cold. Jefferson attempted to look stoic and not at all like he was freezing his balls off.

Shortly after they passed under the blue-painted beams of the Mass Ave Bridge, they came across a small dock used more by Canada geese than boats, judging by the flock that eyed their approach. Shrubs had grown over the small path that would've led to the bike path from the water. Located on a bend in the river, the secluded spot gave the impression that they could be anywhere in rural Massachusetts, not in the heart of a major urban area.

"Here," Jefferson told Finny. "This is the location for Omar Halim."

Finny guided them until they gently bumped the wood planks. Then he looped a rope through a metal ring on the dock, securing them so they wouldn't drift away.

They didn't have very good photos to reference for this victim.

"He wasn't on the dock, right?" Jefferson asked Caroline.

"Under it," she said. Her mouth went flat. "A student was reading here and noticed an arm floating out from the side."

In his peripheral vision, Jefferson saw Finny shudder. Something about that did, bizarrely, seem more disturbing than finding a full body. The dock might've looked fine when the student first arrived before the current shifted.

They could've sat for hours directly over the victim without realizing it.

Okay, he'd even creeped himself out now.

"Omar worked at Biogen in Kendall Square," Jefferson said, changing the subject. "He was last seen at 18:30 exiting the lobby onto Binney Street. His coworkers thought he was catching the Red Line home to Medford, but his CharlieCard was never swiped at a T station. The boys in blue decided he must've walked over to that bridge—" he cocked his head at the nearby bridge. "—and thrown himself off it."

"Remind me why Gilbert and Valdés flagged his case," Caroline said.

"The bridge choice was strange enough considering that the Longfellow is much closer, three minutes from his office and higher off the water at its apex," Jefferson said. He twisted on the boat's little bench, looking toward downtown Boston, and then waved exaggeratedly. Then he let disgust slip into his voice. "But there was *Rohypnol* in his system at the time of death."

In the process of describing the ineptitude of Boston's finest, Jefferson—supposedly in peak physical shape with perfect hand-eye coordination, Jefferson—lost his balance. Caught half out of the boat, he felt his weight tip as he started to fall backwards toward the river. He swore and tensed, bracing himself for impact with murky, frigid water.

A strong hand caught him by the arm, stopping his descent. A calloused finger brushed bare skin at the spot where his polo shirt sleeve had ridden up. Jefferson righted himself and looked up, breath catching, to meet Finny's equally wide-eyed stare. His heart raced, but it wasn't from the adrenaline of the near miss.

"Careful," Finny chided. He released Jefferson's arm.

Jefferson immediately missed that steadying touch. The spot where Finny's palm had been tingled like the aftermath of a new tattoo.

"So . . . so Omar left work . . . . " He had trouble gathering his thoughts. "Cambridge seems out of character for our perp, doesn't it? Why was he over there?"

"Not necessarily," Caroline answered. "Maybe Smiley had a meeting over there. Maybe Omar decided to go on a walk and crossed paths with him on this side of the river."

"Those are two very different scenarios," Jefferson pointed out.

"Yes," Caroline said. "We'll have to ask Valdés and Gilbert what they think. They interviewed the witnesses, I'm pretty sure."

"Fine," Jefferson said. He wrapped his arms around himself, hunching over. Not falling in the cold water had somehow reminded him of exactly how cold he already felt, suffering in this unceasing wind. Out of the corner of his eye, he thought he saw Finny biting back a grin.

The final victim on their tour, Gregory Jackson, had been found floating close to one of the barges used to store equipment overnight by a construction crew working on the restoration of the Longfellow Bridge. He was one of the only victims Jefferson could conceivably understand being initially written off as a suicide or an accidental drowning. Key word: initially.

"The night of his death, Gregory had been out for drinks at the Sevens," Jefferson said, referring to a popular nearby bar. "The BPD determined that Gregory had been heavily intoxicated, had found his way under the Longfellow Bridge to the water, stumbled in, and drowned."

Their final verdict hadn't been worded quite like that, but Jefferson didn't want to share the exact reasoning in front of Finny. In their reports, the police had also made a fuss about Gregory's history with anxiety. They'd suggested Gregory was in a downturn that night, exacerbated by the alcohol. When seeing his friends hadn't helped, he became so overwhelmed that he intentionally "took a walk into the river" (their words, not Jefferson's). Caroline gave him a curious look at his revised summary but didn't contradict him.

"Makes sense," Finny said. He spoke slowly, seeming to realize Jefferson might have left something important out. "The Sevens is only a five minute walk from here."

"Yeah, all that seems perfectly logical," Jefferson said, on a roll now. "If there hadn't been a small, crude *Smiley Face* painted on the side of that barge. That makes three major clues missed or ignored in three separate cases. Incompetent *idiots.*"

The construction site had been dismantled over a year before, so they wound up sitting in the middle of the water, looking at the ball fields and the Mass Eye and Ear tower, instead of the scene of the crime. After floating peacefully, Jefferson managed to get his temper in check.

"Why so close together?" he mused aloud. "There's been separation between where the victims were taken and where they were found in all the other cases."

"Smiley was in a hurry," Caroline answered.

"Which means?" Jefferson prompted.

"He had to dump the body quickly," she said.

Jefferson gestured for her to keep going. "And/or…."

"His base of operations is close by?" Finny guessed.

"Ding, ding, ding," Jefferson said, snapping his fingers. "Correct! So, if we think this might be the center, the other three bodies might represent the edges of his geographical comfort zone."

Finny smiled at him; a simple smile, full of genuine pleasure at being right. Although it was the tiniest of victories, it gave Jefferson a rush of warmth that persisted long after Finny realized what he'd done and schooled his face.

"That would make sense," Caroline said. "Especially since we know he's going into the Harbor as well."

"Sailing for All," Jefferson guessed.

"No," Finny said in a firm voice. "They close at sunset. All the local boathouses do."

"Then where would he be putting into the water?" Jefferson demanded.

Finny asked, "What kind of boat does he have?"

"A little sailboat," Caroline answered. She shifted, digging in her bag again, this time to pull out a laminated still from the security footage. Studying it, she continued, "Big enough for one person and . . . his cargo. Not as big as this boat."

"Something that small could be stored anywhere," Finny told her. "He could be keeping it where he keeps his . . . prisoners and towing it to the water."

"And where would he launch his boat into the river?" Caroline asked.

"There aren't that many places with vehicle access." Finny raised a hand, ticking off fingers. "There's a dock by Kendall Square . . . ."

Jefferson listened to him approvingly. He liked that Finny was being so helpful and Caroline had noticed. He liked seeing Finny in his element, showing his natural athleticism; a true outdoor enthusiast. Most of all, he appreciated how as the hours had gone by, Finny had stopped being so uncomfortable around him; had stopped giving Jefferson those brittle looks that clearly told him Finny wished he could be anywhere else in the entire world. He'd coaxed a laugh out of Finny, albeit at his own expense. Finny had smiled at him, had touched him, and had looked out for him. Every minute they spent together, Jefferson felt a rising giddiness; an addictive kind of hope.

" . . . one at North Point Park in Cambridge, the ramp for the Duck Boats under the Zakim Bridge, and maybe something else on the Boston side, but not that I can think of. I don't know the Harbor area as well," Finny concluded.

Caroline and Jefferson shared a long look.

"I think we're bringing in the City of Cambridge too," Caroline said.

Their Task Force got larger by the minute, but that would give him plenty of reasons to reach out to Finny's office, so Jefferson didn't mind.

Since they'd gradually worked their way east with each stop, the ride from the Longfellow Bridge back to Sailing for All went disappointingly quickly. Once he'd docked their sailboat, de-rigged it, and stored their equipment, Finny escorted them back through the boathouse. He stopped in the little pedestrian plaza where they'd first met up with him, the row of American flags swaying picturesquely behind him.

Caroline offered her hand to Finny to shake, which he did.

"You've been immensely helpful, Fred Ashley," she said.

"Thank you," Finny said, looking pleased by the compliment. "You know, if you'd like I can look into who oversees building occupancy on state lands. It shouldn't take long and might save you some trouble."

"That would be great," Caroline said.

Finny was clearly about to say his goodbye and leave them. He'd taken a step backwards and raised his arm as if to wave.

"Look," Jefferson said, a little desperately. "I'd really like to talk to you when we're not on the job. Could we meet for coffee sometime this week? It could be somewhere near your office."

Finny looked to the sky as if he were calling on the— non-existent, they both agreed—heavens for support. A clump of his hair flopped to his forehead when he looked down again. He didn't meet Jefferson's eyes.

"I would prefer not to see you outside of a professional capacity," he said.

It so greatly contradicted Jefferson's positive impression of how the day had gone, that he flinched, feeling like his chest was being carved out when Finny twisted on his heels to go. Finny's shoes slapped noisily against the concrete as he walked briskly back toward the footbridge. Jefferson couldn't help staring at him, watching every single step Finny took farther away, until a passing cyclist cut into his line of sight, interrupting the spell he'd fallen under. In the absence of the buoyant optimism that had carried him for so much of the afternoon, he felt numb, frozen by a cold that went much deeper than what he'd experienced on the boat.

CHAPTER 8

Wednesday morning, they were midway through a workout when they got the summons. Jefferson had just increased his bench press by ten pounds. Although the addition had been manageable at first, he had trouble completing his second sequence of reps. The front of his gray T-shirt had gone black with sweat. He watched the veins in his arms bulge with each push upwards.

"Eight," Caroline counted. Her hands hovered under the bar, ready to catch it if he dropped it. "Nine. Ten."

"Thank fuck," Jefferson said. He pulled his shaking arms back over his head, knuckles white against the iron, and she helped him set the bar on its stand. His muscles turned to jelly with the loss of the tension.

"We still need to debrief from yesterday," Caroline told him. "We covered a lot of ground."

Jefferson's body was molding into the bench at his back. He forced himself to concentrate as he caught his breath.

"I want to focus on Finny's idea about Mr. Smiley's base of operations . . . As soon as possible we should develop a list of abandoned buildings along the river."

"What exactly are we looking for at those buildings?" she asked. "Mr. Smiley could only be visiting once or twice a year. It's unlikely he's leaving a trace."

"I don't agree," Jefferson countered. "I think he likes to plan things. It's possible we could find a cache of supplies stored on site."

"Okay so we set a priority list. Have agents search them."

"Not in uniform. Maybe dressed as utility workers? We have to be careful. We can't afford to tip him off."

"Agreed," she said. She smacked the bar with the palm of her hand. "You ready for your last set?"

Jefferson groaned. "No," he said, but he lay back to grip the bar. "I can't do ten reps this time."

"Let's see if we can get you to eight."

Hands just past shoulder-width apart, he eased the bar off the rack and bent his elbows to bring it down to his chest in a controlled motion.

"One," she counted.

As he dropped into his second rep, their phones went off in unison, two very different tunes—one Apple, one Android—clashing with every note. Jefferson cursed, losing his focus at the jarring sound. That couldn't mean anything good, not this early, not if people were looking for both of them. He felt suddenly pinned, his tired arms the only thing keeping hundreds of pounds from crushing his chest.

"I've got it," Caroline said, meaning the bar. He let her take it from him.

While he struggled to sit up, she crossed the room and unzipped the side pocket of her gym bag to find her phone.

"Pelley," she answered. After a beat, she added, "Yes, he's with me."

Her face had already looked grim, but it hardened further at whatever the person on the other end of the line had to say. "Where exactly?" She paused. "Okay," she said. "We'll be there in fifteen." She hung up.

"Another body?" Jefferson asked, gut twisting.

"Yes. Close to Sailing for All."

"*Sailing for All?*" Jefferson repeated, astounded. An icy, prickling feeling had started at the nape of his neck and steadily seeped down his spine.

"Yes," she said. "Feels a lot like we're being sent a message, doesn't it?"

"Or being watched," Jefferson said.

Caroline, the heartbreaker that she was, liked to work out in a sports bra and fitted spandex shorts, usually in bright colors that complemented her dark skin. After they jogged back to their apartment, it took her a couple of minutes longer than Jefferson to dress for the chilly morning. That gave Jefferson time to check his own phone. One of his missed calls—the one Caroline had answered—came from the office. The other number had an area code he didn't recognize. He clicked to listen to that message.

"*Jefferson—*" It only took the sound of his name for him to recognize the caller. His chest clenched with apprehension. Yesterday evening, he would have been thrilled to get a call from Finny, but now, based on the timing, this message couldn't bring good news. "*This is Fi—Fred. I'm at the boathouse. There's a body and I don't—*"

Jefferson hung up without finishing the rest, clicking to call Finny back. The line barely rang before Finny picked up.

"Jefferson?" His voice trembled as he spoke.

"Yeah, it's me," Jefferson told him, hand clenching around his phone. He heard Finny release a breath of relief. "Tell me more about what's going on. Are you safe?"

"I'm where we met yesterday," Finny sounded like he was on edge, barely holding himself together. "The police are already here."

"Good," Jefferson said, relaxing a fraction.

"They keep asking me the same questions, but I've already told them everything I know."

"Tell the officer in charge I instructed you to wait until I arrive," Jefferson said. He did a quick mental calculation. There would be no point in driving to the crime scene. By the time he found a spot on Cambridge Street, if he found a spot at all, he could already be there on foot. Sailing for All was less than a mile away. If he sprinted . . . "I'll be there in five minutes."

He ran, taking the exact same route they had less than twenty-four hours before, also going to meet Finny. The cold morning air burned in his lungs.

Unlike yesterday, when he crossed the highway and began cresting down the footbridge toward the park, a large cluster of people gathered along the water's edge. From a distance, Jefferson recognized the uniforms of all the usual suspects: the State Police, the Boston Police Department, and the FBI agent who'd been on call for the night, Special Agent Levenson. He scanned the crowd until he found Finny.

Standing a little off to the side of the crime scene, Finny had his arm around an older woman who looked to be in her mid-fifties and his head ducked down to speak to her. Fear and misery lined both of their eyes. Even from yards away, Jefferson could see the strain in Finny's body; the tension in his back and the hooked shape to his shoulders. Jefferson was helpless to go anywhere but to him.

"Hi," Jefferson said in an undertone, stepping beside Finny. He stopped as close as he could without touching, trying to provide reassurance with the bulk of his body.

"Hi," Finny said in a frayed voice, glancing at Jefferson's FBI jacket, then the pistol at his side. The terror that had taken over his expression seem to ease slightly in Jefferson's presence. That was gratifying. Still, the pitch black orbs of his pupils crowded out the usually warm shade of his eyes.

"This is Special Agent Jefferson Haines," Finny told the woman next to him.

She appeared to be in her early fifties, Caucasian, not pretty exactly, but glamorous looking, well-dressed with her hair kept in a sleek black bob.

"Phyllis Dreegan," the woman said, looking steadier as she spoke. "I'm the Chair of the Boston Neighborhoods Association."

"Nice to meet you," Jefferson said. "Let's have you take a seat over there." He indicated a nearby bench. The gawking college-aged students occupying it cleared off with a wordless wave of Jefferson's hand.

"Thank you." Phyllis followed him the few feet to the side and slumped onto the bench. "I'm going to have to call my Board anyway. Eileen and Reginald are going to have a *fit* when they hear there was another murder. . . . "

She continued speaking, but it was beyond Jefferson's capacity to listen. Increasingly, his attention had focused entirely on easing Finny's visible anxiety.

"You should sit down too." Jefferson took a fraction of a step closer. "You've had a shock."

Finny blinked, shooting Jefferson a startled, cautious look from under his lashes. He didn't move toward the bench.

"Finny?" Jefferson prompted, craning his neck to hold Finny's gaze. He'd forgotten how much taller he was than Finny. For the majority of their meetings so far, they'd been seated, whether in a boat or at a desk. They definitely hadn't been standing this close.

"I was on a walk with Phyllis, gathering her feedback on where the Boston Neighborhoods Association would like to see improvements in the park—and he was just. . . *lying* down there," Finny explained. His breath hitched.

"Wait a minute, okay?" Jefferson said. He wanted to touch Finny in assurance so badly it physically hurt to keep his arm by his side. "Take a few minutes. You'll have plenty of time to talk later."

"Special Agent Haines," Caroline interrupted, in a stern, serious voice.

Experience had conditioned Jefferson to do anything that voice told him: jump, duck, shoot, run. He straightened immediately, turning to the sound.

Caroline stood behind him, holding two cups of coffee from the café beside their gym. She thrust one at him. "A word?"

"Give me a sec," Jefferson answered. He turned back to Finny, passing the cup to him. "Drink this."

"Thanks, Jefferson," Finny said. He took a tentative sip, grimaced, then braced himself and took a much longer pull. The movements of his throat were hypnotic. As he drank, some of the stiffness in his shoulders drained away.

"I'll be right back," he told Finny, then returned to his partner.

She led him over to a granite memorial out of earshot of the scattered first responders and investigators. There she crossed her arms and leveled him with a hard look.

"I like working with you," she told him. "I don't want another partner. So—"

"Do you really?" he interrupted. "You don't look like it."

Her glare intensified. "So, I need you to stay far away from Fred Ashley right now. Don't talk to him. Don't stare at him. Don't go anywhere near him. Leave any questions to Agent Gilbert and I."

Jefferson found himself bristling. "You can't seriously be thinking of questioning him out here in the middle of the park?"

"No, we're taking him in to the office. You're staying here to work the crime scene."

"That's bullshit." Jefferson argued.

"No, you telling Ashley to tell the cops you said he didn't have to talk to them was bullshit. He discovered the body. What the hell, Haines?"

"He and Phyllis Dreegan found the body together."

"And we're taking them both in," Caroline said. She pointed to the crowd near the water. "Now go check in with S.A. Levenson and remember what your job is."

Somewhat cowed, Jefferson obeyed.

The body of Les McIntyre had been left on the crumbling remains of what used to be a set of giant stairs leading to an old concrete boat landing at the water's edge. Jefferson stood at the railing separating the pathway from the slowly disintegrating concrete blocks, studying the scene. Les had been posed completely out of the water, curled on his side, arms and legs arranged to fit on a single block. One of those cruelly mocking smiley faces dripped paint from the block above him. If not for that face, it might have looked like Les was sleeping.

Jefferson immediately figured out why Mr. Smiley had chosen this particular site. From this vantage point, Jefferson had a clear view of the row of flags outside Sailing for All where they'd rendezvoused with Finny the day before.

Les had been a big man, almost 300-pounds, with a football player's build: thick arms and tree trunks for legs. Walking down the street, he would've cut an imposing figure. Based on their profile, Smiley weighed in significantly smaller than his victim. How had the killer gotten the jump on him?

A couple of the past victims, including Henry O'Brien, had tested positive for Rohypnol during the autopsy. Was that their perp's drug of choice? They'd have a better idea after Les's examination.

Footsteps scraped on the gravel beside him, pulling him from his thoughts. Jefferson glanced sideways to see Special Agent David Valdés approaching. Valdés held one of the longest tenures of all the agents in the Chelsea office. When he'd been assigned to Jefferson's case team, Jefferson had known he could learn a lot from the more senior agent. But so far, he hadn't taken advantage, wanting to avoid Valdés's asshole partner, Gilbert.

"I hoped we'd get him before he got anyone else," Valdés said.

"Me too," Jefferson said. He leaned forward, resting his elbows on the balustrade. He found himself musing aloud about some of what had been bothering him since he crossed the footbridge. "We were here yesterday and somehow he knew. This is meant as a taunt."

"Yes, I think so," Valdés said. "But there may be something defensive about it as well. It could be that he's worried you're getting too close."

That idea hadn't occurred to Jefferson. It made him even more determined to keep pushing hard on this case.

"Would that explain the short interval between the killings? Him getting scared and lashing out?"

"Possibly. Or it could be something else entirely. Stressors at home."

"What do you make of the face?" Jefferson asked, gesturing to the graffiti. The thick black line of that twisted mouth smiled over Les's body. Of all the shit Jefferson had seen in his career, this ranked up there with the creepiest. His skin crawled.

Valdés grimaced. "He's a real twisted S.O.B."

"Yes. Hell." Jefferson exhaled hard, squinting in the sunlight as he organized his thoughts. "It's the exact same design we saw on the seawall in Boston Harbor. He's not using the faces to send messages to us."

"No, it's a distinct signature. He wants us to know these kills were his. And he wants us to understand he's happy about what he's done."

A lot of people out there were capable of murder. It was a sad reality of the world. For someone to make a mockery of death like this, they had to be another level of sadistic entirely.

"So, he wants the attention. To be recognized." Jefferson began to form what they knew into a list as he spoke. "He's organized. He planned this enough to be sure he had the paint, the supplies. And he didn't leave any trace of his tools behind."

"Yes," Valdés agreed, eyes fixed on the body in front of them. "I find it unlikely he's a visionary killer."

"No. Or a thrill seeker," Jefferson said. "The murders are too tidy. There's no weapon. No overt violence."

"Then is he drowning these men to gain a sense of power and control over them, or does he believe he's on a mission?"

Jefferson considered it. "It's hard to say. The method of killing—holding them underwater—feels like a way of asserting dominance. But the victims all seem to fit some kind of type . . . at least to him. If only we could figure out *anything* they had in common."

They stood in contemplation for a few breaths after that, seeing yet another man whose life had been cut short by a psychopath. Staring at jagged streaks of paint, Jefferson knew he should feel sad or angry. Right now, he mostly felt empty. Useless. He wished they had been fast enough to save Les's life. The sight of that giant body, awkwardly curled in the fetal position, kept reminding him how badly he'd failed to do his job. Who else might die if they couldn't wrap this case up soon?

They shared a car back to the office. As they pulled up to the curb, Jefferson's phone buzzed with a text from Caroline: *We released him.*

That meant Finny had an alibi that had held. He didn't respond, knowing he would see her soon enough to learn more.

Immediately after he slid his phone back into his pocket, he looked up to see Finny stepping through the Bureau's glass exit doors onto the street.

"Excuse me," he told Valdés, pushing open the car door. He jogged toward Finny. "Finny!" he called. "Hey, wait up."

In a jerky motion, Finny stopped, rocked back on his heels, and turned to face him. He looked pale and tired. He still held the coffee cup Jefferson had given him. By now it either had to be empty or ice-cold. "Do I have to tell you it's Fred again?" he asked. It didn't sound like his heart was in it.

"Are you okay?" Jefferson asked, ignoring the question. The hollowness he'd been feeling earlier had vanished, replaced in equal parts with concern for Finny and his own nerves, which buzzed so violently he almost shook with the need to do something. He started to lift a hand, thinking of resting it on Finny's arm, and then thought better of it, letting his arm drop to his side. For the first time in eight years they were alone together and he couldn't figure out how he was supposed to act.

Finny's eyes had returned to their normal warm brown, although his focus seemed miles away. His eyes weren't particularly beautiful or noteworthy, but when they filled with affection—the way they always seemed to in college—they were incredibly comforting, like a warm drink on a snowy day, or sinking into the couch after a hard workout. Looking down into Finny's face now, Jefferson felt a familiar tug behind his ribs.

"I know what you saw this morning had to be . . . . " Jefferson hesitated, ruling out "upsetting" before finding another word. "Shocking. If you need to talk about it . . . . "

"I don't," Finny said, overlapping with Jefferson's, "I'm here."

That knocked the wind out of Jefferson. Finny ran a—trembling, Jefferson noticed—hand through his hair, which left the short strands sticking up in every direction.

Then, out of nowhere, Finny spoke again. "What do you want, Jefferson?" he asked, with a panicked edge. He scrubbed that hand a second time, mussing his hair even more wildly. "I spent years thinking I would never have to see you again and now it's like you're everywhere. I can't get away from you!"

Jefferson stiffened, fighting the urge to take a step back. "I wanted to make sure you're okay," he protested. "You just saw a fucking body."

"So what?" Finny demanded, voice wavering. His hands clenched in fists at his sides. "You were the biggest asshole in the world but now you expect me to believe you care how I feel?"

Before this conversation, Jefferson would've said he had a pretty good poker face. You had to be able to control your features to interview suspects, considering the nasty shit they'd sometimes say to you. If they landed a blow and you gave it away, your leverage was shot. Caught off guard now, though, he couldn't brace himself and he recoiled.

"You think I don't care?" he asked. His voice came out ragged with hurt. "Four years of friendship and that's it? One bad day and we're done? You think I stopped giving a crap about you overnight?"

"You slammed a door in my face," Finny said. A mottled pink color started to streak his cheeks. His face shifted as he made up his mind to do something. *"You're exactly as disgusting as all the guys say you are,"* he continued, doing a cruel impression of Jefferson. *"That was our room and you ruined it."*

"Stop it," Jefferson said, breath hitching. That wasn't exactly how he remembered it. Not that he remembered much, considering how drunk he'd been. Mostly he remembered feeling more betrayed than angry, so hurt his eyes stung with it, his throat so clogged he could barely swallow. From the moment he'd opened the door to their shared room to see the pale curve of Finny's ass rocking as he moved over the man beneath him, a fog had come over his brain and he'd lashed out with all the raw emotion he'd felt.

"I can't even look at you," Finny continued, throwing Jefferson's words back in his face. *"I never want to see you again."*

"Stop," Jefferson repeated, voice louder this time. "Please."

Finny listened and went quiet, lifting his arms to wrap them around his own chest. He looked as fragile as a pane of glass, standing in front of Jefferson. One wrong word could shatter any hope of reconciliation. This was a terrible time to finally have this conversation, after everything Finny had been through that morning.

It became suddenly blindingly, glaringly obvious to Jefferson that of course the longer they had gone without speaking over the years, the worse Finny would've built things up in his head. Of course, Finny would've gone over and over every terrible thing Jefferson told him, drilling them into his brain. He would've internalized the words, taken them at complete face value, ignored years of evidence to hyper-focus on the one time Jefferson was an asshole to him—a real asshole, not just kidding around. Finny was built that way. He couldn't help himself. Without Jefferson around to correct him it would've been so easy for Finny to convince himself all of it was true.

In an instant, Jefferson's escalating defensiveness died. He deflated.

"I called you a hundred times," Jefferson said, so full of regret he felt nauseous from it. "Texted you even more. Emailed you. Facebooked you. I tried to say sorry every way I could think of." Now that he'd finally been given this chance, he couldn't make himself stop talking. He had so much to say and he'd waited so long to do so.

"I'm so sorry," he continued. "I was . . . so drunk. That's not an excuse. But I was. I didn't mean any of that shit."

Finny made a low noise in his throat. Maybe it was protest; maybe surprise. Although his eyes stayed locked on the ground, the rigid lines of his body, the barely quivering tension in his muscles told Jefferson he had Finny's full attention as he kept speaking:

"I thought about you every day for years. Still do. I used to beg Dan and John to tell me how you were doing. I don't understand how you could think I don't care about you. I really do. You were my best friend in the entire world."

Before he could say anything worse, Jefferson forced himself to shut up. His script had been a lot more elegant than this in his head. The million times he'd rehearsed it, he'd sounded much less desperate. In reality, the words had kept coming out in a torrent. In their wake, he felt stripped raw, like a layer of skin had come off with the bandage. His too-sharp breaths didn't completely do the job. Each one in burned.

His response noticeably stunned Finny. Those long lashes of his swept briefly over eyes gone wide.

"I blocked you," Finny eventually said, very hesitantly. He stared unseeing at the ground, the gears in his head whirling. "Everywhere I could think of. I didn't see any of that. You should've sent me a letter."

Jefferson should've written a letter. He should've hired a *skywriter*.

"This isn't the Dark Ages," Jefferson said—a purely knee-jerk reaction; an old inside joke from some history class they'd taken together, long ago.

He got the barest hint of a smile for that.

Desperately, Jefferson racked his brain for what he should say next. Whatever he came up with undoubtedly wouldn't be good enough, but he had to try something, *anything*, to make this work.

"The truth is, I said those things because I was jealous," Jefferson told him. "I was jealous because I wanted it to be me. And I was angry because you wanted someone else. I don't think you're disgusting and I don't believe you killed those men."

Finny stood motionless, his face unreadable. Only the rush of the cars passing by on the busy highway broke the stretch of strained quiet.

"I'm sorry that these are the circumstances we had to meet again under, but I'm glad I got to say that," Jefferson continued. "I would do anything for a second chance. If you're ever ready to talk, you have my number."

CHAPTER 9

While Caroline and Gilbert met with Phyllis Dreegan, Jefferson continued working with Valdés. They arranged a meeting with Gabby Laposata, Les McIntyre's long-term girlfriend. She lived in Chelsea, close to the FBI offices, which made it easy to coordinate the last-minute interview.

Chelsea contained one of the largest Hispanic populations in Massachusetts. Gabby lived in a neighborhood to the north of the FBI offices, on a street bordered at one end by a church and at the other by a pizza shop. Her apartment was on the first floor of a two-story boxy house with vinyl siding and small windows. It was dark inside the house, even with the curtains open. In the absence of an overhead light, several spindly lamps were lit, staged in different corners to illuminate as much of the living room as possible.

Gabby had long, dark hair, huge brown eyes, and creases in her cheeks that suggested she smiled a lot when the circumstances were much different from today.

"How long have you known Les?" Jefferson asked, once they were seated at the kitchen table.

"F-four years," Gabby began. She opened her mouth as if to say more but then her expression collapsed as she started crying—ugly crying.

Her breath caught twice and then she started wheezing, taking short breaths that sounded like they hurt.

Although Jefferson froze, struggling to regain control of his questioning, Valdés immediately stood to exit the room. He returned with several paper towels and a glass of water.

He passed those to Gabby with a low murmur, and then took the seat beside her instead of across the table with Jefferson, offering his condolences from a respectful distance. Valdés had three teenagers at home. He likely had a lot more practice than Jefferson with what to do when people cried.

Ten minutes later, Gabby's eyes were bloodshot, the skin puffy around them, and she had an irritated red strip of skin under her nose from the rough material of the cheap paper. Whenever she had to speak, she struggled to get the words out, but she looked determined to push through and share what information she could.

"Take as long as you need," Jefferson told her. "You're being very brave right now, speaking with us."

God knew Jefferson wouldn't have been able to talk to anyone in the days after his dad passed. Even a few years out, he still had a hard time discussing it without getting choked up. His dad had been the one who took him to Steelers games when he was a kid; who taught him to throw a baseball; with whom Jefferson spent the most time, growing up an only child. The loss had only come a couple of years after school, before he met Caroline, and in Finny's absence it had been especially devastating, not having anyone to talk about it with.

"When was the last time you spoke to Les?" Valdés asked once it appeared the tears had mostly died down.

"After work Tuesday, Les went out for drinks with some of his brothers." After a shaky breath, Gabby shifted in her chair, putting one of her hands over the other as if trying to comfort herself. "I was already home, but we were texting back and forth. They were having a good time."

"Are you able to confirm if he had anything to drink?" Valdés asked—an attempt to learn if someone might have had the opportunity to slip something in Les's glass.

"He told me he had a few beers," Gabby said.

Like always with this sensitive question, Jefferson was careful to keep his tone neutral. "Was that more or less than usual?"

"About the same," she said. She laughed wetly. "It was always hard to get him drunk."

Considering Les's size, Jefferson could believe that.

"Where did they meet up?" Jefferson asked.

"The Bushwood Arcade Bar. In the Financial District. Les likes—liked," she corrected with a hitching breath. ". . . the games there." That sent her into another burst of crying, tears pooling at the ends of her eyelashes before forming fat globs that slid down her cheeks.

Valdés gave her some time to let it out before asking, "Do you know what Les planned to do after?"

"Yes," Gabby said. Her mouth started to quiver and she forcibly clamped her lips together until the trembling eased. "H-he was going to come here for the night. I drove to pick him up."

"What time was that?" Valdés asked.

"9:15," she answered. "I double-checked my phone before this meeting. I called him when I got close to let him know he should come outside."

Jefferson had known the gist of this before the interview. They'd checked Les's phone records when deciding who to prioritize speaking with. Gabby had been placed on the short list for a reason. Nevertheless, it was one thing to see something written on paper—*Incoming call, 21:15; Estimated time of disappearance, 21:20*—and something else for the scene to start to play itself in his head in HD, as vivid as if it were streaming on his MacBook at home.

"Tell us every detail of that phone call that you can remember," Jefferson said, sitting up straighter at attention.

Valdés gave him a short look that warned: *Watch your tone.*

Jefferson felt like a little kid again, sent to the corner for time out. He rolled his shoulders, attempting to relax.

"Les stepped outside to wait for me. Instead of walking over to Surface Road, he walked deeper into the Financial District. We thought it would be easier for me to pick him up there. Less traffic," Gabby explained. She dabbed at her eyes with a paper towel. It came away black with mascara. "He had a hard time figuring out the name of the side street he was on. There weren't any street signs close by. Eventually, he had to ask someone for help."

Instantly, every hair on Jefferson's arms stood straight up; an immediate, visceral reaction. You could teach yourself the tricks of the job, the techniques that would get you through the day-to-day, but you couldn't teach yourself gut instinct. That was something you either had from the get-go or never learned at all. It set the exceptional agents apart from the average. Right now, his gut screamed at him that he needed to pay attention to this.

At the last moment, Jefferson remembered to heed Valdés and keep it a question instead of a demand. "Who did he ask?"

She blinked, looking surprised. "I don't know. Someone walking by. Not someone he knew."

"What did they say?" Valdés asked.

"I couldn't hear," Gabby said. "It was a short conversation. The guy helped him and Les gave me the address."

"How did Les sound?" Jefferson pressed. He dropped a hand to the arm of his chair, gripping it tightly. Les had spoken to his murderer, Jefferson was sure of it. This reeked of the kind of thing that sadistic asshole would do—another way to torment his victims: help them, and then kill them. There had to be something they could glean from the knowledge.

"Fine," Gabby said. "Normal. *Happy.* I didn't talk to him long. Once we figured out where he was, I hung up to focus on driving. I was close, we . . . " She closed her eyes and inhaled deeply, looking like she was being crushed by the weight of her grief. "I knew I would see him soon."

"How far away exactly were you then?" Valdés asked, softer this time.

"My GPS said five minutes." She answered.

"Where was Les standing?" Valdés continued.

Gabby had to think about that for a second. "He told me he was on the corner of Wendell Street and Broad."

Jefferson clicked on his pen and jotted the address on his legal pad so he wouldn't forget to pull the camera footage as soon as this meeting was over. He made sure to resume eye contact before his next question.

"Walk us through what happened when you arrived," he requested. "Tell us everything you can remember. No matter how inconsequential a detail might seem, it may be important."

"I pulled up where Les said to meet him. There weren't many people around. The street was a little dark, but it wasn't that bad, so I was surprised when I didn't see him right away. I kept my lights on and tried to call him a few times. When he didn't answer, I thought it was because he was so close by he didn't think he had to pick up." She stopped, swallowing hard. "Then I thought maybe he'd forgotten his wallet in the bar and needed to go back."

"But you never heard from him?" Valdés asked.

"No. Eventually I got out of the car. I walked around calling his name. I went into Bushwood and they said he'd already gone outside." Her voice hitched more and more with every word she forced herself to say. "I was *five minutes* away," she repeated. The tears had resumed in earnest. "How could something possibly have happened to him in that time? He should've come home with me!"

She folded her arms and dropped her head until Jefferson only saw a wave of shiny black curls falling across the table. Her shoulders shook with the force of her sobs. He shifted uncomfortably in his seat, feeling the butt of his Luger dig into lower rib before he adjusted the cant of the holster.

Valdés gestured that they should conclude the interview. They could give Gabby a few days and then try again. Jefferson waved his hand in agreement, letting Valdés take the reins on wrapping up.

As they stepped outside Gabby's house, Jefferson felt frustrated and sad and useless and a dozen other things that added up to a foul mood. She'd been crying so hard she'd barely been able to tell them goodbye. All he could do was hope something she told them unlocked the case. His stomach churned with the guilty knowledge that on some level he'd helped create her misery. By publicly investigating the murders, he'd goaded the killer into action. Les had been killed to make a statement to the FBI. Obviously they were doing the right thing—the murderer belonged behind bars—but Jefferson would rather he be the target of Smiley's ire than some innocent person.

This morning while they were in the park, the skies had been overcast and gray but otherwise clear. Now everything in eyeshot was white. It was snowing. In fucking April. He couldn't help but take it as an omen that things would keep getting worse.

The temperature had dropped at least twenty degrees. Flurries stubbornly clung to the landscape around them, coating tiny lawns and rusted mailboxes. They walked quickly to Valdés's car, heads ducked to keep the snowflakes from blowing into their faces. Once inside, they sat for a minute, waiting for the front windshield to heat. The snow had a dampening effect, muffling the usual sounds of traffic on nearby streets. It was like being drowned, Jefferson thought with a horrible lurch of his stomach.

"I don't understand this one," Jefferson said, interrupting the swish of the wipers. Even as the glass cleared, the rest of the view stayed blotted out. "Les had a hundred-fifty pounds on Mr. Smiley. They spoke, I'd stake my career on it. How the hell could Smiley have looked him in the face and decided 'I feel like tackling this linebacker today'?"

Valdés hummed, thinking. "Either our perp didn't see him as a threat or Les fit some other archetype that made him worth the challenge."

"What type?" Jefferson burst out. "None of these victims have anything in common. Not one fucking thing."

"That we know of," Valdés told him. "Maybe we haven't looked closely enough."

That night, after a hellish, traffic-ridden commute home on slippery streets, Jefferson was fresh out of the shower, still scrubbing at his hair to dry it, when he heard his phone ringing in the living room. He dropped his towel on the counter and strode down the hall to answer, wearing only his boxers. His screen showed a vaguely familiar number, although he didn't have the time to figure out where he recognized it from.

He picked up at what had to be the last possible moment. "Haines."

"Oh," Finny said, sounding surprised. "Um, it's—"

"Finny," Jefferson said, alert in a different way than he'd been before, when he thought he might be getting called into the office. "Hey, sorry. I . . . thought this was a work call."

"No," Finny answered. His voice didn't seem quite right. It was tight, not with anger, but the way Jefferson remembered him always sounding before a big test; as if this call made him anxious. "You said we could talk?"

"Yes. About anything you want."

No immediate response came. He listened to Finny taking several breaths.

Jefferson tried to help him. "What do you—"

Finny cut him off. "I want you to explain what happened before graduation."

Now it was Jefferson's turn to take a deep breath, feeling raw and uncomfortable. He'd wished this conversation could happen nearly every day since that night, but he also struggled to relive one of the worst moments of his life.

He wished he'd had time to put some clothes on. He was acutely aware of his near-nakedness.

"You're the exact same guy you were at school," Finny continued. "The same guy I thought was my best friend—"

Thought. Fuck, that hit him like a shot to the chest.

The more Finny spoke, the more decisive he became. "You're being so nice to me right now and I hate it *so much* because I keep wondering when you're going to turn back into that asshole."

His voice went high toward the end of that speech. He sounded a little . . . hysterical wasn't quite the word; but whatever the emotion, it was understandable considering that his nerves still had to be shot to fragments from the morning's discovery. Every word deepened the ache beneath Jefferson's ribs.

"Okay," Jefferson said. How to explain that one disastrous night? "Give me a minute. I want to say it right."

Finny made a faint noise in acknowledgment. So many memories swirled in Jefferson's head, demanding his attention, making it hard to know where to begin. He glanced around while he arranged his thoughts. His apartment was neat and quiet except for the low hum of the Roomba going over the carpet in the living room behind him.

"When did you come out?" Jefferson eventually asked, although he knew the answer—it had been right after winter break senior year, like Finny had spent his three weeks off making up his mind to do it and then taken the first opportunity he could upon returning to school. "Late January?"

Jefferson had spent those same weeks constantly monitoring himself to make sure he didn't talk about Finny too much while sidestepping his dad's comments about all the 'sorority sweethearts' he must be meeting.

"Yes."

Jefferson walked to the fridge to get a beer. He removed the cap using one of the magnets affixed to the door and rested his shoulder against the cabinets there for a while, feeling sick.

"I was so . . . excited when you did. I'd been hoping maybe you were since . . . I don't know, the first time you smiled at me, probably, drunk off your ass on some shitty beer at fraternity rush."

Finny made another sound, not as muted.

"I wish we weren't having this conversation on the phone," Jefferson said with a nervous laugh. "I can't tell how I'm doing when I can't see your face."

After another prolonged pause, Finny said, "Go on, please."

"I was going to ask you out after finals," Jefferson told him. "I had this whole plan." A ridiculous plan that had only gotten more extravagant with time—dinner at a swanky restaurant with leftover Christmas money and then he'd bring Finny back to their room, which would've been decked to the nines with flowers, candles, the works. He'd constantly revised it. Whenever he needed a distraction, that's what he'd thought about: how he'd sweep Finny off his feet. "Except then things were so bad for you with the rest of the guys in the house . . . "

Today, with changes on campus, some of their other roommates would be looking at expulsion for what they'd done: pissing on Finny's clothes; cutting up his textbooks; putting broken glass in his bed. Back then, it had been dismissed as a mostly harmless outlet for so-called 'boyish energy'. With the weight of a badge behind him, Jefferson wished he could go back and scare the shit out of some of them; keep them from ever bullying someone like that again.

Gradually, Finny started spending less and less time at the house and more at the library, where Jefferson could join him, and sleeping at friends' places, where Jefferson couldn't. When he did come home, he spent all his time with Jefferson, using his presence like a shield.

They'd started pushing the dresser in front of the door when they went to sleep. It'd been a small thing Jefferson could do to help make Finny more comfortable. Nothing else had been any use. Finny had tried meeting with the President of the school and talking to campus security but neither had taken any disciplinary action. Eventually, he and Jefferson had paid out of pocket to put a new lock on the door.

My safe space, Finny had called their room during his increasingly rare good moods.

"Why after finals?" Finny asked. "You could've told me right away. It would've helped, knowing you were in it with me."

"I wasn't sure enough that you felt the same," Jefferson explained. Instead of drinking his beer, he held the bottle to his forehead, letting the shock of cold glass against skin clear his mind. "I didn't want to make you uncomfortable in your own room on top of everything else. So, I decided to wait to ask when you'd be free to tell me 'no' and still have breathing room."

"No," Finny said, and his voice went harder. "I think that was the excuse you told yourself. You were starting to get too much attention from the guys for staying friends with me. I think you didn't want to start anything when word could get back to your dad."

Jefferson's throat clenched painfully. He wrestled with what to say next. "Lay off my dad."

"He's the biggest homophobe I've ever met," Finny said furiously. "You couldn't risk one of the guys calling home to one of your dad's old buddies and mentioning that Haines Jr. might be gay."

"My dad is dead," Jefferson snapped.

"Oh, Jefferson." He could hear Finny working through a response. "I . . . shit. I'm—"

The first time Finny came with him, spring break freshman year, Jefferson's dad told them a story about the "faggot" who got kicked out of their fraternity after he got caught with another guy. Then, the next year, when Jefferson's parents visited campus and took the two of them out to dinner, his dad ripped a pride flag out of the planter next to their patio table. After that, Finny started making excuses to get out of Haines family outings.

If Finny apologized to him, Jefferson was going to smash the bottle in his hand. Or start crying. Or both.

"You're right," Jefferson admitted. He found it so fucking depressing that Finny still knew him so well after all this time and yet hadn't known about his dad—indisputably the biggest thing that happened to him in the years they'd been apart. "I was trying too hard to play both sides—to look straight and be your friend. I didn't want to be in bad standing with the fraternity when my parents came for graduation. I should've supported you more."

"Things would have been so much easier if I'd known you were there with me," Finny said. His voice wavered. "And instead you left me out to dry."

"I know," Jefferson said. He felt ashamed of himself. He swallowed hard. "I'm sorry. I was a coward."

He could tell Finny was making a concerted effort to regain his composure.

"So that night. What happened then?" Finny asked.

Jefferson had to retrace the threads of their conversation.

"I . . . I'd been thinking about asking you out for months: what it might be like; what you'd say. Being together, if I was lucky." He took a swig of beer to get rid of the last of the lump in his throat. "That night we were what? Two weeks away? So close. I had like . . . a countdown going. And then I walked upstairs, looking for you—because I was worried about what might happen to you if you were alone in the house. And I walked in to you . . . . "

Fucking someone else. He didn't think he could manage to say that aloud without sounding like an asshole all over again, so he didn't bother to try.

"I just lost it," Jefferson said. The burn of regret sat on his stomach like an oil slick. "I was jealous and drunk and miserable and I massively overreacted and took it out on you. That was all. I'm so sorry. You don't know how many times I've replayed those things I said to you. I hated myself the next day. I would do anything to take it back."

"*Jefferson*," Finny said, sounding faintly incredulous. "I didn't even know that guy's last name. That was just a big 'fuck you' to the house. I wanted to rub it in their faces, have some fun while I was at it. It had nothing to do with how I felt about you."

"Well I thought it meant my chance was over. Which was stupid and selfish, but once I thought that, I didn't give a fuck about much of anything anymore."

"Including me."

"For those few, seriously fucked up minutes, no," Jefferson said. "I was hurt and I lashed out and I never meant a word of it. I tried for years to tell you how much I didn't mean it."

He'd never gotten the chance to apologize. While Jefferson slept downstairs on a La-Z-Boy in the basement, Finny cleaned out every single thing he kept in their small room, leaving his side immaculate. They didn't have any mutual classes that semester, so they didn't take any final exams together, and Jefferson never found him in any of their usual spots on campus.

Overnight, Finny vanished into thin air.

Originally, the plan had been for them to remain in Boston together after graduation. It was only later, after Jefferson completed his FBI training, returning from Virginia, that he'd learned Finny had turned down the Boston job and gone to Philadelphia instead.

"I never thought of that," Finny told him. "I kept thinking you'd tried to be okay with me being gay until you had to actually see it in person."

"No," Jefferson said, low but fierce. "You were my best friend. I would've done anything for you. It was unconditional. Even if you'd turned me down, started dating that guy, I would've taken a couple days to get the fuck over myself, and then I'd have still been your friend."

Finny sounded miserable as he said, "I wish I'd given you the chance to explain this back then."

What a torturous thought. Things would have been so different. Jefferson would have been so much happier, less lonely, those first few years out of school if Finny had stayed with him in Boston. But what mattered, he reminded himself, was that he'd finally gotten the chance to explain himself now.

"You were my best friend," Jefferson repeated. His voice shook too. "I miss you all the time. I wouldn't ever do something like that to you again. If you could forgive me, I would really like to be in your life again, however you'll have me."

Finny swore softly under his breath.

"You're right," he said. "This is a horrible conversation to be having over the phone."

"I—" Jefferson cut himself off, choked by uncertainty. However much he wanted to see Finny, he felt reluctant to do or say anything that might jeopardize this delicate progress. He started to pace back and forth, walking down the hall to his bedroom and then returning to the living room.

"Can we go to dinner?" Finny asked.

"Whenever you want."

"Are you free tomorrow night?"

Jefferson physically ached, feeling like he was recovering from some lingering flu, but at the same time, he felt lighter than he had in a long time. Optimistic.

"*Yes,*" he said.

⁂

There was no chance of Jefferson getting anything else productive done with the rest of his day, let alone any sleep later. He decided it could just be his night for difficult conversations. Once he'd finished his beer, he took the stairs down to Caroline's apartment. In the wake of his knock, he heard the click of the deadbolt sliding ninety-degrees, but Caroline didn't immediately let him in. She peered at him through the crack, one neatly plucked brow arched.

"I know you're pissed at me, but we need to talk," he said.

She nodded. His perspective opened to a nearly identical hallway to his own, only with an opposite-facing floor plan. They had an equal lack of any framed art or other decorations on the wall. The view facing east toward Boston Harbor—including glittering water, the archipelago of islands, and the white spire of North End church—served as the only design element needed in one of their units. Plus, neither of them had the time outside of work to shop for home décor.

He followed, taking a seat on her L-shaped sofa, a piece so large that they both, despite their respective heights, could lay back against an armrest and fully stretch their legs. That, in addition to her 85" TV, explained why they always watched football at her place.

She remained standing, which made her ensuing dressing down even more effective.

"You've had a blind spot in this case ever since we first went to the DPM. You're distracted. You're ignoring evidence. I spent all day with Gilbert and even *he* had more focus than you."

That was an intentionally low blow. It put Jefferson's hackles up.

"But you cleared Finny?" he asked— the closest he'd get to *I told you he was innocent.*

Her eyes went hard. He immediately recognized his mistake. "No, we didn't. But we did verify his whereabouts for part of the night. Guess what he was doing?"

"I don't want to know," Jefferson interrupted, stomach curling.

She ruthlessly continued, "He went to a gay bar in Fenway the night of the murder. Brought home a man. A *married* man. That sound like the guy you were trying to throw away your career for?"

Almost nothing she could have said would hurt him as much and she knew it. Jefferson had to close his eyes. He clenched his fists, taking several calming breaths. Even as he fought it, he kept remembering flashes of that night eight years ago—the way the muscles in Finny's back had been rippling; the loud groans of the man beneath him.

Only thinking of the conversation he'd just had with Finny helped steady him. Finny hadn't said anything to suggest that he ever returned Jefferson's feelings. If they were going to be friends again, then Jefferson had to get over his jealousy. He'd promised he would: *I wouldn't ever do something like that to you again.*

Equally hard to settle was the idea that Finny had been complicit in an affair. Jefferson vehemently hated cheating. There was never an excuse to break a promise to someone who loved and trusted you. If Finny had known the guy was married and gone home with him anyway, then he'd changed substantially from the guy Jefferson remembered.

"Are we even now?" he asked.

She looked a little guilty. The intentional cruelty of her words aside, she wouldn't usually judge anyone for having recreational sex.

"Are you going to get your head back in the game?"

"Yes," Jefferson said. He directed his anger to a new place. "Mr. Smiley staged that attack to get to us after he saw us with Finny. It seems like he knew Finny was going to be walking in the park this morning. That's too fucking close. I'm not letting Smiley get anywhere near him. I want to know how he found out Finny would be there."

"Maybe Finny told him," Caroline said. "Maybe they're partners. In the urban legend it's a group of killers. Not just one."

"I don't see why we should lend that any credence," Jefferson said. "The signature is too distinct. There's one smiley face—one man taking credit for his actions. And we saw one man in that boat."

"That doesn't rule out that he had someone helping. It would explain how he was able to move someone like Les who was so much larger than him."

"We can keep it as a possibility," Jefferson said tactfully. "In the meantime, I think you may have been half right. Maybe our culprit is someone at the Department of Parks Management. They would've known Finny had the site walk. They'd have the same familiarity with the river."

"Maybe," she agreed. "I have been wondering what happened to the person who had his job before him."

"I'll ask Finny for a staff list," Jefferson said. "I'm . . . " he decided to go for broke. ". . . seeing him tomorrow."

She finally took a seat on the sofa, crossing her legs. "Are you?"

"Yes."

"Do that," she said, breaking their staring contest. "Listen to what he says. Maybe he'll reveal something we don't know. Personally, I don't like this Phyllis Dreegan. She's too involved. Her name keeps coming up."

"We already know it can't be *her*," Jefferson countered, emphasizing the gender.

"If it's a group of people then she might be part of it. Or close to someone who is. Who is she married to? Are there any other staff at this Boston Neighborhoods Association? She could have some kind of relationship with the man we're looking for."

"Okay," Jefferson said. He thought it would be hard to fake how shaken Phyllis had seemed, leaning against Finny for comfort, but he also remembered how quick she'd been to pick up the phone and start making calls. "I can help you do some digging tomorrow." He hesitated.

"What?" she asked.

"The married man Finny went home with. It wasn't Dylan Jacobs, was it?"

Caroline looked at him like he'd gone insane. "No, it wasn't."

"You spoke to him?"

"Gilbert did, but no, that wasn't the name Finny gave us."

Since Caroline already thought he was crazy, Jefferson didn't bother holding back.

"It could have been a fake name," Jefferson said. "Do you think we could alibi Jacobs for the last two murders?"

"On *what grounds*?"

"He gave me a bad feeling. And even if it wasn't him with Finny, he's a closeted adulterer."

"How is that relevant?" Caroline demanded.

"If he hates men because he desires them, that's a potential motive right there," Jefferson stubbornly insisted.

She only shook her head, not bothering to play along.

"Okay then, we should look at him for all the same reasons you suspected Finny: he's the right age and build. He has all the relevant knowledge and access."

"He's an appointee of the *mayor*," Caroline told him. "Old money Boston on his mother's side. Oh, and he doesn't sail because he has a phobia of water. I need you to give me a lot more than that before we look like we're going after him. Deputy Director Strait would have our heads."

While true, that left a sour taste in Jefferson's mouth. He gave a jerky nod of agreement.

"We have plenty to go on for now," Caroline said. "I'll see you at 05:30 tomorrow for the gym?"

Just like that, he'd been dismissed. The gap between them right now felt so much wider than it had the last time they were this out of sync—years ago before she dragged him along to Provincetown with her. Normally they'd turn her huge-ass TV on and lounge around after they wrapped up their work for the night. Jefferson hadn't had dinner yet.

Any other day, he'd ask her if she wanted to order pizzas. He thought she was still waiting for him to apologize for challenging her during this investigation and he couldn't bring himself to voice one. Not after she'd thrown Finny's affair in his face like that.

And that was the problem with their friendship—the work and personal were so closely intertwined that they had become impossible to separate. Some days he wondered if they weren't partnered would they even be friends? Right now, he felt depressed to think the answer was probably no.

"Yes," he agreed, turning to go. "Goodnight, Caroline."

CHAPTER 10

U still up?

What r u wearing?

After a week, the FBI had finally been granted access to the dating app Henry O'Brien had been active on a few months before his death. After spending hours reading through hundreds of messages that all followed roughly the same script, Jefferson didn't feel like he'd learned anything new about their victim. The poor sap messaged a new woman almost every day, but from what Jefferson could tell, he rarely progressed to meeting them in person. Jefferson had never tried online dating himself and he was increasingly convinced he hadn't missed anything by going without.

Going back six months yielded nothing of note, so Jefferson switched tactics. They'd also been given the login information for Henry's social media accounts, which were otherwise locked from public view. He started with Henry's own photos. Like many people these days, Henry seemed to consider himself a semi-professional photographer. Most of his recent pictures were either landscapes, mostly early morning scenes from South Boston beaches, or artistic close-ups—like a lone piece of sea glass resting in the sand or a carving of names in a tree trunk.

It took a fair amount of scrolling through the grid before Jefferson reached any pictures with people in them. Then, one of them stopped him in his tracks. The photo showed Henry and his roommate Peter McDonnell standing on the pedestrian walkway on top of the Mass Ave Bridge. They posed on either side of a quirky piece of graffiti that read: *364.4 smoots + 1 ear.*

Both of them looked like they were holding back laughter as the wind ruffled their hair and rowers passed by on the water beneath the bridge.

Jefferson had an almost identical, albeit much worse quality, photo of him and Finny from sophomore year. For several long seconds he couldn't tear his eyes away from those two grinning boys. He felt the same tug of connection to Peter that had knocked him silent during their initial interview the day that Henry's body had been discovered. People generally understood the impact of losing a family member or significant other. But it could be equally devastating to lose a friend.

He struggled more than usual to detach as he kept going through Henry's photos. He didn't want to see any more shots of Henry looking happy, surrounded by people who would never see him laugh again.

Several dozen photos in, Jefferson reached one of Henry in a Bruins jersey. It predated the night he'd been taken but was almost certainly the same jersey he'd been wearing when he died. In a flash, he remembered something Henry's friend Bo had told him: *There was a girl a section over from us. Henry stood up to wave to her a little into the first period. He'd been on his phone before that, scrolling through Instagram.*

Could Jefferson find that woman? Maybe she'd noticed someone in their section that Peter, Bo, and Julie hadn't? Or maybe there'd been someone with her at the game who'd noticed Henry . . . .

Henry's account only followed about a hundred people. And most people didn't post more than once a month or so on this platform. Back-reading through Henry's feed, Jefferson quickly reached a sequence of black and white photos memorializing Henry. Shortly after he saw it: a panorama of T.D. Garden, the arena a sea of black and gold under bright lights with a pristine, white sheet of ice in the center of it.

Below the picture Henry had commented: *Are u at this game? Me 2!*

A back and forth followed where the two accounts shared their respective seat numbers, realizing how close they were sitting.

I'm standing up. Look 4 me! was Henry's final comment, and the last of his life.

One click later, Jefferson landed on the profile of one Amber Collins. Her profile picture contained a group of women posed together in lime green tank tops, so he couldn't immediately see what she looked like. Most of the photos on her main feed showed groups as well, but after some scrolling, he pieced together that she had curly dark blonde hair, a heart-shaped face, and blue eyes. She was pretty. No wonder Henry had made a point to say hello. Jefferson sent her a message asking for a meeting.

That small victory buoyed him as he entered one of the Bureau's conference rooms for a late-afternoon check-in with their full case team. Caroline, Valdés, and Gilbert were all in the cramped room, in addition to several junior agents Jefferson didn't know well. They primarily assisted with research and surveillance. Until just recently he'd been just like them—on the periphery, waiting for a chance to prove himself by being tapped to lead a major investigation. The sense of triumph he'd felt finding Amber evaporated under the weight of expectation that rested on his shoulders.

Jefferson hesitated in the doorway, looking for a seat. Caroline caught his eye and nodded once, pushing aside the briefcase marking the spot beside her. He felt a wave of relief that objectively he knew was stupid. They were co-leads in this investigation. Professionals. She wouldn't shut him out here. He slid in beside her.

"Cutting it close," she murmured.

"I caught a new lead on Henry O.," he said. "I tracked down the unidentified woman he saw at the Garden the night he died."

Her eyes widened. "Nice, Haines. Who is it?"

"Amber Collins. She's a senior at Boston University." He gave her a tight smile. It looked like everyone they were expecting sat in the room now. "You want to kick us off?"

Caroline opened the meeting with a lightning round where each person in the room spent a minute sharing their major updates since the last group check-in.

Valdés described their interview with Gabby Laposata, and Jefferson added on his recent research into Henry O'Brien. The junior agents spoke to their surveillance of abandoned buildings along Boston Harbor and the Charles River. So far, they hadn't noticed anything more suspicious than teenagers sneaking around after curfew.

Then, Caroline briefed the room on her and Gilbert's interview with Phyllis Dreegan. Since Caroline and Jefferson last spoke, she'd been able to do more digging into Phyllis.

"She's fifty-seven. Married to Wade Dreegan, the founder of a successful venture capital firm, now retired. They own a brownstone in Beacon Hill, a lakeside home in New Hampshire, and a home in Florida."

"Any flags so far on Wade's record?" Valdés asked.

"Not yet," Caroline said. "Although he bikes nearly every day along the Charles River, which I found interesting."

That left Gilbert to cover the meeting with Finny. As he spoke, he absently rubbed at his beer gut, where it strained two buttons on his shirt. Jefferson was struck again by the difference between Gilbert and his partner. Valdés was a serious athlete who had recently completed his first Ironman. When Valdés went home to his family for the day, Gilbert went out with some of the other single agents, usually to one of the breweries or distilleries in Everett. Back when they were partnered, Jefferson had never enjoyed riding along with Gilbert while listening to him bitch about his ex-wives.

Jefferson had to grit his teeth throughout Gilbert's update. Gilbert's words alone didn't piss him off. Right now, Gilbert was mostly on his best behavior, knowing he had an audience. But as Gilbert spoke, he sounded so fucking condescending, like Finny was the dirt beneath his shoes. Jefferson remembered that Gilbert had questioned the man Finny slept with two nights ago. Gilbert now knew Finny's sexuality and had adjusted his opinion of him accordingly. What a homophobic jerk.

Afterwards, they dedicated most of the meeting to try to put together a profile of Mr. Smiley's ideal victim type. Caroline tasked one of the junior agents with taking notes on the white board while they compared Les and Henry across demographic characteristics.

"Relationship status," Caroline prompted.

The dry erase marker squeaked as the agent wrote that and drew a thick black line underneath.

"Henry was single," Jefferson said, thinking of all those messages.

"Les was in a serious relationship," Valdés added.

"Age," Caroline said.

"Henry was 27," Gilbert answered.

"Les was 24," Jefferson said.

Caroline looked down at her outline then said, "Ethnicity."

"Les was Latino American. Henry was Caucasian," Valdés said.

"Family," Caroline cued.

"Neither had any children," Jefferson said. "Henry had a brother and sister."

Gilbert added, "Les was an only child."

"That can't be right," Jefferson told him. "The girlfriend said he was meeting his brothers that night at the Bushwood Arcade Bar." He looked to Valdés. "Didn't you set up interviews for two of the brothers tomorrow?"

Instead, it was Gilbert who responded. "Whoever they are they aren't his brothers by blood. I'm confident of it."

"*Are* yo—" Jefferson began, jaw tight. Midword, he remembered one other common usage of "brother" and broke off. "Les must have been in a fraternity. Omar Halim was too. Was Henry?"

He met Caroline's eye, feeling a burst of excitement as he said it. Only two other markers—skin color and religious beliefs—had connected three or more of the past victims, and those had already been ruled out as relevant. She didn't share his smile.

"He wasn't," she said.

Jefferson blew out a frustrated breath. They kept going from there, discussing jobs, hobbies, neighborhood of residence, and more. There was no clear link between the two most recent victims, let alone between Les and Henry and the remainder of the Smiley Face Killer's presumed victims.

"So, all we have is just what we had before," Jefferson said. "Geography."

"And gender," Caroline added. "There are no female victims."

"And they're all attractive, muscular men. I think we can assume our killer might be homosexual." Gilbert said. "A man who *hunts men* and knows the Charles River. We've interviewed at least one guy who fits that description."

"Says the guy who thinks our victims are attractive," Jefferson snapped. It pissed him off even more to realize he'd had a similar theory when leaving DUP Director Dylan Jacobs's office.

Gilbert gave him a look that said he'd like to make *Jefferson* the next victim.

Caroline quickly adjourned the meeting after that. Jefferson made his escape, only stopping long enough to grab his wallet from his desk drawer before heading straight to his car. He'd agreed to meet Finny at a speakeasy-inspired bar near the State House and would barely have time to change after his drive home.

As the sun set, the temperatures dropped below forty -degrees and the wind picked up with a force so strong it rattled Jefferson's side mirrors. After he parked, he ducked up to his apartment so he could throw on a pair of snug dark jeans, a Henley shirt, and a fleece vest for the walk.

The name *Finny Ashley* flashed on his screen as he stepped out of the elevator into his building's lobby.

"Hey," Jefferson answered.

He halted so close to the automatic entryway doors that his weight triggered them and they slid open with a *whoosh*, hitting him in the face with a blast of frigid air. He braced himself while he waited for Finny to speak. It wasn't like Finny to cancel. Not this late. But things had changed a lot in the years they'd been apart. Finny had a very demanding job, he reminded himself. If Finny had called to say he couldn't make it, the reasons might not even be personal.

"Hey, Jefferson," Finny said. The sound of a gust blowing across the speakers nearly drowned out his words. "I was just at Carrie Nation and it was closed for a private party. I'm headed back your way. Would Ward 8 work?"

A wave of fondness hit Jefferson, humming through him, effervescent. No, Finny hadn't changed at all. Of course Finny—details are everything, compulsive-planner, Finny—had arrived early and scoped out their destination.

An enormous smile split his face. God, he'd missed Finny. He couldn't believe this was actually happening—that after all this time he was finally getting to sit down to dinner with Finny again.

"Sure," Jefferson said. He'd heard of the place but had never been before. It was fancier than the sports bars he and Caroline tended to frequent. "That's closer for me anyway."

"Great, I'm about five minutes away."

"I'll be there a few minutes after you."

"I'll wait outside for you," Finny said. It sounded like he was smiling too. He didn't say goodbye.

"How was your day?" Jefferson asked, starting to walk in that direction.

"Not too bad," Finny said. "A lot of meetings. How about you?"

"I just had one very long one," Jefferson said. "I've never been to Ward 8. How's the food?"

"I'm not sure. A coworker recommended—" Abruptly, Finny's tone changed. "What the hell?"

"What?"

Finny dropped his voice, speaking just above a whisper. "This guy ahead of me is giving me the creeps. I'm going to see if I can cross the street."

"Describe him to me," Jefferson said. "I can—"

He only heard the sound of heavy breathing in response. Then Finny said, "Hey, stop!"

Jefferson demanded, "Are you okay? Finny, what's going on?"

He caught a high-pitched whine. Then, the line went dead.

That horrible noise had left the hairs on his forearms standing up. He immediately tried to call Finny back.

One ring, two rings, three rings . . . the line kept ringing until Finny's voice clicked on. *You have reached Fred Ashley—*

Jefferson hung up. Then, he immediately redialed. He needed Finny to pick up and tell him he was safe.

Click. You have reached—

Jefferson raised his left hand to his hair, tugging at the short strands. His heart had kicked into another gear. He drew on years of training and counted five steady breaths in and out to steady his nerves. Ruthlessly, he made himself put aside his worry for Finny so he could think clearly.

If Finny was as close as he'd said, and he'd come from behind the State House, then the mostly likely route he'd taken would've been via John F. Fitzgerald Road. Jefferson started sprinting in that direction. He made a right on Canal Street, dodging the Celtics fans piling into the row of bars there. Then, shortly after, he turned left onto Valenti Way, which would spit him out where he thought he needed to be. Valenti Way typically remained quieter than most of the surrounding area, with more offices and residential buildings than shops and restaurants.

Jefferson ran so hard that he had a fucking side stitch. With each step, his loafers clapped loudly against the sidewalk. This was so much faster than his training speed at the gym. He didn't think he could replicate this pace under normal circumstances, even if he wanted to.

One block up Valenti Way, Jefferson skidded to a halt. Forty-yards ahead a dark sedan had pulled over to the side and turned its emergency lights on. The driver's side door was open. A man wearing a black ski mask with a grotesque smiley face painted on slid behind the front wheel.

Jefferson stood too far away to stop the man and because he hadn't wanted to be armed on what he thought might be a date, he didn't have his Luger to try to shoot out the tires. He started forward again, only to hear the door slam and see the headlights click on. The car's engine revved.

When the car began to drive forward, Jefferson instinctively threw himself behind one of the big metal trash compacters beside the road, hiding from view. If the killer was brazen enough to act at this time of the evening, near a game day at T.D. Garden, he wouldn't have any qualms about mowing Jefferson down. The sedan quickly reached fifteen, twenty miles an hour, passing Jefferson. In the backseat, Jefferson saw a slumped figure and a flash of light brown hair.

A sharp pain lanced through Jefferson's chest. He tore his eyes from Finny and looked to the license plate, taking note of the numbers there.

"8VX-476," he read out loud.

Then he took off in pursuit, doing his best to keep the car in sight. He was grateful for his dark shirt and jeans, which hopefully helped him blend into the background.

"8VX-476, 8VX-476," Jefferson repeated, until he felt confident he had it in his head.

As he ran, he lifted his phone to his face, even though he knew it slowed him down not to have the use of one arm. At the top of his contact list, he'd saved the Bureau's emergency line, meant to be used after hours or when major issues arose in the field under *00Emergency*. He clumsily dialed.

A woman answered his call midway through the first ring. "This is Agent Raswell. What's your situation?"

"This is Agent Haines," Jefferson said, breathing hard. "I'm in active pursuit of an individual who I believe is the SFK. He's kidnapped a civilian."

In response, he heard the immediate clatter of a keyboard. Deputy Director Strait had made it clear that apprehending the Smiley Face Killer was the number one priority for his staff. Anyone still at the office would be reassigned to help with this and all the agents on call for the night called in to assist.

"What do you need?" Agent Raswell asked.

Another of those biting gusts of wind hit and Jefferson barely felt it, completely focused on the problem at hand. The person behind the wheel drove strangely respectful of the law for a serial killer. They continued at the speed limit and used the turn signal to make the right onto Merrimac Street.

"I need an APB on a black Audi with license plate 8VX-476. It's about to go through the camera at the intersection of Merrimac and Lomasney. I'm following on foot."

She started to say something else, but he didn't have time to talk further. He made the turn himself in time to see the car stopped at the light he'd mentioned, waiting in the right turn lane. He hung up, shoving his phone in his back pocket. After so much running, Jefferson had returned to where he'd started, near the entrance of his apartment.

Off the back streets, the sidewalks were more crowded with people leaving work, heading home, visiting the bars, or funneling into the Garden. After a few seconds of dodging slow-moving clusters of pedestrians on the sidewalks, Jefferson leaped over to the mostly-empty bike lane and put on a burst of speed, trying to make up some of the ground he'd lost while his perp halted at this enormous, snarled intersection.

He heard the squeal of brakes as a cyclist came to a screeching halt behind him.

"Hey dickhead, get out of the bike lane," the guy yelled.

Jefferson became so impatient over being forced to stop that he craned his head to take a look at his new friend instead of ignoring him like he should've. It was some college kid with no helmet on, riding one of those ubiquitous blue-glossed rideshare bikes with stations all over town. Before he could respond—and it sure wouldn't be a nice response—an idea struck. The bike belonged to the *city*.

"FBI," he told the kid in his hardest voice. "I'm in active pursuit of a suspect. Hand over the bike."

The kid went wide-eyed, glanced down at his bike, and immediately began to dismount.

The seat was adjusted for someone several inches shorter than Jefferson, which forced his knees to bend at too-sharp angles. The fabric of his already tight jeans stretched to the point of cutting off circulation.

Almost as soon as he got on the bike, the light changed, and he kicked off, bursting onto Staniford Street, then following the car as it merged onto Nashua Street. Jefferson pushed the slow, heavy bike to its limits, furiously pumping his legs. He didn't have to work hard to stay back out of sight of the car's rearview mirrors. Nashua Street took a long, slow, curving route toward the Charles River, avoiding the highway exit ramps and the commuter rail tracks. Under the highway overpass, it was dark to be on a bike. Jefferson could barely see the road in front of him in the weak beam of the light affixed to his handlebars.

For now, Jefferson kept up with the presumed Mr. Smiley, but the only advantage he had for the moment was the clog of post-work traffic. If the driver continued straight onto Storrow Drive at the end of this loop and picked up speed, Jefferson would lose him.

Instead, the Audi made a right turn onto Charles River Dam Road, heading in the direction of the Museum of Science. One small kink in the enormous mass of tension in Jefferson's shoulders came unknotted.

Within a few minutes, the car passed the front edge of the Museum of Science property, then stopped in the middle of the road, its left signal on. Jefferson frantically scrolled through his mental map of streets in the area. The car neared the Cambridge city line, possibly headed in the direction of Kendall Square. Several blocks back, Jefferson got stuck at a light. He ran it, weaving through traffic. The angry honks of car horns followed him after he cut into their paths.

Once again, the driver surprised him. Ahead, the car made a left turn into a small lot near the turn to the Gilmore Bridge.

When Jefferson reached the Museum's parking garage a few minutes later, he started watching for the break in the sidewalk to his left. There, after a long stretch of concrete, he saw a turn-in to a small parking lot and two dilapidated brick buildings. In the gap between the two buildings, mostly out of sight from the street, Jefferson could barely make out the bumper of a black sedan, blending into the shadows. Finny had guessed that the murderer would use an abandoned building like these as his base of operations. He'd been spot on.

Finny. Please, please let Finny be okay. Jefferson was so close now. He'd gotten here as fast as humanly possible. Sweat drenched the front of his shirt. They knew that the Smiley Face Killer kept his victims alive before killing them, although they weren't sure how long. That meant Finny might still be alive. Jefferson couldn't bring himself to keep moving forward if he considered the alternative.

It'd been one hell of a break that he was on the phone with Finny when Mr. Smiley took him. Otherwise, Jefferson might've waited fifteen to twenty minutes for Finny to arrive before sounding the alarm and he would've missed his window to follow the car. On another night, if they weren't already scheduled to meet, Jefferson might not have known something was wrong until the next morning, by which time he definitely would've been too late.

It was almost too lucky a draw. A traitorous part of Jefferson's brain reminded him about Caroline's theory that Finny might be helping the killer. If true, Jefferson could be heading directly into a trap.

He was willing to take that risk. He couldn't live with himself if something happened to Finny.

At the edge of the parking lot, Jefferson made the sharp turn onto crumbling asphalt. There he ditched the bike, laying it gently on its side. He crept toward the second of the two buildings, hugging the shadows of the Museum garage.

As he drew close, he heard the soft but unmistakable sound of something heavy being dragged along the ground. His heart thundered in his ears.

When the crunch of his shoes on gravel proved to be too loud, he stepped out of them and sped up, ignoring sparks of pain as rocks dug into the soles of his feet. In his peripheral vision, about a half-mile up the road, he saw a silent flash of blue lights. The police weren't using their sirens, attempting not to give away their position, but they were close, trying to force cars to move so they could break through the traffic.

Good. At least if Jefferson got killed, someone would be along soon to hopefully save Finny.

After what felt like an eternity, but could probably be counted in seconds, Jefferson rounded the back of the first building. He ducked behind the black sedan, took several steps, crouched low along the side, then peered over the hood. A heavy-duty bucket that had to be weighted with something . . . sand, maybe, propped open a rusted metal door on the side of the second building. Halfway between the car and the building, a man dragged Finny by both arms, shuffling backwards toward the open doorway.

The sight was like unexpectedly being plunged below the surface of a frozen pond.

Jefferson made a low, involuntary sound of pain that—luckily—got masked by the slide of the body and the low roar of the wind shearing off the water. He felt a spike of agony so intense he had to close his eyes for a moment, seeing flares of red burst at the edges of his vision. It wasn't necessarily a body, he tried to convince himself. Finny could be unconscious or conscious and staying still—so eerily still—in the hopes of avoiding notice. Nonetheless, for a split-second Jefferson couldn't force his muscles into action because he grew so terrified by what he might see if he moved closer.

The man gave a particularly hard yank, drawing closer to the building, and Jefferson saw Finny's head smack against the ground. In an instant, he had straightened to his full height and rounded the car.

"Freeze," he said in a vicious voice. "FBI."

The man did freeze, obviously surprised by Jefferson's arrival.

For the span of one heartbeat, the man stood still, his gaze locked with Jefferson's. Although the man's hair and most of his face were covered by that grotesque painted ski mask, Jefferson saw a flicker of shocked recognition pass through the man's body. The man knew him, Jefferson felt certain, which meant he would assume Jefferson was both armed and not alone.

Jefferson pressed the advantage. He held his hand over his hip, bluffing as if he had his pistol. "It's over. Show yourself."

At that, the man burst into action, dropping Finny's arms so abruptly that Finny's back slammed into the ground.

"Hey!" Jefferson shouted, bursting forward.

The man fled on foot, scrambling toward the Charles River. The lack of streetlights nearby made it difficult to track his progress. The man ducked through an overgrown patch of shrubs and half-slid down the short slope that led to the stone dust path that cut under Edwin H. Land Boulevard to the CambridgeSide Galleria Mall. There he disappeared into the night.

In his wake, Finny lay still on the sidewalk.

Sick with dread, Jefferson took four heavy, unsteady steps and dropped to his knees on the ground beside Finny's torso. With a shaking hand, he reached forward, placed his fingers on the curve of Finny's shoulders, and traced the dip along bone and sinew to his neck. He caught the collar of Finny's shirt. With an adjustment, he found skin and pressed inward.

Thump. Thump. Thump.

The indescribable sense of relief he felt at finding a pulse washed over him, easing tense muscles from head to toe. His eyes stung with unshed tears. For the first time in twenty minutes, he could breathe again.

With both arms Jefferson reached forward, raising Finny's back off the ground so he could pull him against his chest. Finny's head dropped to rest below his collarbone as Jefferson held him close. He turned his face into Finny's hair, inhaling deeply.

Finny was alive. Somehow, despite all odds, Jefferson had averted the unthinkable. His fingers went tight, pulling on the fabric of Finny's shirt.

The crunch of tires entering the lot came unexpectedly loud, a jarring contrast to the short stretch of peace before. The glow of headlights bathed them as one car, then another, pulled in. Jefferson looked up only long enough to confirm that they were, in fact, the BPD and then turned his attention back to Finny. In this new light, he could watch the rise and fall of Finny's chest. His own breathing started to follow that rhythm.

A door slammed. "Police. Identify yourself."

Jefferson had to look up again briefly to acknowledge the request. "Jefferson Haines. FBI. My badge is in my front pocket if you need to see it."

"We're here on report of a kidnapping," the officer said.

"Perp fled on foot," Jefferson told him. He craned his neck toward the tunnel under the bridge. "That way. Caucasian. 5'8 or 5'9. One hundred sixty pounds. Dressed in dark colors."

"How long ago?"

"One minute? Less than three."

The man put a hand behind his back and gestured at the other officers who'd climbed out of cars to join him. He barked an order and his three colleagues moved in unison toward the water, heavy with purpose.

In the wake of all that noise, Finny stirred in his arms.

"Jefferson?" he asked, in a soft, groggy voice. Faint terror still clung to the edges. "I feel so . . . drunk."

"Hey Finny," Jefferson said, trying to keep his voice gentle. He raised a hand to cup the back of Finny's head. One of his fingers brushed against a damp spot, which hopefully wasn't a deep wound. "You're okay. I'm here. I've got you."

Finny gasped, a thick, wet sound, and pressed closer until his nose dug into Jefferson's sternum. With his other palm, Jefferson smoothed the line of Finny's spine, offering wordless comfort.

"He needs medical attention," Jefferson barked, twisting to face the officer who'd come forward to verify his identification.

The beams of the headlights shone as bright as a spotlight on him. He felt exposed. Every ounce of what he was feeling had to be plastered across his face. The urge to cry spiked briefly again, followed by a seeping exhaustion that made him grateful to be sitting on the ground already. Finny didn't speak a second time, falling back into a semi-consciousness not unlike a doze.

Through it all, Jefferson kept holding him, stroking his back in one endless circle until an ambulance came bursting into the lot and an EMT hopped out of the side door to take Finny from him.

CHAPTER 11

The EMT lifted Finny from his arms, moving inside the warmth of the ambulance to tend to him. Jefferson remained at the periphery of the busy parking lot. He fell into a kind of trance, staring fixedly at the light spilling out of the ambulance interior.

"You're shivering, you reckless *idiot*," someone told him.

His view briefly became cut off by the drape of fabric over his eyes. After Jefferson pulled the material down, he found himself holding a heavy winter jacket. He *was* shivering, he realized, shaking violently in the now arctic air.

"Thanks," he said.

It seemed like too much effort to stand up straighter from the wall, so he put the jacket on backwards, sliding his arms inside until his chest pressed flush against what would normally be the back. The weight of the material comforted him even if he didn't exactly feel cold, detached from most physical sensations.

Then, he finally looked to the source of that voice. Caroline stood beside him, wearing a sweatshirt under her FBI windbreaker and a fleece headband across her ears.

"Where are your shoes?" Caroline asked him. The strain in her voice was matched by the deep grooves at the sides of her eyes and mouth.

Confused, Jefferson glanced down at his feet. His once navy socks were now coated in a fine layer of dust.

"I took them off," he said. His voice sounded as rough as the pebbles grinding against his heels whenever he shifted.

"No shit. Where?"

He waved vaguely in the direction of the driveway, now packed with vehicles. There was a good chance his shoes had been run over. She huffed and stalked off in that direction. After a minute or two, she returned, both of his loafers dangling from one hand. She dropped them unceremoniously at his feet and he stepped into them on autopilot.

"Thanks," he repeated.

"Did you lose your mind?" she demanded.

Her jaw clenched into a hard line. Her eyes glinted from all the bright staging lights surrounding them.

"I had to do it," he said

"You should have called me."

His throat clenched. He remembered again that frantic period when he hadn't known if Finny was alive or dead.

"I had to get out the APB."

"You shouldn't have gone in alone," she said. The words shook.

"Finny could've died," Jefferson said, voice flat.

"So could you!"

Jefferson didn't know how to respond. That hadn't mattered to him, not when it was Finny's life on the line. And he would've done the same for her, too, even if she'd be pissed at him for saying so.

They stood in silence, watching the buzz of activity around them. Agents were cleaning out the vehicle, as well as the second of the two buildings, going back and forth to FBI vans carrying strange objects, everything from a small stool to thick metal chains. There would be an endless number of things to sort, catalogue, and analyze tomorrow.

"This night didn't go how you wanted, huh?" she asked after another stretch of quiet, voice almost gentle.

He surprised himself by laughing weakly. That giddy happiness he'd felt early in his call with Finny now felt like it was a lingering memory from a dream. It seemed too pleasant for the way he currently felt, drained and scraped clean, empty of all emotions.

Caroline shuffled closer until her arm bumped his. She dropped her head to his shoulder. Jefferson let his own head fall against hers. Her hair tickled his temple. Slowly, he began to feel steadier. He closed his eyes and let Caroline take some of his weight when he sagged sideways. The hum of busy people surrounding them became as soothing as white noise.

After a few minutes, the press of her elbow into his side told him to open his eyes. He blinked several times and the EMT came into view, a big man, taller than both of them, Black, heavy, but muscular.

"You know the victim?" he called to Jefferson as he came into range.

"Yes," Jefferson managed, as he was hit with a renewed surge of fear.

"He's asking for you," the man said. "Do you have a few minutes?"

Relief flooded Jefferson. "Yeah, I do."

"Follow me."

Jefferson obeyed, sensing Caroline close behind. The man led to the back of the ambulance. This close, it was impossible to look anywhere but toward Finny, who sat upright, staring at a row of cabinets built into the ambulance wall. Jefferson wanted to be talking to him directly, not listening to someone else explain what was going on.

"He's doing well," the EMT told Jefferson. "Some bruising and minor cuts aside. It's lucky you came when you did." The man had a deep voice that made him sound older than he looked. The tenor and his steady confidence were able to briefly capture Jefferson's attention. "Whatever he was drugged with will take a while to work its way out of his system. He'll be groggy when you speak to him."

"It was likely Rohypnol," Jefferson said. "Based on past autopsies, we believe our perp has been dissolving the tablet and then injecting it into his victims."

The EMT looked briefly surprised. "Yes, my suspicion was something similar. There's an injection mark at the back of his neck."

The idea of Finny being stabbed with a needle made Jefferson even more impatient to see him. He took the first step up into the ambulance. "Can I?" he asked, waiving to the interior.

"Yes," the man said. "Watch—"

Jefferson had already climbed the rest of the way inside, ducking to clear the frame. Finny didn't seem to hear him approaching until Jefferson took the final step toward the gurney. Then, his head turned upwards and he blinked several times, squinting into the light.

"Hi, Finny," Jefferson said, voice going soft. He tried for a friendly smile, certain he wasn't pulling it off. His hand clenched while he fought off a wave of anger at the man who'd done this to Finny. "I heard you were looking for me."

Washed out by the harsh lights overhead, Finny looked alarmingly pale. Even though he was sitting up of his own ability, he kept listing sideways. In a few minutes, he'd be lying down again. "Jefferson, you're still here. I was . . . ."

He trailed off, not finishing the sentence.

Jefferson put a hand on the thin mattress, wanting to be near but not confident his touch would be welcome.

"I'm not going anywhere," he promised, keeping his voice soothing. "What can I do?"

Finny's eyes were so wide, pupils enormous. They broadcast his every emotion, so different from the careful filter he'd maintained for all of Jefferson's recent conversations with him to date.

"I'm supposed to sleep this off," he said slowly, like he struggled to get every word out. "They said I'll feel better tomorrow."

"That's great, bud," Jefferson told him. He thought he knew where this was going. Yes, he'd absolutely make sure Finny got home safely.

"I don't . . . ." Finny broke off, looking miserable and very tired. "I can't stand the thought of being alone tonight. Do you think . . . could I stay with you?"

Oh. *Oh.*

"Yes," Jefferson said immediately, barely waiting for Finny to finish the question. Looking at Finny, who could barely keep his eyes open, he didn't think he could bear to leave Finny alone either.

"Are you—"

"Yes. Absolutely." His voice had a ferocious edge to it. On his second attempt, he did a little better at sounding normal. "It'll be just like old times."

A fraction of the tension in Finny's body lightened.

"Thank you, Jefferson," he said sincerely.

Jefferson let his hand close the gap between them, laying it so his fingers just barely brushed Finny's elbow. "Anytime."

Since he'd already done an initial debrief with one of the agents on call for the evening, he would be able to leave to take custody of Finny. In the morning, he'd get to work to make sense of this clusterfuck of an evening. For now, the plan for the preliminary processing of Mr. Smiley's base satisfied him.

"He's coming home with me," Jefferson announced, leaning out of the vehicle.

"Which car is yours?" the EMT asked. He sounded weary, like someone who knew he had a long shift ahead of him, where Finny might be in the most stable condition of any patient he saw. "I'd like to escort him there."

"Uh," Jefferson said. He looked helplessly at his stolen bike, still resting sideways on the ground several yards away, and then pleadingly at Caroline.

"I ran here," she told him. "I was in a hurry to go after some *asshole* who tried to get himself killed tonight."

Jefferson swore loudly. "*Shit.*" He patted at his pockets, looking for his phone.

Caroline stepped forward, putting herself mostly in front of Jefferson. Her voice took on a quality he'd only ever heard when they went to bars and she was on the prowl for her newest man-of-the-month.

"His building is only a few minutes away. You can see it from here." She waved toward the enormous tower they lived in, the tallest building in this portion of the skyline. "Is there any way you could give us a ride?"

The EMT looked uncertain, but also—as Caroline was going for—reluctant to say no to a beautiful woman.

"I could never do something like that for a civilian," he told them.

"We know," Caroline said. "And we appreciate you considering doing so for us—what's your name?"

"Bill," the EMT said.

"Thank you, Bill," Caroline said. She smiled at him.

"I have to confirm with the patient," Bill said, visibly caving.

Bill returned to the interior of the ambulance, where he did another check of Finny's pupils, then his pulse. His voice carried to the outside.

"Mr. Ashley? Are you okay if I take you to stay with these two agents?"

Jefferson couldn't hear Finny's response, but it must have been in the affirmative, as Bill stuck his head out of the back of the ambulance.

"You two can come with me," he told them.

After less than five minutes they pulled into their building's garage. The ambulance stopped at the base of the gently-sloping ramp that led to the elevator bay. While Caroline continued chatting up Bill, comparing notes on the Celtic's season, Jefferson went to stand next to Finny's gurney. Once the vehicle started moving, Finny had fallen into a deep sleep, curled on his side, head on a tiny, piti-ful-looking pillow. Coming to a stop in the garage hadn't roused him.

Looking at him, Jefferson could almost pretend that this long, horrible night had never happened. Finny's breaths came and went evenly. For the first time, Jefferson noticed the clothes he wore: a green and blue checkered, button-down shirt, tailored to emphasize wiry arms and a narrow waist equally, a dark blue cashmere sweater, slim-fit khakis, and brown leather ankle boots. Those weren't work clothes—Finny had put in an effort specifically for him. At that thought, Jefferson felt a strange sensation, like a fan whirling behind his ribs.

Free from the torment of the evening, Finny looked as fragile as he did handsome. The idea of moving him seemed wrong, no matter how much better it would be for him to be lying down in a real bed, behind a closed door where no one could bother him.

Bill had Jefferson sign a form releasing Finny into his care for the evening. Then, he unfolded a collapsible wheelchair from a rack underneath the bed and set it out on the floor of the ambulance beside the gurney. Together, they lifted Finny into it. Bill wheeled Finny down the ambulance ramp, up a parking lot ramp, and into the glass waiting area that housed the elevators.

"I can take it from here," Jefferson said.

"You sure?" Bill asked. "That's a lot of dead weight."

"Yeah, I've got it."

Carefully, so very carefully, aware of how tender Finny's back had to be after being dragged across the ground, Jefferson leaned forward, sliding one arm underneath Finny's knees and the other under Finny's shoulders. Warmth radi-ated through Finny's clothes.

After a deep breath, Jefferson pushed through his legs to stand, focused on keeping the motion steady so he wouldn't jostle the figure in his arms. Finny was much lighter than he expected, eight inches shorter than Jefferson with whipcord muscles instead of bulk. It was easy to carry him like this.

Once his weight settled, Finny's head dropped to Jefferson's chest, the way it had in the parking lot. Jefferson glanced down at him when he felt the pressure. Finny's face had gone slack, free from disturbance. Jefferson had never felt like this before, so protective, like he would do anything—including filling in the entire fucking Charles River with dirt—to prevent Finny getting hurt again. He took two wary steps forward, feeling like a newborn colt, worried his knees might give out at any moment. Caroline noticed the movement and turned her head, giving Jefferson a quick nod of acknowledgment as she reached to press the button.

"Goodnight, Bill," she said.

"Thank you," Jefferson said, eyes on Finny's face.

"Take care of yourselves," Bill told him. "And him."

On the elevator trip up, Jefferson didn't dare speak. Every time he exhaled, Finny's hair swayed. There was a strange kind of parody to the ride—he held Finny like the cliché of a groom with his . . .groom, ready to step over the threshold with him. The flashing light above the door that marked the elevator's progress took forever to click between each floor.

Caroline didn't press the button for her level. When the doors opened on Jefferson's, she followed him to his apartment.

"Keys?" she asked, keeping her voice low.

Finny still stirred, making a muffled sound that froze Jefferson in place. Jefferson hesitated before answering, eyes locked on him, waiting for further signs of consciousness. Only once it became clear Finny wasn't going to wake did he whisper, "Front pocket."

After fishing them out, Caroline let them inside, following behind him to place his keys on the counter. Jefferson continued past her into his bedroom, bending over to gently place Finny on his bed. Still all too aware that Finny had been drugged, with the fucking date-rape drug, of all things, Jefferson didn't linger in the room. The only thing he did to make Finny more comfortable was ease off his boots and drop them on the floor by the nightstand.

As his weight settled, Finny's head tipped to one side against the pillow. His lips parted, letting out slow breaths. His long lashes fanned against the delicate skin under his eyes. For now, he seemed to be at peace. Jefferson had to fight the urge to lean forward and brush his thumb through the short, soft-looking hair at Finny's temple.

Before turning to go, Jefferson took one final look, assuring himself once and for all of Finny's safety; that he'd somehow survived his brush with death incarnate. Then he walked to the doorway, switched off the lights, and swung the door closed to a crack. He headed back to his living room for a debrief with Caroline, who'd been remarkably restrained so far in not asking him to recount the events of the evening. An undoubtedly long, sleepless night stretched out before him.

He spent over an hour sitting in the living room with Caroline, talking in hushed voices so as not to wake Finny, going over every detail of the night for the second time. She took notes in her phone for a future record. His eyes turned gritty and dry and he started to feel a pulse at the bridge of his nose.

"Mr. Smiley *knew* me," he told her. "He recognized me."

"You mean you think we've interviewed him?"

"Right. Or at least spoken with him."

He could see her turning that over, thinking through everyone they'd met with so far in the course of this case.

"There's something else I haven't told you yet," Jefferson said. "You know how in the video footage we've seen his mask was black? Now he's *painted* it."

"With a smiley face?" she guessed.

"Yes. It's fucking creepy."

"He's starting to own the identity more and more," she reflected. "It's not just a calling card he leaves on a wall, but he's also made it an outward manifestation of himself."

"It's *bold*. He was parked just outside the North End looking like that. Anyone could have seen him." Jefferson said.

"I think he's suffered a major stressor. Maybe a death in his main support system has made him increasingly unhinged. To fill that void, he's focused on us—it seems especially on you."

"I understand the two of us," Jefferson said. "But why me in particular? Why *Finny*?"

"If Mr. Smiley sees you and him as having some kind of relationship, he might be jealous of Finny," Caroline said. "This could have been Smiley's attempt to get him out of the way."

Jefferson thought again of Dylan Jacobs—that squeeze of his hand and the lingering eye contact that followed. It was possible Jefferson had given off some signal in that meeting that he hadn't been aware of. Maybe Jacobs felt that they'd made some kind of connection that day. The timing certainly made sense—it had only been two days later that they found Les's body.

"Gilbert could also be right that Mr. Smiley's homosexual," Caroline continued. "You and Finny might be appealing targets because you openly share the sexuality that he's inwardly ashamed of."

"It doesn't fit the pattern. Only one of his past victims before this was gay," Jefferson said, growing frustrated. He still hated this theory; mostly because of the homophobic backlash that would surely follow if that aspect of a killer's identity were made public.

"Yes, but men alone might have satisfied him before. Now that he's shaken, it may be more imperative that he have the perfect victim," she said.

They spoke a while after, continuing to speculate about their suspect. At 00:15, Caroline headed downstairs for the comfort of her bed.

That single thought kept running through Jefferson's head in her absence: what if she was right? What if this whole evening had been staged for his benefit? If so, then if Finny had died tonight, it would have been for the single, horrifying purpose of getting Jefferson's attention. The killer just hadn't expected to have Jefferson's eyes on him so quickly.

He struggled to fall into uninterrupted sleep. Every time his eyes closed, he found himself dreaming that he'd been too late; that in the morning he'd wake to a call with news that they'd discovered Finny's body facedown, draped on some dock off a wharf in Boston Harbor. In total, he caught a couple of restless hours, constantly shifting to get comfortable on his couch, which was a simple leather piece about half the size of Caroline's.

Around 04:30, he realized that he was awake for the day, gave up, and got up to do work. Today, oversight of the processing of evidence from Mr. Smiley's building would revert back to him and Caroline. A wave of initial reports and photos had already hit his inbox. As he sipped a mug of coffee, Jefferson spent some time reading through them and trying to organize his own fractured thoughts.

Now that he'd been pushed back a step, Mr. Smiley should, in theory, need to retreat for a few days. They'd discovered his base of operations and taken it over, which would be a hurdle to him acting again anytime soon. It had been unbelievably daring of the man to go after Finny, knowing Finny held ties to the Bureau office; that he'd been tapped to consult on the case. Not much else he could do would make a bigger splash.

When the last streaks of sunrise pink had disappeared from the sky outside his window, Jefferson gave Valdés a ring, hoping to learn how much further the pursuit had gone after he'd taken Finny home last night.

"The BPD was able to follow footprints along the Lechmere Canal," Valdés told him. "They also found traces of blood on a rock on the slope to the water."

"He was bleeding?" Jefferson asked, surprised.

"Yes," Valdés said. He made a slurping sound, like he'd taken a sip of his own coffee. "The perp appeared to have badly cut his hand in a fall."

"How far did the trail go?"

"We lost him near the entrance to the Galleria."

"No idea where he went after?" Jefferson guessed.

Valdés sounded regretful. "No."

"Hell," Jefferson said. He smacked his fist hard enough on the surface of the table that it stung after.

Noticing a flicker of movement in the corner of his eye, Jefferson turned his head to see Finny emerging from his bedroom, still wearing that blue and green shirt, now crumpled, as well as his dirt-stained khakis. A line from a pillowcase creased one cheek which was more endearing than it ought to be, considering the circumstances. Finny glanced around the apartment, taking in the big windows with far-reaching views, the plush sofa and moderately-sized TV, and the gleaming, immaculate kitchen. All the appliances had been state-of-the-art when the apartment was first constructed only a few years ago and Jefferson didn't use his kitchen enough to put visible wear on it.

"Thanks, David, gotta go," Jefferson said, ending the call.

Finny held himself with enough stiffness that Jefferson worried about how sore Finny must be from his rough treatment at the hands of Mr. Smiley. Jefferson's own legs ached from his frantic sprint and impromptu bike ride. When Finny's gaze landed on Jefferson, his posture relaxed in a series of incremental changes to the line of his shoulders and the arc of his spine. He looked relieved, of all things, to see Jefferson.

"Morning," Jefferson said. Even sleep-deprived and stressed about the work ahead of him, it wasn't hard to smile at Finny.

Finny gave him a strained smile in return. He didn't immediately step out of the bedroom doorway. A ray coming through the window from the rising sun bathed him in soft light, catching on the lighter streaks in his hair. After everything last night, he was alive. It was a miracle that he stood here in Jefferson's apartment.

"Good morning," Finny said, sounding tired. He started to cross his arms, grimaced, and stopped, letting them fall back down.

Jefferson began to rise, knocked his knee on the underside of the table, then dropped his ass back into the chair.

"How are you feeling?" he asked.

"Like I'm covered in dirt," Finny said, making another face. "Or worse. I must have ruined your comforter, I'm sorry."

"I can get another," Jefferson told him, unconcerned. He waved a hand toward his bedroom. "Shower is wide open if you want to use it."

"Yeah, thanks. And could—do you have any clothes I could borrow?"

"Definitely," Jefferson said. He did get up then, less abruptly than on his first attempt, easing back his chair.

On his feet, he became conscious of his own outfit. Since he hadn't wanted to disturb Finny by going into his bedroom, he hadn't changed out of his clothes either, even though they were sweat-soaked and covered in dust. To get comfortable for bed, he'd stripped down to his boxers. Only this morning, when he'd gotten up to work, did he put back on his crumpled white dress shirt and lazily do up a few buttons. Half of his chest showed. Once Finny was taken care of, Jefferson thought he should probably put on pants.

In his hall closet Jefferson dug out his lone spare towel, fortunately clean. He handed that to Finny then continued into his room, rifling through his dresser until he found one of his smallest T-shirts and a pair of ratty sweatpants.

"Here," he said, passing those to Finny, as well. "Shower's in there," he said, gesturing at the bathroom. "There's soap, shampoo, everything you should need. Leave your dirty stuff out. I'll have to take it for evidence."

"Thank you, Jefferson," Finny said. The quiet way Finny said his name did funny things to Jefferson's stomach.

As Finny disappeared into the bathroom, Jefferson went back to the kitchen. He busied himself preparing a new pot of coffee: rinsing the carafe, refilling the water tank, and scooping grounds into a clean filter. The only sugar he had in his apartment was a small stash of Dunkin' Donuts packets stuffed in the back of a drawer. He fished those out and put them on the counter, hearing the muted sound of the shower starting through the wall.

While he waited for Finny to finish, he texted Caroline: *Will likely drive Finny home. Go in without me*

What a gentleman, she sent. Shortly after, she added: *Schedule a time for him to come in for an interview about last night. Doesn't have to be today, but soon*

K, Jefferson sent.

He okay?

Think so, Jefferson sent. He could only hope so.

The shower clicked off. Jefferson turned his phone over, facedown. The coffee had mostly finished brewing so he got out a mug from his cabinet, along with some food in case Finny felt hungry. While he was at it, he threw together his lunch for the day, making two ham and cheese sandwiches and grabbing an apple and a protein bar. He was searching for a plastic grocery bag to carry it all when Finny reappeared in the doorway.

Jefferson's sweats fell so long on him that Finny'd had to roll both the waist and the bottoms of them. The shirt fit a little better, but not by much; a lot of extra fabric hung around the arms and chest. In college, he'd teased Finny endlessly about how much shorter he was, while secretly liking that Finny had to tip his head back to meet Jefferson's eyes. To keep himself from staring, he rose and returned to the coffee pot.

"All set?" he asked, pouring a cup.

Finny nodded, another movement Jefferson only saw in the periphery of his vision.

"You hungry?" Jefferson asked. He brought over the mug and several of the sugar packets, placing them at a seat at the table in the hopes that Finny might come closer so Jefferson could get a better read on how he was feeling.

"No," Finny said, making a face. "I feel nauseous."

"What about just toast?"

"Maybe toast," Finny agreed uncertainly.

"Can do," Jefferson said. He grabbed two pieces of bread before Finny changed his mind.

Moving like a skittish animal, Finny finally left the sanctuary of the doorframe and took a seat to claim his coffee, fingers curling around the ceramic handle. Absently, he took a sip, eyes following Jefferson around the kitchen as he moved back and forth from the toaster. A second later, Finny spit the liquid back, looking at his mug like it had betrayed him. Jefferson hid a smile while Finny dumped all three of the nearby sugar packets in his drink. There was a quiet lull while Finny slowly downed the caffeine, some of the color returning to his face, and Jefferson got out a plate, knife, and butter.

When he finished prepping the toast, Jefferson carried it over and slid it across the wood to Finny, who eyed it with a queasy expression, making no effort to take a bite.

"You might feel better with something in your stomach," Jefferson reminded him. Then he inwardly grimaced. He sounded like his *mom*.

Finny only stared at him, his brown eyes swirling.

"You saved my life last night," he said, with a tremor to his voice. He glanced around the living room wide-eyed and disbelieving, as if assuring himself of his security.

Jefferson wanted Finny to relax, not to scare him further, but he also didn't want to lie to him. "Likely, yes."

"How did you find me?"

"I followed the car you were taken in," Jefferson said. "Good thing we were on the phone together, huh?"

He tried to catch Finny's eyes; to share a smile, get him to stop looking quite so terrified. Finny's gaze looked a million miles away, head tilted down, so Jefferson only saw the curl of his eyelashes. Finny's mouth twisted with something Jefferson had to study for a moment before he could place it—Finny was thinking hard.

"I don't remember most of the night," Finny said slowly.

"That's okay," Jefferson said when Finny didn't continue. "That's normal. You were drugged."

Finny's frown deepened. He thought further, nose crinkling with the familiar pattern of lines that Jefferson always wanted to trace with his finger.

"Was anyone with you?"

Jefferson hedged, "Backup was on the way."

"You came *alone*?" Finny asked. That heartfelt look of concern was a million times more effective than Caroline's dressing down had been, even if both of them might've been coming from the same place.

"The police were right behind me," Jefferson assured him.

The troubled look on Finny's face didn't ease. The way Finny stared at him, barely blinking, made it hard for Jefferson to think.

"Did you catch him?" Finny asked, glancing back at the table.

"No," Jefferson said regretfully. "He's . . . he got away. We're looking for him now."

The news obviously alarmed Finny. He swallowed, the newfound color draining from his face.

"We're bound to catch him soon," Jefferson promised. It killed him that he couldn't reach across the table and put his hand on Finny's to offer some kind of wordless comfort. "We know where he was working. We've got his car. And he's hurt. He doesn't stand a chance."

"Okay," Finny said, after a long pause. "Why did he take me?"

"To challenge the authority of the FBI. Or . . . maybe to get my attention," Jefferson admitted. "Could be both."

"Wouldn't it have been easier for him to kill me right away?"

"I think he likes for his victims to be alive when he drowns them," Jefferson explained. "Which is lucky, because it gave me time to get to you."

"Why *drowning* in particular?" Finny asked. "That's not a common way to murder someone, is it?"

Despite the gruesome topic, Finny had a naturally inquisitive mind. Jefferson got the sense that Finny had even more questions he wanted to ask to help him make sense of the night before.

"Dumping bodies in water happens often enough," Jefferson said. "Murder by drowning . . . less so. If he's religious, he could see it as a way of cleansing his victims. A lot of cultures around the world think you can be reborn from water as a new person. Or, and this is very different, the killer could feel overwhelmed by the world around him. The kills could be something that makes him feel like he's in control again.

"There's something very intimate about killing someone that way," he continued. "It's similar to strangling, but more peaceful. There's no weapon in the way between the killer and his victim. Just his hands on their shoulders, pushing them under and holding them there."

For a minute there, he'd forgotten where he was and had gone off like he spoke in the midst of a briefing. He only realized he'd gotten carried away when Finny shuddered.

"Sorry," Jefferson said quickly. He dropped his hands, from where he'd been demonstrating the technique in mid-air.

"I asked," Finny said. He started fiddling with the toast in front of him, tearing it into tiny pieces. His breathing had accelerated to match the harried pace of his fingers.

Jefferson watched him with a thickness like a cotton pad at the back of his mouth, hating the lingering distance between them more than ever before.

CHAPTER 12

While Finny picked at his breakfast, Jefferson took a quick shower, appreciating how good it felt to finally wash the dried sweat off his skin. The pounding hot water helped loosen tight muscles and woke him up in a way the coffee hadn't. Afterwards, seeing Finny alert and seemingly in good health, Jefferson knew it was time to head into the office.

When he presented Finny with Caroline's question about scheduling an interview, Finny chose to come in with Jefferson instead of being driven home.

"Let's get it over with," Finny said, shrugging.

As they sped along Route 1, Finny seemed to relax, letting go of at least some of his fear from the night before. He folded one leg so his heel pressed against his thigh, his right knee to the side door of Jefferson's Nissan.

Jefferson broke the quiet, asking, "Where do you live?"

"Southie," Finny said. "Between Andrew and Broadway."

That was far from Finny's office, on the complete opposite side of Boston Harbor from Jefferson's apartment. It was actually pretty close to where Henry O'Brien had lived. Some of those photos Jefferson had been scrolling through on Henry's social media accounts must have been from near Finny's neighborhood.

"What's that commute like?" Jefferson asked.

"Not too bad. When there's bad weather I can transfer Red Line to Green. Otherwise, I walk."

"That must be five miles," Jefferson said. He didn't do much walking in his day-to-day life.

Finny shrugged again. "Under three. It helps me clear my head. A lot of days I combine it with my run."

"Of course you do," Jefferson said, grinning. "Do you have any roommates?"

"It's just me," Finny said. He hesitated. "And I have two cats."

"You have cats?" Jefferson echoed, charmed to learn that fact. He didn't know why it surprised him. Finny'd had one growing up, he remembered. Fall break sophomore year, he'd gone home with Finny and it had been there, alternating between ignoring Finny for hours and sprawling possessively across his lap whenever they put a movie on. "What are their names?"

"Oreo—he's black and white, obviously—and The General." Finny said both names like he knew how ridiculous they were but liked them anyway. "Or Gen."

Jefferson didn't have to think on it long. He grinned and quoted, "'Take a shower and shine your shoes. You got no time to lose. You are young men, you must be living.'"

Their mutual favorite band back then had been an obscure group called Dispatch and they'd listened to one song in particular—The General— a million times over. Every pregame. He still knew it by heart. The opening chords started playing at full volume in his head as he thought about it. The chorus would be stuck in his head for the rest of the day.

"Yes!" Finny said. They shared a look that told Jefferson he remembered similar nights sitting on the edges of their beds, four feet apart, sipping Natty Light from Solo cups while music played from the speakers of Finny's laptop. "She's a Maine Coon so she's very large. She likes to lord over me from high up and regularly orders me to feed her."

Jefferson laughed. "I look forward to meeting her one of these days."

"I'm sure you will soon," Finny said.

When Jefferson glanced at him, feeling a rush of happiness, a streak of red blotched Finny's throat. Jefferson had to jerk his attention back to the road when he felt the buzz of the rumble strips under his tires.

The miles passed quickly. They reminisced about some of the restaurants they'd loved as undergrads that were no longer in business. Jefferson asked about Finny's time in grad school, his sister, and some of their mutual friends from school he'd lost touch with. Finny asked about his mom and Jefferson's experience living in Boston as a real adult, not a student.

It had always been like that with Finny—they could talk about anything for hours and Jefferson never got bored. With Caroline, it wasn't quite the same. He felt completely comfortable with her when they were together, but they also had their particular things: work, sports, lifting weights, boxing. When he spent time with Finny he found himself discussing everything from childhood memories, to a recent behavioral economics study Finny had read, to their favorite New England breweries.

They were five minutes from the office, going over the Tobin Bridge with its spectacular views in both directions, when Finny said, "Can I ask you something personal?"

That made Jefferson want to laugh. Nothing that Finny could ask him got more personal than their conversation two nights ago.

"Of course," he said.

"Do you consider yourself bisexual?"

"Gay," Jefferson said. "I . . . any women you saw me with in college were for show."

There had been a couple of those—women he slept with to fit in at the frat house, only to wind up throwing up in the bathroom after. Granted, he'd felt that way with men, too, a couple of times—shitty afterwards, like in Provincetown—so he didn't know what, exactly, that made him.

Uptight? Because he'd never found casual sex *fun* the way so many other people seemed to. With strangers, he got too caught up in trying to read them—monitoring every flex of muscle and intake of breath, trying to make sure his partner enjoyed themselves—while at the same time monitoring himself, making sure he didn't say anything stupid or make any weird sounds. Only when he knew someone well could Jefferson relax and really enjoy sex as an experience beyond the basic physical release it provided.

"Are you dating anyone now?" Finny asked.

"No."

"Not Caroline?"

Jefferson couldn't help it—he started laughing. "God, no."

"I thought you were at first. You're very close."

"She's my ride or die," Jefferson said, in the way they always did, sarcastic but with a tiny bit of pride. For the time being, he put aside his worries that that wasn't necessarily still true. "As we would say it. I'll admit we have a very strange relationship."

"I like her," Finny said. The beginning of a smile tinted his voice.

"She's pretty awesome," Jefferson agreed, feeling a pang of loss. How funny to have Finny sitting next to him again, but not feel confident that if he asked Caroline out to the bar after work that she would say yes.

Not long after, Jefferson pulled into the lot of the FBI offices, swiped his badge to get through the gate, then raised his hand in greeting at the guard. He parked in his assigned spot. Turned the car off. He didn't make a move to climb out, leaving his thumb resting on the power button, so Finny, who seemed to be following his lead, didn't either. Jefferson's pulse stuttered.

"What about you? Are you dating anyone?" Jefferson dared ask.

"No," Finny said.

When Jefferson glanced quickly at him, brimming with a wild kind of hope, Finny had his bottom lip between his teeth, tugging at the plump flesh there.

It felt like Jefferson had been waiting his whole life to ask his next question.

"What would you have said, before, if I'd asked you out in college?"

Then it was Finny's turn to laugh, a sound less amused than Jefferson's had been and more dumbfounded.

"I had the biggest thing for you at school," Finny told him. "Like you said—probably from the first moment I saw you. No question—I would've said yes."

While they waited at the security desk in the Bureau lobby to sign Finny in, they stood close together, elbows brushing whenever either of them shifted their weight. A new energy ran between them. For the past week, Jefferson had been aware of Finny, able to pinpoint his exact location in any space, but now that awareness was being reflected back at him. Waves of energy crackled over his skin with each glance Finny sent his way.

Once the person standing in front of them was granted access to the building, Jefferson moved forward to greet the uniformed guard, sensing Finny a half-step behind.

"Hey, Greg. I'm checking in Fi-Fred Ashley for an interview."

"Mornin', Haines," the guard said, lifting his chin in greeting. He reached forward expectantly. "You know the drill. ID."

Jefferson had his badge ready. Finny had to twist to dig through the pockets of those ridiculously loose sweatpants to find his wallet, which somehow hadn't fallen out of the back pocket of his jeans when he got pulled across the parking lot the night before. The motion made the pants slide two inches down his hip, revealing a flat, pale strip of skin below a sharp hipbone. Jefferson swallowed, pointedly looking back to the front desk.

After entering Finny's information into the system and scanning his ID, Greg printed a temporary visitor's badge for him, a white label with Finny's photo, his name, and the date.

"Keep this on until you leave," Greg instructed Finny, handing it over.

Finny nodded, then smoothed the sticker flat against the chest of his borrowed T-shirt.

Any other morning, Jefferson would've shared the elevator to his floor. Instead, he pulled an admittedly dick move and hit the *Door Close* button to make sure the woman he could see walking briskly across the lobby in their direction wouldn't have the chance to step in with them. He had something he'd made up his mind to say and he wanted a few moments of privacy to speak to Finny. The elevator jerked as it began to rise.

"Hey look," Jefferson started. At the sound of his voice, Finny glanced up at him. The way Finny looked at him now was completely different than it had been last week in the Department of Parks Management offices—his expression radiating trust and affection, a throwback to a very different period in Jefferson's life. He never wanted Finny to stop looking at him like this again. "I'm going to work on calling you Fred," Jefferson continued, fighting hard to keep any lingering reluctance from showing on his face. He mostly managed to keep his voice neutral. "I know you hate being called Finny. It'll take me a while to get used to it and I'm sorry if I screw it up, but I'm going to stop."

"Oh," Finny said. He looked down at his feet where he began rolling one ankle, digging the toe of that shoe into the carpeted floor. "If we're together for work, like this morning, I'd appreciate that. Otherwise, actually, I, uh . . . I like it when you call me Finny."

The multiple times Jefferson had been told otherwise made it hard to take Finny's words at face value.

"You don't have to tell me that just to spare my feelings," he said.

Finny flashed Jefferson a quick, lopsided, and wholly disarming smile. "I like it. Before I was only . . . trying to keep some distance between us."

"Making me suffer," Jefferson guessed. The fact that he was able to shoot Finny a wry grin as he said it made clear the extent of the progress they'd made in the last forty-eight hours.

"A little," Finny admitted.

"But you like it? Really?"

"Coming from you, yes. You must be special."

The attempt at sarcasm fell flat. They were too busy grinning at each other, transported somewhere else entirely. They stood so close together that Jefferson could see every fleck of color, from the darker, burnt red streaks, to the warm browns, that all combined to make up the rich sepia shade of Finny's eyes.

There were definitely cameras in the elevator. There were cameras everywhere in this building. Jefferson *worked* here. He reminded himself of all these facts, but the knowledge they had to be under surveillance didn't stop him from wishing he could lean over and press a kiss to the center of Finny's smile.

A pinging sound as the doors slid open helped him hold on to his restraint.

Midmorning on a weekday, the office was at its busiest, nearly every cube occupied. A rush of sound hit them as they stepped out onto the floor, the hum of a dozen separate conversations going interrupted by the shriek of phones ringing on two different desks. The open floor looked much brighter than the elevator. The floor-to-ceiling windows that flanked the outer walls brought in plenty of natural light despite the overcast skies outside. As he escorted Finny to Caroline's desk, Jefferson had to step aside several times to let another agent pass.

"Delivery for you," Jefferson announced, ushering Finny into Caroline's cube.

Caroline spun around in her seat.

"Perfect timing," she said. She was too good at her job. Even as she spoke, addressing Finny, Jefferson could see her eyes moving, observing the changes in their body language respective to each other and their close proximity. "Fred, I'm going to take your statement from last night in a private conference room. We appreciate your willingness to come in and speak with us after everything you went through."

"Whatever it takes to catch this monster," Finny said.

Jefferson had gotten the message loud and clear that he couldn't join in these meetings. After this morning's car ride, he no longer had any grounds to deny his enormous conflict of interest when it came to Finny.

"Return him in one piece," he told Caroline, taking a step back.

"I'll try my best," she said.

"Hey," he remembered, lingering in the gap between the divider. "Did we get a match on the registration for the Audi yet?"

"Yes," she said, even as she started to shake her head. "It was reported stolen from the valet at the Aquitaine Restaurant on Tremont Street about an hour before Fred was taken."

"What about the restaurant cameras?"

"The restaurant didn't have any out front," she answered, frowning in disapproval. "They didn't want to worry the customers."

"Did the valet remember anything?"

"Nope."

"The *fuck*," Jefferson said. At once, he remembered Finny and glanced his way. "Sorry."

"Don't mind me," Finny said.

"I'll see if I can spot anything from the cameras farther up Tremont," Jefferson told Caroline.

Turning to go, Jefferson laid a hand on Finny's upper arm. His fingers rested on the worn fabric of Finny's—*his*—shirt. The base of his palm touched warm, bare skin where the sleeve ended.

"Come find me after," he requested. He gestured at the wall to his left. "I'm just next door."

"I will," Finny said, holding his gaze for a moment too long.

Jefferson left them to it, taking the six steps around the cube to his own desk. He sat in his chair, logged onto his computer, and opened his email server. Third from the top of his inbox sat a short note from Deputy Director Strait's assistant: *DDS would like to see you as soon as you're in.*

Jefferson immediately rose again.

The deputy director had an extremely square jaw—a face not unlike the boxer dog Jefferson's neighbors had, growing up—that, combined with the streaks of white in his hair, gave him a perpetually serious air. Most days, though, Strait amused Caroline and Jefferson more than he intimidated them. He tended to be nitpicky about the smallest of things, like how agents formatted the date in memos, which tended to give off the impression of a high school English teacher instead of the head of a large regional office. But he was levelheaded, open to his subordinates contradicting him if they provided well-reasoned arguments, and fiercely protective of his agents when they came under outside scrutiny. All in all, he made a pretty good boss.

The man had his own office with all the old-school trappings of power: a large, mahogany desk; awards hanging on the wall in heavy frames in rich shades that complemented the furniture; a signed picture of the governor; even an American flag in a stand in the corner by the window. When

Jefferson knocked lightly on the door, the thick Oriental rug on the floor absorbed the sound.

"Special Agent Haines," Strait said, glancing up from the stack of documents he'd been signing. He stood, reaching forward to shake Jefferson's hand when Jefferson approached his desk.

"Sir," Jefferson said. "You wanted to see me?"

"Please have a seat." As if in illustration, Strait returned to his own seat.

Jefferson obeyed, dropping into the harshly stitched chair across from the deputy director, feeling the imprint of several buttons woven into the chair against his back.

"You had an exciting night last night." Strait folded his arms on the desk and gave Jefferson his full attention.

Jefferson forced the smile that remark had been intended to produce.

"Somewhat," he said.

"Your actions last night were a testament to the Bureau," Strait told him. "You thought quickly and logically and took decisive action, saving a life in the process."

"Thank you, sir." Jefferson resisted the urge to fidget in the uncomfortable seat. "Agent Raswell should also be commended. I couldn't have done it without her support. Nor without the officers from the BPD who arrived on site shortly after I did."

"They should," Strait agreed. "Agent Haines, your actions last night are exactly the kind of thing that led me to name Agent Pelley and yourself to lead this investigation."

Jefferson tried to look suitably grateful and not as awkward as he felt. Sure, he was used to being praised—a sentence or two of acknowledgment at the start of a staff meeting, not this focused positive feedback in such an intimate setting. He didn't know what to say that wasn't repeating *Thank you, sir*, like an idiot.

He almost felt relieved when Strait continued. "You are personally acquainted with the victim, I understand?"

Now this made for a landmine of a conversation topic. Jefferson didn't hide his sexuality at work, but he didn't broadcast it, either; especially not after the terrible few months he endured after he came out to Gilbert. He had no idea if the deputy director knew he was gay. He had no idea what Strait's political views were. Although they worked in Massachusetts, the first state to legalize same sex marriage, the older agents tended to be more conservative. The governor in that photo above Deputy Director Strait's desk had backed candidates for office who vehemently opposed gay rights.

Just in case, Jefferson made the conscious decision to pander to the *good ole boy* mentality. "We were roommates at MIT."

"*Hm.* Watching you two come up in the elevator you seemed very close."

"We haven't seen each other outside of work in several years," Jefferson said.

"Yet you were scheduled to meet last night?"

"We were going to have a couple of beers. Catch up."

"I see," Strait said. He didn't say anything else on the subject, and yet Jefferson got the pervasive sense that Strait *knew*, not only about his sexuality, but also exactly how much Finny being taken had affected him. Someone who'd been early on the scene, when Jefferson still held Finny in his arms, must have talked. Which probably meant everyone in the office would know by end of day. *Fuck.*

Jefferson's face grew suddenly hot. He could feel a patch of dampness in his undershirt low on his back. Regardless, he pushed on. He had something more important he wanted to talk to Strait about.

"Sir," he said carefully. "After last night I believe the Smiley Face Killer may be someone I've spoken with in the course of the investigation. I'd like your approval to question DUP Director Dylan Jacobs again."

That visibly surprised Strait. He shifted in his chair, watching Jefferson carefully as he considered the request.

"*You* would like permission?" he clarified. "How does Agent Pelley feel?"

"This is not her recommendation," Jefferson said.

To Strait's credit, he didn't immediately order Jefferson to drop it.

"Why are you making a recommendation to me that your partner doesn't agree with?"

"Because I looked our suspect in the eye last night and he knew me," Jefferson told him. "My gut keeps telling me that we're close. Director Jacobs is the right height and build."

"Apart from that, do you have any concrete evidence to support questioning him?" Strait asked.

"No sir," Jefferson said.

Strait breathed out softly, a tired sound. When he next spoke, however, he sounded completely certain.

"While I trust your instincts, Agent Haines, I'm afraid I can't authorize that. The DUP is too essential a partner for us in Boston. Jacobs himself is too well-respected in the city. Until you can place him near the scene of the abduction, I need you to direct your attention elsewhere."

"*Sir,*" Jefferson began, in protest. He cut himself off at a warning look from Strait. He clenched his fists tightly under the cover of the desk. "Understood," he said.

They talked for a few minutes longer about next steps in the case, especially how Jefferson and Caroline planned to continue to oversee the processing of evidence. Strait requested that Jefferson make himself available for any media inquiries regarding his "heroics" the evening before. The more they could keep the public eye on this case, the more likely it would become that the Smiley Face Killer could be located via a tip from the community.

"That's all for now," Deputy Director Strait said, shortly after. He stood, offering his hand a second time. "Again, good work last night, Agent Haines."

Jefferson thanked him as graciously as he could manage, although it came out stilted to his ears, and then made the retreat back to his desk.

He started by spending half an hour going through the security footage from the businesses that bordered the Aquitaine Restaurant at the approximate time the Audi was reported stolen. Two of the cameras, both located across the street, showed a steady stream of people passing by on the sidewalks, either heading to the many townhomes and apartment complexes in the area, or one of the dozens of other restaurants. Jefferson stared hard at those tapes, looking for anyone who resembled Dylan Jacobs. Then, when he hit a dead end there, he switched to a camera on the same side of the street as Aquitaine. He watched those tapes until he saw the Audi drive by, its driver barely visible through the passenger-side window.

Jefferson decided to give the footage another shot later, with a fresh set of eyes, and turned his attention to an inventory from the cleanout of the abandoned building behind the Museum of Science—

Duct tape, rags, pliers, a lime-green baseball cap . . . .

He paused in the middle of the list. Could that be significant?

There weren't photos of each individual item on the inventory, but there were plenty of the inside of Mr. Smiley's . . . lair? Whatever the hell you would call it. Last night, Jefferson hadn't ventured inside that open door their perp had been dragging Finny toward. The pictures gave him a pretty good idea of what he would've seen.

The building held roughly the same size footprint as Jefferson's office floor. Most of the vacant space appeared to be used as some kind of scrapyard. In the background of the photos, heavy machinery loomed out of the darkness. Stacks of wood accumulated dust, rat droppings, and even the tip of a feather, striped black and brown.

Mr. Smiley had cleared a small area for himself near the doorway. There, sat a standing lamp, two sturdy-looking wooden chairs, and even a coffee table—a living room showroom set, transported to a much less welcoming setting. The scene made Jefferson's gut lurch. He suspected these photos provided their answer to the gap between when the victims disappeared and when they died.

Although Finny had been drugged, he'd been lucid for stretches, he'd *talked* to Jefferson. So, what would've happened if Jefferson hadn't arrived when he had? Would Mr. Smiley have taped Finny's arms to that chair? Sat with him? Had some kind of fucked-up conversation? Was he that starved for company?

The consideration put into staging the scene suggested it was somewhere Mr. Smiley spent a fair amount of time. That bode well for their investigation. He could easily have left trace evidence while arranging his victims. Had he slipped up and left any fingerprints? Perhaps on the furniture, which looked nice enough to have been used in someone's home. Most promising of all was the fine layer of soot on the ground. Had the agents been able to recover shoe prints?

The sound of someone tapping on the wall of his cube with their knuckles broke Jefferson's rumination. He sat hunched forward with both elbows on his desk, leaning very close to the screen, the edge of the desk digging into his stomach. To turn around, he had to brace a hand on either side of his waist and push his computer chair backwards. As he straightened, his spine cracked. Finny stood a step inside his cube from the corridor.

"Hey," Jefferson said. "All done?"

Finny ventured deeper into Jefferson's cube and said, "Yeah. Caroline says I'm good to go for the day."

Only a few personal effects decorated Jefferson's desk: a MIT pennant flag, a framed photo of him and his parents at his graduation from the Academy, the gym bag on the floor at his feet, his coffee thermos, and the few holiday cards he'd received from coworkers that he really needed to purge soon, considering how quickly May approached. Finny's eyes swept over each item in turn.

"Great," Jefferson said, rising to his feet. Mostly kidding, he asked, "You tell her everything we need to know to nail this guy?"

"I wish," Finny said. He frowned, forehead wrinkling. "The only thing I really remember is realizing you had come to save me."

Finny said it absently, a passing observation with no particular inflection. The words disproportionately affected Jefferson, making his knees go weak.

"Oh well," he said, trying for a similarly casual tone. "You're safe now. That's what matters."

The words garnered him a pleased smile. Then Finny's gaze fell on the graduation photo and he ventured within arm's reach, lifting it to examine.

"This is a good photo of you," he said, turning the frame to show Jefferson.

"Thanks." In it, the sun shone on Jefferson's dark hair and he was smiling more genuinely than he usually did in photos, enough to show a hint of white from his teeth. He looked particularly tall compared to his mom, whose head only came to his collarbone. He didn't have the photo out because of his looks, though; but because it was the last family photo he had with his dad. He planned to keep it on his desk for the rest of his life.

"I wanted to say bye." Finny set the photo down. "And, uh . . . I'll see you soon, right?"

"Yes," Jefferson agreed, too quickly. "But—how are you getting home?"

"I was going to call a car."

Finny hid his anxiousness at the thought well. Someone who didn't know him as well as Jefferson did wouldn't have picked up on Finny's nerves about traveling alone.

"No, I'll take you," Jefferson told him. He wasn't going to sit here reading reports while Finny sat in a car with a stranger, reliving his ordeal from the night before the whole way home. He patted at his pants to make sure he had his keys and phone. Since he'd barely been at his desk today, they were still in his pockets.

"You don't have to do that," Finny protested.

"I don't mind," Jefferson said.

"You've barely been at work today."

"Work will still be here when I get back. I want to take you."

"Okay," Finny said. His relief bled into his expression. "*Thank you.*"

"Just one minute," Jefferson told him.

He rapped on the wall of his cubicle that he shared with Caroline, and then went around the corner to see her face-to-face. She'd definitely been listening in on his conversation with Finny. She'd already turned her chair around to wait for him.

"You're leaving," she observed, crossing her arms over her chest.

"I won't be more than forty-five minutes," he told her. "I'll have my phone on me."

Her eyes said, *You owe me big time, Haines.*

"Come see me the minute you get back so we can plan for Amber Collins," she instructed.

"Yes ma'am. And then we'll head to the site for the rest of the afternoon?"

"Yes," she agreed. "I want to walk it in person. Get a feel for it."

Finny and Jefferson both remained quiet in the elevator and on the walk through the lobby to Jefferson's car. On

Jefferson's side, it was an effort to remain professional until he'd left the office. His filter kept slipping the more time he spent around Finny. Based on his conversation with Deputy Director Strait, there were already rumors swirling about him in the office. Jefferson could make his peace with those—what people thought of him hadn't mattered anymore from the moment when he'd heard the beautiful sound of Finny's pulse in that gravel driveway. That said, he didn't need to make them any worse.

He didn't realize it was different for Finny until a mile or so into the drive. Jefferson was meant to be an expert in body language, but he still couldn't quite read the strange tension in Finny's body; what it meant that his hands had gone white, the right clenched on the door handle, the left on his knee.

"What's wrong?" Jefferson asked. "Did I—"

"I'm sorry," Finny said, interrupting him.

"*Nothing* about last night is your fault," Jefferson told him.

No," Finny said, shaking his head. "I'm sorry I shut you out for so long. I should've heard you out. Given you some chance to explain. I just . . . couldn't stand the thought of hearing again how much I disgusted you. Not from you."

"I promise that disgusted is the last thing I'd ever feel about you," Jefferson said.

Finny's breath caught. His voice dropped. Jefferson could barely hear him over the steady thrum of tires on the highway.

"You know I get kind of cra—worked up sometimes . . . always fear the worst."

At his earliest opening, Jefferson made an abrupt turn into the abandoned parking lot of a former mechanic's shop. He put the car in park, parallel to the road, and twisted to meet Finny's eyes. Finny's mouth had fallen open, chapped lips parted in an expression of surprise. His cheeks had darkened, the color settling high on his cheeks.

"I remember," Jefferson said. He reached out tentatively and brushed the pads of his index and middle fingers against the bare skin at Finny's wrist—a quick, comforting motion. The corner of Finny's mouth just barely curved upwards. "And I understand why you didn't. All that matters to me is we're talking now."

"It's not just that," Finny insisted. "I shouldn't have said what I said about your dad."

This conversation was too draining after the night they'd just had. The lingering aches Jefferson had mostly pushed to the background—his throat, his chest—came rushing back, hurting even more than he remembered.

"It was true," Jefferson said, feeling himself go tense.

"I know how much you loved him and how much he loved you."

"Yeah, but . . ." Jefferson trailed off. *He wouldn't have loved me if he'd known.* There was no way he could say that out loud.

"Did you ever tell him about you?" Finny asked.

Jefferson couldn't possibly meet his eye and answer that, so he stared far off in the distance, at a rusty sign advertising $10 oil changes. "No."

"Do you think he would've cha—"

"No," Jefferson repeated. "I never thought that would be a positive conversation. So, I kept putting it off. And then it didn't matter anymore."

The words sounded bitter. Jefferson didn't expect sympathy from Finny on this particular subject, so it surprised him when it arrived. Finny reached out to take Jefferson's right hand. He swiped his thumb across Jefferson's palm, then interlaced their fingers. Finny's palms were warm and a little calloused, presumably from all his recent sailing. It felt nice. Jefferson tried to remember if he'd ever held hands with someone in his adult life and came up short.

Strangely enough, it did help ease some long-ago hurt inside Jefferson. He stared helplessly at the place their fingers interlocked.

"I'm sorry," Finny repeated softly.

Jefferson had the ridiculous urge to lift Finny's hand and press a kiss to the back of his knuckles.

Instead, he almost jumped at the sound of a far-off car alarm blaring.

"I should—" he reluctantly said, moving his hand in the direction of the steering wheel.

"Oh right," Finny relinquished his grip. His cheeks flushed.

Jefferson put the car back in drive and pulled onto the road, feeling an echo of Finny's touch as he took the steering wheel in a firm grip.

After what seemed like no time at all, Jefferson exited the highway and began to approach Finny's street via Dorchester Avenue. As distinctly different as their neighborhoods were—Finny's low, to Jefferson's high—their apartments were only a short trip apart by car. The route took a straight shot via I-93.

"Here you are," he announced, pulling in front of a three-story painted white triple-decker with light blue shutters marked with the number Finny had given him. Finny's apartment was likely only one floor or half of a floor inside. So few people owned full homes in Boston anymore, not when landlords could subdivide and make a fortune in rent.

No response came from Finny, who didn't move to climb out of Jefferson's car. When Jefferson turned to look at him, Finny's face had gone the color of his house.

"Finny?" Jefferson asked, stomach lurching. After hesitating briefly, he reached over and placed a light hand above Finny's knee, feeling the dampness of Finny's skin through the thick material of his sweatpants.

The touch got Finny to look at him. His breaths had become sharper in the last few minutes. His pupils had dilated. He was panicking.

"Hey, Finny," Jefferson said, low and gentle. "What's up?"

"What am I supposed to do all weekend?" Finny asked, each word rushed. "I can't—I have to go to work on Monday. I can't stay in my apartment forever. And I'm going to be—I'm so scared, Jefferson. What if he comes after me again?"

The more he talked, the more labored his breathing became. He kept having to pause, needing to inhale so his voice wouldn't give out.

"Hey," Jefferson repeated, tightening his fingers. He waited until Finny caught his eyes, seeing expansive black pupils and little else. This wasn't new exactly—he'd seen it play out dozens of times in school. But it was different when the stakes were life and death. He found it a lot easier to reassure Finny when he only felt anxious about a test score.

Jefferson spoke slowly, enunciating every word. He didn't look away from Finny.

"I've asked BPD to put an officer at your door for the next few nights. You should stay inside this weekend. Get some rest—you need it more than you think after last night. Can you do that?"

He waited for Finny to nod.

"I'm going to do everything I can to catch him before he hurts anyone else," Jefferson said, in a fierce tone. "I'll work my ass off to be sure of it. Until then, if you ever feel unsafe, if a single thing ever seems wrong to you, off in some way, give me a call. I'll get to you as quickly as I can."

"Okay," Finny said finally. His voice was strangled but his gaze locked on Jefferson's, unwavering. He looked like he believed everything Jefferson was telling him; more than that—like a man leaving a desert and finding a river, desperately drinking the words in.

On impulse, Jefferson lifted his hand to Finny's face, thumb resting on the curve of Finny's cheekbone.

"I'm not going to let anything happen to you," he vowed.

Finny nodded jerkily, making Jefferson's arm bob, but not dislodging his hand. Gradually his breathing slowed.

"Does that help?" Jefferson asked. The words came out hoarse.

"It does," Finny said, after a long moment.

Something told Jefferson not to move his arm.

"I'll do anything to keep you safe," he said, very seriously. He'd never meant anything so much. "Whatever it takes."

In a single abrupt motion, Finny leaned across the center console, closing the gap between them. He pressed his mouth to Jefferson's, off-center, clumsy with insistence, almost frantic. It happened so suddenly that it took Jefferson's brain a second to catch up and realize, *this is a kiss. Finny is kissing me*—something Jefferson had envisioned a hundred times over, in varying levels of detail. The thought of kissing Finny had kept him up at night in school, listening to the even sound of Finny breathing across the room, while his heart thumped in his chest.

The rational part of his brain telling him, *Finny is freaking out,* was firmly overruled by the part of him that had wanted Finny since freshman year. He raised his other hand to Finny's face, cupping both of his cheeks. He kissed back, adjusting the angle, soothing some of Finny's freneticism. His knee knocked against the console and he barely felt the sting. For those few seconds it lasted, the world narrowed to Finny's tongue, silken against his; the press of his soft lips.

"You have to get back to work," Finny said, as he pulled away, sounding more like he needed to tell himself than Jefferson. His lips looked slick and so very pink.

"Yes," Jefferson said. He had claimed some of Finny's shortness of breath. He didn't want to let Finny go, but he made himself, intentionally laying his palms on his thighs, knowing that the best thing Jefferson could do for him was stay on the case.

"I'll call you on my drive home tonight," he promised, fighting to keep his gaze from dropping to Finny's mouth. Even though he'd been increasingly hopeful throughout the morning that something like this would happen, it was also momentous, something that would've seemed impossible a month ago. For most of his adult life he'd believed that he'd blown his chance with Finny for good and yet here he was, still able to taste Finny on his lips. "I'm here for you, whenever you need me."

Finny nodded. He looked better than he had a few minutes before, satisfyingly dazed.

"Bye, Jefferson," he said, finally moving in order to raise a hand to the door handle.

"Bye, *Finny*," Jefferson said, putting an emphasis on the name that garnered him a quick quirk of a smile. He waited in his car until Finny crossed his short lawn and let himself into his building before driving away.

CHAPTER 13

On the way back from Finny's house, Jefferson hit what ended up being a thirty-minute slowdown caused by a lane shutdown for construction; traffic stopped as dead as leads on their case. It gave him plenty of time to think about his upcoming interview with the young woman Henry O'Brien had waved to at the Bruins game. Had Amber Collins been someone special to Henry? Or was she just one in a seemingly long line of women Henry pursued? Jefferson hoped she would have some new insight to give them.

By the time he made it back to his desk, Caroline stood in the doorway of his cube, practically vibrating with impatience.

"Forty-five minutes my ass," she told him.

"I know, I'm sorry," he said. He chugged several quick sips of coffee from the cold thermos at his desk.

"Ms. Collins is waiting in interview room two."

"Okay, let's go," Jefferson said, putting down the coffee to follow her there.

A curvy young woman sat in the small room waiting for them, wearing black yoga tights and an oversized sweatshirt with three triangles on the front—sorority letters, *Delta Delta Delta*. She'd pulled her blonde, curly hair into a loose braid.

"Ms. Collins?" Jefferson asked, stepping inside. "I'm Agent Haines."

While Caroline verified Amber's full name and confirmed the night Amber had been at the Bruins game,

Jefferson reviewed the notes scrawled on his yellow legal pad, trying to organize his thoughts after his frantic sprint from his car to his desk, then here. A short silence descended as Caroline waited for him to take over. He glanced up to find the two women watching him.

"How did you know Henry?" he asked.

"My mom is friends with his mom," Amber explained. "We used to hang out at their dinner parties. He was always really sweet to me. So, when I needed someone to come with me to Tri Delta's annual 'Let's Glow Crazy' neon party a couple of weeks ago, I decided to ask him to be my date."

She then launched into a minute-long description of that night. It sounded like it had involved a lot of glow sticks, highlighters, and neon clothing. From what Jefferson could tell, although Henry and Amber had enjoyed their time together, they hadn't met up again until they ran into each other at the game. He listened as Amber talked about who she'd been with at the game and who else she'd noticed in her section.

"One of my sisters is dating a guy who works for the team and he gave us the tickets," Amber said. She liked to talk, Jefferson noticed. Now that she'd gotten used to the idea of an interview, she spoke longer and longer in response to each question. "Four of us went together. It was my first time at a game. Hockey is a cool sport. I didn't completely understand what was happening at first, but the guys in front of us explained it to me so I could follow along. It was a nice surprise when Henry commented on my Instagram."

"Did you see Henry speaking with anyone or see anyone who looked like they might be watching him—following him?" Caroline asked.

"No," Amber answered. "He was sitting pretty far away. I was only able to find him in the stands because he was wearing a bright hat."

"Do you have any pictures from that night on your phone?" Jefferson asked.

"Of course," Amber said.

"May we see them?" Jefferson asked.

"Oh, sure," Amber said. She reached below the table and pulled up a large, black designer purse. She had to dig around in it for a while to find her phone. Then she spent some time scrolling on it before sliding it across the way to them. "Start on that picture and swipe right to go through them."

Jefferson scooted his seat over to Caroline and they looked through the photos together. There were an astounding number of pictures considering the game had only lasted a few hours. He saw dozens of selfies—Amber alone, Amber with friends, Amber with Blades, the Bruins mascot—crowd shots, pictures of drinks and food, and pictures of the rafters. Anything Amber could have possibly photographed, she had. A love of photography might have been something she had in common with Henry.

Nothing in any of the crowd shots jumped out at Jefferson, other than one photo where he was convinced he could see a spot of bright color that must have been where Henry sat. Caroline didn't ask him to go back to any pictures, either. When they reached a change of scenery—photos taken of the sunrise outside a window, possibly the next morning—Jefferson thanked Amber and passed the phone back to her.

The moment the interview concluded and Amber had been placed back in an elevator to the ground level, Jefferson left the room and took the stairs two at a time, jogging to the basement. He could feel Caroline following close behind.

"Where are you going?" she asked. The soles of her sneakers smacked loudly with each of her steps.

"There was a neon green hat in Mr. Smiley's hideout," Jefferson said. "I want to see it in person."

"*Why*?"

"Because I think it had sorority letters on it," Jefferson said.

The evidence from Mr. Smiley's corner of the abandoned building was still being processed, so it hadn't yet been placed in a secured storage facility. For the time being, it was laid out on a table in a conference room, being meticulously catalogued. Jefferson checked in with the junior agent in charge of the work, then started scanning all of the materials.

He spotted the hat in seconds. The bright color stood out like a beacon at the far end of the long table. Heart racing, Jefferson walked around the edge of the room to look more closely at it. Stitched into the front panel were the same three Greek letters that had been on Amber's sweatshirt, with the words *Highlighter Party 2020* below.

"Henry O'Brien was wearing this hat the night he died," Jefferson told Caroline, staring down at it. "I saw it in the camera footage."

"Okay," she said. She didn't get it. In college, she'd been a varsity athlete. She hadn't had time to rush a sorority.

"What if Mr. Smiley saw this on Henry and thought he was in a fraternity," Jefferson said. "I think I guessed it right a few days ago. He's hunting men who were in Greek life. Like Les. Like Omar."

Caroline eyed the hat with a new light in her eyes.

"You can't just see that by looking at someone," she said. "You think they were all wearing hats?"

"Or something else branded," Jefferson said. "Let's go find out."

This time, they took the elevator up. When Jefferson got back to his desk, he opened the portable drive of past cases and began clicking through the most recent of the files.

Looking at photos of bodies was never an easy task. According to Valdés, you didn't ever get used to it, either.

Within each folder, Jefferson focused on the victim's clothes so he wouldn't have to see their bloated, water-logged faces and think about what they might have looked like in their prime.

Randall Allen had been running in a T-shirt that advertised a fraternity clam bake to benefit a local charity while Omar Halim had been wearing a dark jacket with large white Greek letters embroidered on the front left side.

Les McIntyre took a little more examination. He'd been dressed in work clothes, a white dress shirt and navy blue suit top. Only after looking through several different angles of pictures did Jefferson finally notice the gold pin affixed to Les's lapel.

The only recent victim Jefferson couldn't find anything for was Gregory Jackson. The night he died, Gregory had been wearing a deep green V-neck shirt, dark jeans, and nothing else.

Jefferson made a low, frustrated sound in the back of his throat, and shoved his mouse away. Caroline had pulled in a chair and been watching him quietly, letting him work uninterrupted, but at that, she finally spoke.

"It may not have mattered what he was wearing. Gregory was out at a bar with friends. They could have been reminiscing together about the good old days and have been overheard."

"True," Jefferson agreed. His shoulders remained hunched. "We still have no solid evidence. Just conjecture."

"Can you verify that Gregory was in a fraternity, at least?" Caroline asked.

After a few different searches, Jefferson found Gregory's name on a Northeastern University fraternity's website page for the class of 2017.

"Yes," he said, turning the computer to show her.

"There you go," she said. "So, we are looking at a common victim type. Even Fred fits, right?"

"He definitely wasn't wearing anything branded," Jefferson said. He suspected that Finny had burned all the fraternity shirts he owned after school.

"Fred's different though," she said. "He was taken to make a point to *you*, so his abduction had to be planned in advance. It wouldn't have taken Mr. Smiley much research to figure out where you two knew each other from."

"I keep trying to figure out what it means," Jefferson said. "Did Mr. Smiley try to rush a fraternity some odd thirty years ago and not get in? Did someone in a frat steal his girlfriend? What does this actually tell us about him? Why does it matter to him that his victims be in a fraternity?"

"I don't know," Caroline said. "But it's something about him we didn't know before. I'll take it."

In the wake of that realization, they took a field trip to Mr. Smiley's base. Two buildings sat perpendicular to one another off the gravel lot where Jefferson had faced off with the killer. One, shaped like a large U, faced outward toward Edwin H. Land Boulevard and East Cambridge. The other rectangular one took up the back of the lot, directly on the banks of the Charles River.

Although the buildings had clearly fallen into disrepair, in broad daylight the exteriors showed some signs of what they might've looked like when in active use. The walls were all brick. The roof tiles and doors appeared to have once been painted an olive green. The gutters, although now rusty, still had flecks of a brighter red paint. The complete package would've been something almost festive.

Mr. Smiley had worked out of the second building, which was easily accessible from two different roads, but still lay largely out of sight, hidden by the first building and a copse of trees. Close by was a ramp that led directly to the water. Although most of the doors on the building were large and rounded, designed for cars to drive through, Mr. Smiley had chosen a smaller one; a pedestrian side entrance.

The forensics team remained on site, still scouring for trace evidence, so that door jutted open. Jefferson and Caroline stepped inside, entering a space much darker and colder than the one they'd left behind. Even with staging lights placed at regular intervals, Jefferson found it difficult to see. Most of the—it wasn't quite a warehouse, but that was the best word Jefferson could think of to describe it—was packed with snowplows, lawn mowers, backhoes, and other machinery, all branded by the Commonwealth of Massachusetts. None of them appeared to be in working order. Collectively, the machines blotted out the windows. That had given Mr. Smiley an additional layer of privacy.

So many agents coming and going had stirred up the heavy layer of dust blanketing everything, making the air thick and hard to breathe. In the distance, Jefferson heard an animal scurry across the floor. This wouldn't have been a welcoming place to be in alone late at night, setting up for an abduction.

He turned his attention to the part of the space he felt most curious about—the bizarre sitting room that he'd studied so closely in the photos. There it was, just inside the doorway: two chairs facing each other at an angle, a little table in between them, and a lamp to offer some much-needed illumination. Next to one of the chairs rested a light metal chain. A tea-party set where only one of the guests wanted to be there.

The atmosphere inside this building didn't invite conversation. The oppressive darkness and looming shapes made every word sound too loud. Jefferson and Caroline were both quiet as they made their observations. Jefferson tried to make sense of it.

Only two kinds of people would set a stage like this: someone lonely, so desperate for company that they could overlook the harsh surroundings, or someone so assured in themselves and what they had to say that they barely noticed it.

So, which was Mr. Smiley?

And how did it fit with the fraternity angle? Did Mr. Smiley lecture his victims about the dangers of hazing before killing them? That didn't seem fucking likely.

Even though the skies were overcast, both Jefferson and Caroline winced against the change in brightness when they finally stepped back outside. They maintained that same pensive silence they'd had inside the building on the return trip to the office.

By the time Jefferson left for the evening he'd beaten his own personal record for the latest day he'd ever clocked. The cumulative effects of two back-to-back nights with little sleep were getting to him. His eyes burned from tiredness. It felt like particles of sand ground under his eyelids whenever he blinked. The vast emptiness of the lanes ahead didn't help him resist the desire to close his eyes and put his head down. Even as he actively focused on keeping the wheel level, he jerked, catching himself drifting across lanes. The rumble of gravel under his tires in the emergency lane startled him enough that he sat up straighter, fighting harder against his exhaustion.

He wanted to talk to Finny.

A mile or two passed while Jefferson debated with himself. It was late, the first hours of Saturday morning, later than Jefferson would be awake on a regular night, let alone when he was running on fragments of sleep, feeling shoddily glued together. How likely was Finny to still be up? If he called, would Jefferson risk waking him? Or was Finny up too, jumping at every sound? It couldn't hurt to try, could it? Didn't everyone sleep with their phones on *Do Not Disturb* nowadays?

Being so drained, Jefferson's willpower was completely shot. Having someone to talk to might help him stay awake, he justified. Plus, Jefferson had promised to call after work and check in, so he should keep his word.

A very selfish part of him didn't care if he woke Finny, as long as Jefferson got to hear his voice one more time before bed. He wasn't too tired to recognize how sappy that sounded. That moment in the car felt like it had happened a hundred years ago. They had *kissed* this morning. At the memory, he immediately found himself smiling, briefly able to forget the weight of stress and exhaustion pressing down on him. It only took three touches on his dashboard screen to call Finny.

Once the system dialed out, his car speaker clicked on, blaring the ringing chimes. The sound jarred Jefferson fully awake. It reminded him too much of that frantic, hellish period last night where Finny's phone had gone to voicemail over and over again. He stiffened, going suddenly, unexpectedly cold. After two rings, he didn't feel worried about falling asleep at the wheel anymore.

A split-second before he would have started to panic, whether rational to or not considering the time, the line clicked.

"Hi," Finny said. He sounded as tired as Jefferson felt, voice low and rasping, but openly fond, with a long-forgotten but familiar note that said he was hearing from one of his favorite people and couldn't be happier about it. "I was worried you were pulling an all-nighter."

"Not quite," Jefferson said. He risked taking a hand off the steering wheel to scrub at his eyes. "I had to get out. I was falling asleep at my desk."

"No kidding, it's 1:30."

"I didn't wake you, did I?"

"No," Finny answered. "My schedule is all out of whack. I slept half the day so now I feel like I could go out and run a half-marathon."

"Don't," Jefferson said, sharper than he meant to, hands clenching on the wheel.

"I'm not." Finny sighed, an absent sound he probably didn't realize he'd made. "I'll be stir-crazy by the end of tomorrow, but I'm not going anywhere alone until this is over, I promise. You don't have to tell me not to."

Jefferson focused on the calming sound of Finny's voice, letting himself pretend that Finny was the final destination at the end of this infinite-seeming stretch of highway, not his empty apartment. "Do you work out every day?"

"Most. I run five or six days a week."

"That's what I try for too."

"It shows," Finny told him, in a tone that thrust Jefferson right back to that morning's kiss.

Any time someone he was actually interested in flirted with him, it felt like being smacked upside the head—every thought went flying out of his mind as he struggled to remember how to form words. *Finny* flirting with him was even worse. He hadn't had the chance to build up any tolerance to it.

"Not running," he clarified instead of returning the compliment. "Lifting weights, mostly. And I like to box."

Anything time and distance might have done to diminish the strength of his feelings for Finny was erased as they spoke. Finny had been through a horrific ordeal last night and yet now he was laughing again as he listened to Jefferson stumble his way through this conversation. In so many ways, Finny was the bravest person Jefferson knew. Even when something scared him, he ultimately found the strength to move past his fears and keep going. When he couldn't do it alone, he didn't hesitate to lean on someone else. And he always reciprocated that support two-fold when you needed something from him in turn.

"If you wanted to get in a run, I would go with you," Jefferson found himself offering. "You don't have to go the whole weekend without."

"Would you?" Finny's enthusiasm for the idea shone through in his voice.

"You're going to leave me in the dust, but yeah. It'll be nice to have a break."

He heard Finny hesitate before he said, "I don't mean to keep taking you away from your job."

"You're not," Jefferson said. "What if I pick you up at 08:00 tomorrow?" He remembered the time and corrected, "Today?"

"Do you mean eight o'clock?" Finny asked. "That sounds so weird."

"That's how you tell time."

"If you're a robot. Do you talk to anyone who's not in the FBI?"

Jefferson hadn't much lately—at least not until the twist of fate that brought Finny back into his life.

"I'll see you at *oh-eight-hundred*," he promised pointedly, just before hanging up. He was still smiling as he swiped his fob to get into his building's garage.

When he parked his car and could check his phone again, he had a text from Finny that said: *You're a NERD*, followed by a single red heart.

It became immediately evident to Jefferson how over his head he'd already gotten in this thing with Finny. He stared at that innocuous symbol way too long, his own heart clenching. He couldn't bring himself to look away from it.

✳✳✳

After a brief night's sleep, Jefferson picked Finny up and then drove for twenty minutes to the west of Boston to a reservoir with a mile-and-a-half loop around it. Finny hopped out of Jefferson's SUV on a side street they'd found near the trail, looking particularly youthful in his delight as he jogged in place waiting for Jefferson. His enthusiasm was contagious. Jefferson paused, pretending to double-check that he had his keys long enough to steal a few seconds watching him. He liked being the one to make Finny smile like that. Also, he liked the way Finny's legs looked in his running shorts, which were borderline indecent, too short for Finny to be wearing boxers.

There wasn't an ounce of fat on Finny's body. Lean muscles dusted with a fine layer of light brown hair stretched from the very high hem of his shorts to the ground. A narrow belt at his waist held two miniature water bottles clipped on either side. It kept tugging at the fabric, revealing a band of white skin less tanned by exposure to the sun.

"Are you wearing anything under those?" Jefferson asked, less as a come-on and more in the way he used to talk to Finny, affectionately giving him shit.

Finny gave him a particular kind of look, glancing up under his eyelashes. "Wouldn't you like to know?"

Jefferson swallowed, mouth suddenly gone dry. With a thrill he remembered that things were different between them now.

"Lead the way," he said. The words had a hint of scratchiness. "I'll do my best to keep up."

After shooting him a knowing grin, Finny spun and started jogging down the sidewalk in the direction of the water. Jefferson tapped at the tracker on his wrist to activate it, and then followed. They emerged from a low-lying mixed-use area to an elevated lake with a spectacular view of Boston to the east and more residential neighborhoods through the trees to the north and west. They hopped on the dusty running path and Finny started to move his legs much faster.

With the advantage of his height, Jefferson kept up for the first two laps. Anyone in decently good shape could run a 5K if they put their mind to it. It was all a mental game— one foot after the other. Since he'd left his headphones in the car, Finny's voice became his soundtrack for the run as

Finny maintained a steady, mostly one-sided conversation, never once getting out of breath.

As time passed, the route changed from pretty and interesting, to boring in its repetition, to peacefully monotonous. Jefferson began to notice the smallest of reference points, like tree roots sticking out of the ground, while being fascinated by every little change, like a turtle sliding off a log into the water. In the middle of the third lap he started to lag behind. Then he kept himself entertained watching the view in front of him.

Halfway through the fourth lap—around the six-mile mark—Jefferson slowed to a walk.

"Finny," he called ahead.

Finny twisted to look at him, jogging in place. Three yards ahead of him Jefferson saw a bench shaded by a stand of trees.

"I'll wait for you there," Jefferson told him, pointing. "Go as long as you want."

Frowning, Finny jogged forward and stopped beside him. "You okay?"

Jefferson found himself grinning, the high of the workout making him buzz from head to toe, even along his leaden legs. This had been fun, albeit torturous.

"Just tired. We can't all have your stamina."

"I can stop," Finny offered. His eyes said he wanted to go another fifty miles.

They began to walk together, falling into step. Their knuckles brushed as their arms swung.

"No, keep going," Jefferson urged. He dropped onto the bench with a satisfied groan and spread his legs, sprawling against the boards. "Enjoy the beautiful day. I'll be right here." Although the reservoir was packed, he made sure to add, "Stay on the trail and around people."

"I will," Finny said. Instead of turning to go, he moved forward, stepping inside the vee of Jefferson's thighs and knotting a hand in Jefferson's T-shirt. Using that leverage, he leaned forward to press a kiss to Jefferson's mouth. Jefferson's pulse had already been accelerated from the run, but it gave a valiant effort to speed up further. "Thanks for today," Finny told him.

When Finny pulled back, Jefferson caught a whiff of sweat on flushed skin. The scent hit him hard, making the attraction that had been simmering low in his attention all morning spike in heat. The combination of Finny's hand at his chest and Finny's masculine smell made his mind wander. He found himself fantasizing about it: Finny's lean body stretched out against his sheets; a drop of sweat curling over Finny's perfectly flat abdomen; running his hand up that soft-looking skin high on Finny's thighs. Jefferson had to shift on the bench, tamping down on his arousal before it became physically apparent.

It was a brisk day, good for running, but cold when sitting still. Over the next thirty minutes, Jefferson entertained himself tracking Finny's loops shamelessly, taking every chance he could to stare at his old friend. Jefferson liked a lot of things about Finny in particular, but generally he had always liked competence and Finny ran very well. This was Finny in his element, eyes locked ahead, arms and legs pumping; a well-tuned machine. Apparently he'd been holding back while he ran with Jefferson. On his own, he went even faster. About every ten minutes he passed by, shooting Jefferson a bright grin or a wave. In between, a constant stream of people crossed in front of Jefferson: other runners, families with strollers, friends out for a walk, and dogs. So many dogs.

In the middle of his second additional lap—at close to nine miles—Finny gradually started to slow. He walked the final stretch back to Jefferson's bench, letting his body cool.

"I'm done," Finny said, breath hitching on the word. He beamed at Jefferson, face flushed pink with effort.

"Come sit," Jefferson scooted sideways to give him room.

Finny dropped next to him, close enough that the bare skin of their upper legs pressed together. His light brown hair had gone dark with sweat. He tugged at his damp shirt, rippling it to let air between his chest and the fabric. This close, the smell of his exertion was even stronger, still so strangely appealing.

"How was it?"

"Incredible," Finny said. He unclipped one of the tiny water bottles in the belt at his waist and squirted it into his mouth from several inches outside his parted lips. It made a loud *squelch*ing sound. Jefferson got a little fixated on the way Finny's throat worked while he drank. After several long gulps, Finny had emptied the bottle. "I think I PR'ed a mile toward the end there."

Jefferson tried to keep up while Finny talked about pace, splits, and Garmin data, but his mind wandered elsewhere. As Finny began to wind down his observations, Jefferson made his move. Copying Finny's earlier action, he clenched his fingers in Finny's shirt, pulling him into another kiss.

This wasn't the quick brush of lips Finny's kiss had been. Finny made a low, satisfied sound, opening up for him right away as he put a hand on each of Jefferson's biceps, fingers gently digging in. His mouth felt cool from the water. He kissed the way he ran: confident, settled in for a long haul, but careful that every step along the way be good.

In an effort to bring Finny even closer, Jefferson lifted Finny's right leg and draped it across the tops of his own legs. Between the way Jefferson felt about him . . . emotionally, which already overwhelmed him in its own right, and the sweet curl of Finny's tongue, kissing Finny was a bit of an onslaught. Jefferson slid his hand up Finny's chest, curled it around the back of Finny's neck, and held on tight, enjoying every minute.

Kissing wasn't even the right word for what they were doing. No, they were making out on a bench in broad daylight like a couple of teenagers, too impatient to wait for the privacy of one of their homes—which they both had, because they were *adults*.

Their bodies curved toward each other. Every single place Finny touched him seared into Jefferson's skin, from the damp underside of his knee on Jefferson's thigh to the hand that had shifted to the collar of Jefferson's shirt, thumb resting in the hollow above Jefferson's collarbone. On every inhale, Jefferson breathed Finny in, that combination of sweat and deodorant driving him crazy. When Finny shifted, tipping his weight further onto Jefferson's lap, Jefferson dropped a hand to Finny's leg, sliding his palm under those flimsy shorts.

His heart raced. His body felt like it was on fire. They kissed, open-mouthed and wet, and he still wanted more; wanted Finny so badly he thought his chest might explode from it.

"Finny," Jefferson gasped as he pulled back. He felt wild, brain out of sync with his actions. On hot summer days in college, they used to drive out to a quarry in Western Massachusetts with a swimming hole. He'd been transported back there—taking that first step off a 40-foot ledge, trusting that he would hit the water the right way. This gave him the same rush. "Fuck. Wow."

Finny was breathing harder than he had been when he finished his run. "Yeah," he agreed, equally incoherent. His eyes were huge. Looking into them from so close reminded Jefferson again of standing in front of a painting—a canvas that at first appeared to be a single sheet of rich color but changed with light and movement, nuances of shading coming out.

Without him consciously deciding to do so, Jefferson's hand slid an inch higher up Finny's thigh, fabric brushing over his knuckles. Soft hairs tickled his palm. He felt the point where muscle met bone. One inch to the left those hairs would thicken noticeably . . . .

"I have to go to the office," he said, trying to remind himself.

As if he couldn't help it, Finny leaned forward, pressing his mouth to the edge of Jefferson's jaw.

"Do you?" he asked, lips moving against Jefferson's stubble.

Jefferson had to think about that. What he wanted to do was take Finny home and taste salt on the flat plane of his stomach. He wanted to see how Finny's running stamina translated to bed. He wanted Finny to keep sucking on that spot under his jaw. There were so many things he wanted to do and the thought exhilarated him, making him feel human in the rawest sense of the word, fully alive.

Alive. It was like someone had dumped a bucket of ice water over his head. He remembered the horrible sight of Finny's motionless body in a heap on the ground and felt cold to his core.

With enormous reluctance he said, "I do."

Before he could change his mind, he freed his hand from Finny's shorts. Then he lifted Finny's leg off his knee, gently placing it back down on the bench.

"*Jefferson,*" Finny pleaded, emphasizing each of the three syllables, the particular way only he said Jefferson's name—a sound Jefferson hadn't heard in eight years.

Jefferson's chest went tight. In a kind of apology, he swiped his thumb over the flush on Finny's cheeks. As he did so, Finny closed his eyes, face going soft. Watching him, Jefferson felt a fierce spike of protectiveness. No matter what it took, he was going to keep Finny safe. He would protect Finny—and protect this special, delicate thing burgeoning between them—at all costs.

It gave him the willpower to heave himself to his feet and hold out his hand to help Finny up.

"Let's get going," he said.

Finny kept hold of that hand as they retraced their steps around the reservoir back to Jefferson's car. While they walked, Jefferson kept an absent eye on the shallow water near the shoreline. In a dense stand of reeds, he noticed something and came to an abrupt stop.

Finny broke off in the middle of a story about one of his coworkers to ask, "What is it?"

Jefferson made a soft *shh*ing sound. He crept two steps closer to the water, paused, waiting, then took another two, pulling Finny with him.

"What?" Finny repeated, much softer this time.

Jefferson pointed. Mostly hidden by some rocks at the water's edge squatted a bird a little over a foot tall with a long, sharp beak like a pair of scissors, blue-green wings, yellow legs that darkened to orange where they were submerged, and a plum-colored chest.

After a moment of searching, Finny saw it too. "Whoa." He smiled, glancing quickly at Jefferson before returning his attention to the water.

"That's a green heron," Jefferson told him in a low voice. "I've only ever seen a few. They're very shy around humans."

"It's a beautiful bird."

"I think so too," Jefferson said, as pleased as if he'd been the one complimented. With his free hand, he fished in his pocket for his phone, bending down to take a photo.

When he finished, he tugged at Finny's hand to let him know they could keep going.

"You have a good eye," Finny said, falling into step with him. "I wouldn't have seen that."

"Thanks. I have a lot of practice," Jefferson said.

"At . . . birdwatching?" Finny clarified.

"Yes."

"Are you a *birder*, Jefferson?" Finny asked, sounding delighted.

Jefferson wasn't used to people understanding what that was. He hadn't fully put two-and-two together that Finny worked for the parks department, and therefore likely got a lot of birdwatchers on the properties he managed.

"A casual one," he said.

"You're a man of hidden talents," Finny told him. He waved at the water. "Could you tell me what everything out there is?"

"Not everything. Probably most."

That led to Finny playfully testing him for several minutes, pointing out different ducks on the surface of the water. Jefferson identified one of dozens of ubiquitous mallards, then a couple of American black ducks, then finally, a lone, spectacular greater scaup, identifiable by its dark head, neck, and tail that bookended gray, spotted wings and a white underbelly.

Soon after, they left the dusty trail and turned onto the paved sidewalk that would lead them to Jefferson's car.

A few minutes after they'd taken Finny's exit, and approached the point where they'd have to part ways, Finny asked, "Are you doing anything tomorrow night?"

"Only hoping to get out of the office at a reasonable time," Jefferson said. He didn't want to discourage Finny initiating anything—and he couldn't imagine anything Finny might ask that he would want to say no to—but that was the reality of the job right now: work had to come first. "Why?"

"I have this thing," Finny said. "A gala for the Boston Neighborhoods Association. I'd like it if you'd come with me as my date."

The invitation threw Jefferson. He'd been expecting Finny to ask him over for dinner. His car screeched in protest when he waited a second too long to start to brake for a red light.

"So . . . it's a work thing?" he asked.

"Yes, you've met one of their members—Phyllis Dreegan," Finny explained. He quickly added, "But if you can't make it, I understand."

Jefferson opened his mouth to gently decline, when he reconsidered, pausing to think it over. Phyllis Dreegan had been walking with Finny the morning they discovered Les McIntyre's body. When he first met her, Jefferson had assumed it was bad luck on her part—that, like Finny, she'd been in the wrong place at the wrong time. Looking back, he felt less certain.

The *day after* that, Finny had been taken. That morning, Phyllis had been so quick to pick up her phone to make a call. She'd been watching Jefferson and Finny interact—had she flagged for their killer that Finny was someone important to Jefferson?

Their case team still hadn't ruled out the possibility that the Smiley Face Killer had an accomplice. The possibility still existed that the local legends had it right and someone aided Mr. Smiley in his quest. Maybe Phyllis, or someone close to her, who she might have told about her experience finding the body. If he went to this event, Jefferson would have a unique opportunity to watch her outside of an interview, better understand her personality, and see who she might be close to.

"I'll go in early tomorrow morning so I can get out in time," Jefferson promised.

"The gala is black tie. Do you have a tux?" Finny asked.

"I do." Was it clean? Jefferson really didn't think so. If he remembered correctly, he'd shoved it back in the garment bag and left it hanging in his closet after the last formal wedding he'd gone to. But he'd figure something out. "I'll be there."

CHAPTER 14

There were so many details to get right when dressing in formal wear. Were both suspenders hooked, the straps straight? Yes. Were his shirt cuffs folded evenly, his cuff-links securely fastened? Yes. Had he remembered to drop his collar down in the back after putting on his bow tie? Yes, good.

In a slightly compulsive gesture, Jefferson lifted his arms to smooth the front of his jacket as he studied himself in his bathroom mirror. Not too shabby. The dry cleaner had turned his tux around in time for him to pick it up on the way home from work. It fit a little too snugly, but there was nothing he could do about that; he'd put on muscle since he last wore it. At least the way the fabric strained at his shoulders appeared more flattering than not. If he weighed five pounds more, it might have been a different story.

Altogether, he could admit he looked good. His dark brown hair was neatly styled and held with a pomade, combed a little higher off his forehead than he would normally wear it. Instead of giving himself his usual morning shave, he'd waited until an hour ago and had been especially thorough. His skin felt silky smooth.

He grabbed his keys from the kitchen counter and headed out the door. This time, he didn't need the GPS to get to Finny's place; he had the route memorized after so many trips back and forth. The triple-decker house Finny lived in had been divided into five apartments off a central staircase, with two on the first floor, two on the second—Finny's floor—and a single unit on the third. After Finny buzzed him in from the ground-level door, Jefferson jogged up the stairs and knocked on the door to Finny's unit.

"Jefferson?" Finny called from deeper in the apartment.

"Yeah, it's me."

"One minute," Finny yelled, the sound muffled.

Jefferson heard footsteps moving around, then a latch clicking, before the door in front of him swung open. The effect created by Finny's tux, tailored to fit his very lean body, was much different from Jefferson's. The dark material brought out the blonder streaks in his hair. The same muscles in his legs that Jefferson had been admiring yesterday while they ran were showcased by careful stitching.

"Hey, Finny," Jefferson said, drinking in the sight.

"Hi," Finny said. "Sorry, I had to shut the cats in the bathroom so they wouldn't get hair all over your tux. Come in a few minutes?"

Jefferson reflexively checked the time. The event started soon, but he said, "Sure," anyway. Finny stepped back to let him inside.

"I realized something today," Finny told him. He gave Jefferson a quick once-over, warm eyes darkening with approval.

"What's that?" Jefferson asked.

"That I've missed you," Finny said. Once again, his gaze skittered to meet Jefferson's then dipped away. "A lot."

"You too," Jefferson said, voice dropping, going softer.

Finny reached for him and it was already instinct for Jefferson to reach back. They started kissing, kissing like they had on the park bench: desperate, the precursor to something more. Finny's grip grew tight on Jefferson's hips, fingers digging in. He had to be on his toes to catch Jefferson's lips when they were both standing. The position left his body flush against Jefferson's. Once Jefferson wrapped an arm around Finny's waist, there wasn't an inch of space between them. The way Finny kissed him, all-consuming, made it impossible to focus on anything but him.

Finny gave a great, gasping breath, dragging his hand down Jefferson's chest, the pads of his fingers catching on the buttons of Jefferson's shirt.

"You look amazing," he said, breathing hard. He toyed with the second-to-last button down, twirling it on its threads. Then he skipped a button, going straight to the metal hooks fastening Jefferson's pants.

A tremor shook Finny's hand, at odds with Finny's deft fingers. Jefferson wondered if maybe he should slow this down, ask about it. He was about to try to catch Finny's hand, when Finny leaned in closer and he felt the hot line of Finny's erection hardening against his body. His gaze dropped to the single finger Finny had hooked on his waistband and his pulse thudded.

"I thought all week about this," Finny told him, sounding almost annoyed by it. His chest kept rising with his rapid breaths, pushing against Jefferson's sternum. He slid that finger sideways, knocking one of the fastenings out, then moved on to undo the second hook. The flies of Jefferson's pants popped apart, spreading into a vee. Finny took hold of the zipper pull, starting to tug at it. At once, his gaze had the intensity of a flame building on a match. The knuckle of one finger brushed against Jefferson's cock on its journey down and Jefferson felt himself start to swell.

"Can I suck you, Jefferson?" Finny asked, voice gone rough.

Jefferson swallowed hard, feeling a tingle building in his groin as he said, "Yes."

Finny slid his hand fully into Jefferson's pants, pushing them an inch down Jefferson's hips in the process. In a smooth motion, Finny went to his knees. There, he pulled Jefferson's pants the rest of the way to the floor. They fell in a rumpled heap at Jefferson's ankles. Finny's head dipped and he mouthed at the front patch of Jefferson's underwear. At the press of Finny's mouth and fingers, Jefferson went so rigidly hard he thought he might burst a blood vessel. Finny left a wet trail from tip to hilt along the cotton. Simultaneously, he raised his hand, gently massaging Jefferson's balls with his knuckles.

Jefferson's head fell back with such force that it *thunked* against the door. He barely noticed the sting. He started to laugh, a quiet, pleased sound. Every touch made him giddy with arousal. He lifted a hand, tangling his fingers in Finny's hair.

"This feels so good," Jefferson told him, sounding winded; the way he did after several reps of a new weight at the gym. He grinned at the words, unable to help it.

"I've barely started," Finny said, tipping his head back to smile at Jefferson. The force of that smile was brilliant.

"I *know.*"

With a new determination, Finny peeled back Jefferson's boxer briefs to free his cock, shoving them down too. Jefferson became essentially trapped there, legs bound, one of Finny's hands still tight on his waist. That didn't bother him at all, especially not once Finny took him into his mouth.

The mood shifted. Jefferson went quiet, transfixed by the sight of his glistening cock sliding through Finny's parted lips. Each bob of Finny's head brought wet, tight pressure—pressure that Finny ruthlessly maintained. His mouth clamped around Jefferson, a heat that Jefferson fought the urge to press farther into. He felt a little like a teenager getting his very first blow job, amazed by every swipe of Finny's tongue. Finny was single-minded in his efforts, breathing solely through his nose, prolonging the torment. Saliva built in his mouth, making the slide of Jefferson's cock that much smoother. A drop of it formed at the corner of Finny's lips and Jefferson wiped it away, brushing his own cock by accident in the process. He sucked in a sharp breath.

Jefferson was so focused on not thrusting forward, it took him several seconds to realize Finny was encouraging him to do just that, opening his throat. Unable to speak, Finny tugged at Jefferson's hip, coaxing him to move with a hum. Cautiously, Jefferson let his hips shift. The head of his cock slid into a new heat, a tight, constrictive space that he realized had passed the initial resistance at the back of Finny's throat.

Jefferson made a loud, guttural sound that he would have been embarrassed by under any other circumstances. He could tell the sound pleased Finny, though, which made him want to do it a hundred times over. Finny hummed again, satisfied, then pointedly swallowed, increasing the tightness. Pressure built to an almost unbearable degree.

"I'm going to—" Jefferson warned, breathing hard.

Finny eased off only slightly. That last move undid Jefferson—the drag of the tip of his cock as it popped free of Finny's throat. The world went briefly white as he started to spurt. He came in waves, panting with it, and Finny swallowed every single drop.

When he finally finished coming, Jefferson slid his softening erection from Finny's mouth with a long groan. His knees were giving out on him, so he let his legs slide, dropping to the floor beside Finny. The aftermath of his orgasm left him weightless, tingling all the way down to his toes.

"God, Finny," Jefferson said, stupefied by how good he felt. He started laughing again, soft but a little wild, completely unable to stop. Finny caught his gaze and started laughing too, such a happy sound.

"So, you liked that?" Finny checked.

In response, Jefferson kissed him again, tasting the salt of himself on Finny's tongue. He barely recognized himself, he felt so consumed with the desire to share with

Finny the same pleasure he'd been feeling. Their tongues met sloppily. As they kissed, Jefferson's hands moved in clumsy, near-frantic motion. He pushed Finny's tux jacket off his shoulders, undid the suspenders, rucked up his shirt, pulling it from his pants, and undid every single one of the buttons. Finny's shirt came completely off, except at both of his wrists, where the fabric caught, the cufflinks attached. Finny's chest began to rise noticeably. His blush showed on his throat.

"I want to kiss you all over," Jefferson said, voice low.

Finny shuddered, lashes fluttering as he said, "You can."

Jefferson tipped him backwards onto the floor. Finny's own weight held his shirt against the wood, trapping his arms on either side of him. He couldn't reach for Jefferson without breaking one of the eyelets where the cufflinks were attached. Jefferson didn't feel the need to free him. He figured they were even. His own pants still confined him by the ankles.

Finny helpfully spread his legs, biting his lower lip when Jefferson knelt between them and raised his hands to Finny's waistband. Jefferson didn't make a show of it, the way Finny had. He hurried to undo Finny's pants, and then shoved everything, pants and boxers, several inches down Finny's corded thighs. The muscles in Finny's abdomen jumped in anticipation. Jefferson leaned in, breath hitching at the sight of Finny's cock, already leaking. Several filmy droplets fell onto Finny's smooth skin and Finny groaned, hips canting. Jefferson swiped his tongue across his lips, wetting them. Finny's enlarged pupils tracked every move.

"*Jefferson*," Finny begged. Forgetting, he tried to raise his arms and the fabric of his shirt pulled taut. "Wait."

Jefferson froze, feeling a pit forming in his stomach.

"Take off your shirt," Finny told him, gaze so intent it felt like a physical caress. "I want to see you."

"Yeah," Jefferson agreed. He shrugged out of his jacket, not caring if he wrinkled it, and threw it away to the side. Then he quickly tried to undo the row of buttons on his dress shirt. In his hurry, he missed two and had to return to them.

Finny stared at him the whole time he did so, making Jefferson feel sexy in a way he wasn't used to, but was rapidly coming to like. They had to make quite a pair, both of them in various stages of undress, pants at their ankles, sprawled out on the floor just inside Finny's apartment.

Finny's arousal was palpable. He grew thick against Jefferson's tongue, hard as a rod, sliding in and out from Jefferson's lips. And he voiced his enthusiasm, making soft, pleading sounds that urged Jefferson on. Jefferson had a good angle to use his weight to keep Finny's hips from snapping up, which he needed since he unfortunately didn't have Finny's talent for deep throating.

Jefferson grasped the base of Finny's shaft, adding pressure where his mouth couldn't reach. As he sped up his grip, he started to feel the little spasms under his fingers that told him how much Finny enjoyed this. He pulled away for a second, taking in a gulping breath of air in preparation to push Finny across the finish line. In that same moment, Finny gasped his name and started to erupt. Hot come splashed Jefferson, catching the underside of his jaw, smearing his chest, and even landing on his abs.

After one look at Jefferson, Finny started laughing again, sounding delirious. Jefferson felt the same: elated after the release of almost ten years of pent-up desire. Finny rested his head on the floor and threw an arm over his eyes while his chest heaved.

"That's not very nice," Jefferson said. He sprawled out next to Finny, boneless and grinning, tipped onto one side, the hardwood cold on his bare ribs.

"You're going to have to shower before we go," Finny said.

"In a minute."

Their breaths gradually evened out as they lay there. The hairs on Jefferson's chest became increasingly stiff as the streaks of come started to dry, but he didn't move. His eyes slid closed.

"I don't want to go outside," Finny said, his quiet voice breaking the brief spell of contentment.

"We don't have to go," Jefferson said drowsily. That sounded appealing—falling asleep here with Finny in his arms.

"No, I do," Finny said. "And I want to be there. But . . . I hate being scared to leave my apartment. It's worse when it's dark."

Jefferson opened his eyes. Finny was looking at the ceiling, jaw held so tight that a tic had formed in his cheek. Jefferson hesitated, then placed his palm possessively in the center of Finny's bare stomach, feeling something painfully tender open behind his ribs as he did so.

"Do you have any idea who he is?" Finny asked.

"More after this weekend than we did before," Jefferson said, stealing the line that had worked to assure him. "Every day we get closer."

"I'm glad you're coming with me tonight," Finny said.

So was Jefferson.

Getting up and moving seemed to help Finny relax. Finny let his cats out of the bathroom so Jefferson could take a quick shower. While Jefferson cleaned himself up, Finny gave their clothes a quick iron. Then, Jefferson drove them to the Park Plaza Hotel.

The building, which dated back to the early 1900s, sat fourteen stories high and was shaped like a lopsided triangle, as if it had been designed to fill every inch of the gap between the surrounding streets. The sleek black awning that proclaimed the hotel's name provided the only bit of color in the understated facade at the entrance. This kind of place didn't need flashy signs to attract its guests.

"Tell me about this event." Jefferson said, carefully navigating the narrow streets approaching the parking garage.

"It's the Boston Neighborhoods Association's biggest fundraiser of the year," Finny explained. "Usually only my director and her husband get free tickets to come but the BNA gave us a couple extra this year, so I got the invite. There'll be dinner, drinks, speeches, that sort of thing."

"What kind of work do they do?" Jefferson asked.

"A lot of things," Finny said. He scrunched his nose as he thought, making one of Jefferson's favorite expressions. "They work in neighborhoods all over Boston, giving grants for things like tree plantings, sidewalk improvements, new lights, and signage. A lot of their work involves parks, which is how I know them. They also help spread the word to Boston residents about things happening near them. If we know we're permitting an event that might close a road or renovating a playground, we'll ask them to share the news."

"Interesting," Jefferson said. "Will you know many people there?"

Finny made a face. "A few. Not many I want to see. Usually they're calling to yell at us for something."

Jefferson had a sudden memory of standing in the DPM offices, seconds before his world had been upended and Finny had come back into his life, listening to the phone ring over and over again. Coming from a large bureaucracy himself, he thought he could understand what the problem might be.

"Do they wish you were doing more?"

Finny gave a quick, slightly strained laugh, then asked, "How'd you know?"

"Federal agency," Jefferson reminded him, pointing at his own chest.

"Right," Finny said.

"Too many people making decisions and not enough money to get everything done."

"Exactly," Finny said, with another chuckle. "The BNA has the money to fund the work we both would like to see completed, which is a good thing . . . most of the time. If we had the staff to knock out every project they wanted, we'd be in great shape."

They parked and made their way into the hotel. No party Jefferson had ever attended had been anywhere near as dazzling as the setup in the Park Plaza grand ballroom. The room would've been impressive even if it wasn't decorated for the gala. Giant crystal chandeliers spanned the ceiling, each holding fifty or more twinkling lights. At one end of the room, the distance of a football field away, a stage spanned the full length of the wall, draped by a velvet curtain. Viewing boxes lined the long opposing side walls, each with a private balcony backlit in a light purple. The carpet below their feet swirled with intricate patterns.

Everything brought in for the evening made the setting more opulent. Dozens of round tables spread across the floor. At the center of each sat a trio of flower arrangements in tall, glass vases of staggered heights. Jefferson didn't need to know anything about flowers to appreciate that the ones he saw were expensive. The sole kind he could name were the orchids bursting from long stalks. Hundreds of people packed the room, every single one of them dressed to the nines, the men in well-tailored tuxes and the women in floor-length gowns. When the overhead light hit just right, it glittered off the diamonds draped on one woman's neck.

"Wow," Jefferson said, stopping just inside the doorway, momentarily stunned by the sight.

"Champagne, sir?" a well-dressed server offered, appearing next to him. The woman's footsteps were so soundless, Jefferson hadn't noticed her approaching.

"Yes, thanks," Jefferson answered, wanting to have something in his hand to better blend in. The server passed him one of the bubbling flutes with a white-gloved hand.

Finny accepted one as well.

"What the fuck?" Jefferson asked under his breath while he surveyed the room. He absently raised the glass and took a sip. "Damn, that's good."

Finny laughed, low and fond. "I can't take you anywhere."

They spent a lot of time people watching as they did a lap around the ballroom. Jefferson kept his eyes peeled for Phyllis Dreegan. In the meantime, he recognized a couple of Red Sox players and Finny noticed the mayor. Whenever they ran into someone in Finny's network, Jefferson smiled and shook hands, steering the conversation away from what he did for a living, or giving a generic answer, like, "I work in law enforcement."

The table of auction items captured their attention for a while. It included everything from a round of golf with a famous actor from the Boston area to a one-week stay in an apartment directly overlooking the Duomo in Florence. The recommended starting bids began at $1,500 but a few items already listed at over $5,000. Neither of them could afford anything being offered, but they enjoyed comparing what they'd most like to win.

Jefferson tried to stay alert but a couple of times he felt himself slip up and get distracted by the feel of Finny's fingers pressed gently at his lower back. The emptier Finny's glass of champagne got, the more he absently touched Jefferson, using the hot pressure points of his fingertips to guide him between tables. In periodic flashes, Jefferson remembered earlier: Finny's mouth so perfectly satisfying. It felt like the flush on his cheeks must be broadcasting to the entire world what they'd done.

About an hour after the event was originally scheduled to start, a series of bells chimed through ceiling intercoms, cueing them to take their seats. They found their names and assigned table numbers painted in silver on a large mirror near the door where they'd entered the ballroom. Their table, table number fifteen, was toward the back of the room, away from the stage, so they didn't have to walk very far to locate it.

They appeared to be at the 'government' table. There were six other places set. Finny's boss and her husband claimed two. The seat next to Jefferson held a woman who worked for Boston's Transportation Department, and her daughter sat beside her. One pair of chairs remained empty long after they started eating.

Throughout dinner, a fleet of servers moved unobtrusively among chairs to deliver the three-course meal. First, came an artfully plated salad, with a small tower of Bibb lettuce leaves, mandarin orange slices, fresh fennel, and avocado. For dinner, their choice of a piece of beef tenderloin with shrimp, or a quarter-chicken in a maple glaze. Between courses, a heaping breadbasket featured a variety of warm rolls for them to select from. Finally, the dessert arrived, three layers of yellow cake with alternating vanilla buttercream and strawberry jam.

While they ate, and therefore were a captive audience, a presentation began, projected onto a screen lowered in front of the drapes lining the stage. An older man, introduced as a member of the Boston Neighborhoods Association's Board, stood at the podium and summarized the Association's work throughout the previous year. During his remarks, photos scrolled, showing playgrounds, flower beds, holiday wreaths on lampposts, and more. Although the man speaking had a crackling, monotone voice and he spoke slowly, looking frequently at the printout of notes in front of him, it gave a helpful overview of the group's work for Jefferson. He paid close attention to the various faces that appeared in those scrolling photos.

When the man finished his speech, Phyllis Dreegan stepped up to the podium. She looked almost unrecognizable as the woman Jefferson first met in the park except for her bobbed hair. Her dress started in a pale gray at the neck and gradually darkened to black where it met the floor. She wore a three-tier strand of pearls with matching earrings.

"Thank you, Monty," she said, pausing until the man reclaimed his seat. "I'm Phyllis Dreegan, Chair of the Boston Neighborhoods Association. Tonight, you've heard about the essential work we were able to do last year with your support. Now I want to look ahead and share how you can help make Boston a better place to live in the years to come. Under the leadership of the BNA's Grant-Making Committee—" Phyllis glanced up.

"Where are all of you? Please stand." She gestured with an outstretched hand and four people seated at the center table closest to the front of the room rose to their feet. She pointed out each one in turn. "Eileen, Tanya, Dick, and Reginald all volunteer for what is essentially a full-time job much of the year, evaluating the proposals we receive for funding. There are so many projects of need across Boston and our goal is to *double* our annual budget. Will you help us get there tonight?"

And so it went, on and on. Once he'd finished eating, Jefferson settled into full surveillance mode. What a strange world of money and power this was. This whole benefit seemed ultimately so self-serving. These people could raise money then put pressure on the city to do work in their own neighborhoods. If Jefferson and Caroline had theorized correctly, and the Smiley Face Killer was someone with ties to the Boston Neighborhoods Association, then what did

Mr. Smiley get out of his membership? Did it amuse him to bring death to the same streets he helped make so beautiful? Did belonging to this group give the man another way to feel like he had control over other people?

The speaking program came to an end and Phyllis encouraged guests to place their bids in the silent auction before it closed. A good number of people throughout the room rose to their feet, heading to the bathrooms or to other tables to say hello to friends.

"Excuse our tardiness," a familiar voice said.

Jefferson looked away from the front of the room. He was surprised to see Dylan Jacobs standing with a blonde woman who must be his wife behind the open chairs at their table. The wife absently put her hand on the director's arm, gesturing at another table where a woman waved to her. Jacobs nodded in acknowledgement, leaning over to kiss her cheek before she walked over to say hello.

Jefferson moved with purpose, coming around the table to greet him. "Dylan, good to see you here."

"Jefferson," Jacobs said, sounding genuinely pleased.

Jefferson held out his hand for a shake.

When Jacobs took it, Jefferson held on a fraction of a second longer than necessary, copying Jacobs's move from their earlier interview. He thought of his call with Valdés the morning after he rescued Finny: *The perp appeared to have badly cut his hand in a fall.* The Smiley Face Killer had been clothed from wrist to ankle when Jefferson saw him that night, only wearing what looked like thin nitrile gloves on his hands. The only place he could've cut himself badly enough to leave the amount of blood detected on the rocks would be his hand. And the blood streaks had been consistent with someone throwing out a hand as they fell, sliding down the steep embankment.

Jacobs's right hand felt perfectly smooth against his. What about the left?

"These things can be painful, huh?" Jacobs asked, as Jefferson let go.

"They aren't so bad with the right company," Jefferson said, adding a hint of suggestion.

"True," Jacobs said. His eyes were searing in their intensity. "And I'd been hoping we could meet up again."

An empty wine glass sat at what would be Jacobs's place setting and near the center of the table, Jefferson spied a bottle of red wine left by the servers for their table's enjoyment.

"Buy you a drink?" Jefferson asked Jacobs, already reaching for both.

That got him a chuckle.

"As long as you have one with me," Jacobs said, playing along.

"I can do that," Jefferson said. He tipped the glass on its side, watching it fill with the rich burgundy liquid.

When he passed the glass to Jacobs, Jefferson made a point to hold it to the left side of Jacobs's body so Jacobs would reach with that hand he'd been so casually keeping in his pocket. Jacobs took it easily, curving another unmarred hand around the stem. Not only was there not a cut on either palm, Jefferson realized, but Jacobs's hands lacked any roughness; nothing like the thick callouses he'd noticed on Finny's hands, which suggested that Jacobs had told the truth about not being a sailor.

"Thank you," Jacobs said, taking a sip. "So, what brings you here tonight, Jefferson?"

Fuck. Jefferson felt stupid, infuriatingly so. He'd been entertaining the fantasy that Jacobs would slip up in conversation and reveal something that gave Jefferson the cause to go to Deputy Director Strait. No matter what Caroline and Strait said, Jacobs had always made the most sense to Jefferson as a suspect. Now, once again, he was back to square one. If it wasn't Jacobs, then who?

"Excuse me," Jefferson said, dropping the hint of flirtatiousness. He didn't reach for a second glass.

Confusion flickered across Jacobs's face, followed shortly after by disappointment. It was, annoyingly, close enough to how Jefferson felt that he experienced a pang of commiseration as he stepped past Jacobs.

Across the way, Finny gave him a searching look, a hint of something hurt in his eyes. Jefferson shook his head, hoping that conveyed *Don't worry about it.* If anything, Finny's confusion only intensified. In need of a few minutes to clear his head—and a break before he had to go sit across from Jacobs for the rest of the night—Jefferson went to the bar. He ordered a Stella Artois to bring back to Finny in a kind of apology.

As he stepped away from the bar, bottle in hand, he paused, took a deep breath, and allowed himself a single sip. He focused on tamping down his rising irritation. The Stella was light on his tongue, easy to drink. When he snuck a second sip, his eyes landed on Phyllis Dreegan at the front of the room. In her remarks, Phyllis had pointed to her table, containing a group of some of the Boston Neighborhoods Association's most influential members—the grant-making committee.

Jefferson decided he would go over and thank Phyllis; get a sense for the players of the group in the process. Should he ask Finny to go with him, since Finny could facilitate introductions with several of the BNA's members? No, Jefferson didn't think that was necessary. He didn't want to get Finny any more involved than he'd already been.

Instead of returning to his table, Jefferson moved down an open aisle, heading toward the stage. A small group of people waited to talk to Phyllis before him; other partygoers wanting to congratulate her on a successful evening. Jefferson stood nearby, studying Phyllis's companions out of the corner of his eye. Everyone seated at table one appeared to be in their sixties or early seventies. There was an even mix of men and women, paired in what seemed to be couples, except for the ninth guest, a lone man, the only other person at the table Jefferson knew—Reginald Shapiro, who'd had that strange, likely fabricated, story about an attempted abduction.

Phyllis excused herself from her current conversation and greeted the person in front of Jefferson—a woman with white hair pulled back into a low bun.

"This whole night has been exquisite," the woman told Phyllis. "Another feather in your cap, my dear."

Feather in your cap. An expression hunters used to cheer each other on when they killed their first game bird. It reminded Jefferson, suddenly, of sitting in Reginald's apartment for their interview, admiring the pheasant feathers he had displayed on his mantel. The Ring-necked pheasant was so commonly hunted in Massachusetts that the state actually stocked thousands of them a year. The bird's tail feathers had a distinct pattern with severe brown and black stripes at half-inch intervals. He'd seen that pattern somewhere else too—on a fallen feather in the Smiley Face Killer's hideout by the Charles River.

Every piece of the profile fit, Jefferson realized: the familiarity with Boston. The wealth. If Reginald spent most of his time volunteering on this board, then he likely had a schedule flexible enough to allow for everything from early afternoon kidnappings to middle of the night boat rides.

Admittedly, Jefferson and Caroline had written him off during their interview, when Reginald had seemed so frail. Looking back, he'd been wearing an oversized sweater and loose pants—clothes that masked his weight and made him look skinnier. Seeing him now in a well-cut tux, Jefferson gauged that Reginald was almost the exact same height and weight as Dylan Jacobs.

Reginald kept his hands below the table. Both his water glass and wine glass were still full to the brim. His plate of food sat mostly untouched. Jefferson gave up on waiting to talk to Phyllis and made his way around the table to the other side, pasting on a friendly smile. On the way, he deposited his beer bottle in an open space between plates.

"Reginald," he said as he approached.

Reginald twisted in his seat, craning his neck.

"Agent Haines," he greeted.

Jefferson pulled the exact same move he had with Jacobs and extended a hand.

"Nice to see you again," Jefferson told him.

Several of the other guests at Reginald's table watched them now, openly curious. Reginald couldn't shun him without looking rude. Jefferson could see Reginald's reluctance even as the man rose from his chair and raised an arm. A black, leather driving glove covered Reginald's right hand.

Jefferson felt a rush of something like triumph as he took that offered hand. Through the material, he couldn't feel if there was a gash. He squeezed, putting pressure on Reginald's palm and heard the man inhale sharply as pain flashed across his eyes.

"Reginald Shapiro," Jefferson said, keeping his voice quiet, not wanting to cause a scene. "I'm wondering if you might accompany me to answer a few questions."

Reginald didn't immediately move. He quietly considered Jefferson.

Jefferson quickly thought through his plan for next steps. He would escort Reginald to the front desk. There, he'd have assistance. The hotel manager would help keep Reginald under supervision until the Bureau could send a car to escort Reginald in for questioning.

Then, Reginald opened his mouth.

"Let go of me," Reginald said in a high, tremulous voice. Every head at his table snapped their way. "You're *hurting* me."

"This isn't a game," Jefferson told him. "Please come with me."

"Why won't you leave me alone?" Reginald asked, sounding every bit a frightened old man.

"Come with me, Mr. Shapiro," Jefferson repeated, giving a little pull at Reginald's arm.

The woman seated closest to Reginald rose to her feet. She wore an elegant blue-green dress embellished with thousands of sequins. Every time she moved, it shimmered in a continuous wave.

"What is going on here?" she demanded.

"This man is trying to make me leave with him!" Reginald said. He made a show of trying to pull out of Jefferson's grasp, causing Jefferson to have to yank Reginald's arm back down. A murmur of disapproval sounded behind him.

"Ow!" Reginald said pitifully.

"Let him go!" The woman exclaimed.

Another man at the table, wearing a tartan suit, stood and asked, "Who do you think you are?"

"My name is Agent Jefferson Haines," Jefferson said, clenching his jaw. He didn't want to take his gaze off Reginald for a single second, even if these people were demanding his attention. "I'm with the FBI."

He expected for that to be it—for the weight of the badge to lend this situation the gravity it needed. No one at the table reacted with the respect he was used to from most members of the public.

"This is neither the time nor the place for this sort of thing," said the man in the tartan suit.

Jefferson had forgotten that these people were the elites of Boston—that they considered themselves above everything else; including, apparently, the law. The woman in the green dress came closer and actually put a hand on Jefferson's arm, trying to get him to let go.

"Dick is right," the woman said. "This is a very important event for us. Whatever you think Reginald has done, this can wait."

"What's going on here?" a new voice—Finny—asked.

Jefferson turned to look at him. Dylan Jacobs appeared to have followed Finny and stood a few feet behind him.

"I've asked Mr. Shapiro to follow me so I can ask him a few questions," Jefferson told Finny, as evenly as he could manage.

Finny's expression changed as he went alert with understanding.

"Eileen," Finny said, looking to the woman in the green dress. "Can you let go of Agent Haines, please? Let him do his job."

"He's *ruining* our gala, Fred," she complained.

"This man is the Smiley Face Killer," Jefferson snapped.

Jacobs sucked in a startled breath and took a step closer to Finny.

The woman in the green dress only laughed incredulously. "Our Reggie? You've clearly got the wrong man."

Jefferson had had enough.

"You're coming with me *now*," he told Reginald, twisting the arm in his grasp to give himself better leverage.

"Go with him, Reginald," the man in the tartan suit said. "Let's not have a fuss. We'll have you free of this bully soon enough."

In that instant, while Jefferson's focus was torn between pinning Reginald's arm behind his back and keeping the woman clutching his forearm at bay, Reginald reached with his free hand and took hold of one of the flower vases at the center of the table. He brought it up in a violent swing toward the side of Jefferson's head.

Someone screamed. Someone else chided, "*Reginald.*"

Jefferson tried to duck. He managed to take away some of Reginald's angle, but the heavy glass container still hit him so hard against his temple that his teeth clacked. Spots of red, then black, danced across his vision. Frigid water splashed against his collar and dripped down the back of his neck.

While Jefferson fought off a wave of dizziness, Reginald pulled free of Jefferson's grasp and took off running.

The chaos that unfolded in the room around him didn't help the pounding of Jefferson's head. The tinkling of glass breaking. Chairs clattering as they were pushed back in a hurry. More people screaming. Jefferson blinked furiously, fighting off the blackness. He felt a hand at his back, steadying him.

"God, Jefferson, are you okay?" Finny asked.

His vision cleared enough that he could see the table in front of him. Jefferson jerked his head up, fighting another sickening slide of the room, in time to see a figure disappearing through a side door. He was supposed to be following that person.

"Stay here," Jefferson told Finny, and took off in pursuit.

Someone, incredibly, tried to stop him, stepping into his path. "Reginald clearly needs—"

Jefferson pushed the man aside, almost falling over in the process. His steps still felt like he was on a moving ship, the deck rocking, but he fought the sensation and made it across the room, shoving at the iron bar to open the door the man had disappeared behind. He stepped out of the pandemonium in the ballroom and into the shocking silence of an empty corridor.

CHAPTER 15

Jefferson blinked several times until the blurry room in front of him came into focus. He stood in a long—maybe a hundred yards—hallway, with a series of four or five pairs of doors on both sides. It was sleekly designed, with dark paneling and little nooks to sit in along the way. The blue and gold geometric carpet resembled a never-ending honeycomb. Bright lights shone from square fixtures arranged in clusters at even intervals along the walls. Looking at them made his head throb.

His head hurt so much he could barely think.

Where was he? Why was he here? He had the fleeting sense that he'd been searching for someone, but he couldn't remember who or why. His heart thundered in his ears.

He took two steps farther down the hallway, hoping he might get some kind of hint from his surroundings. His legs seemed to have forgotten how they were meant to work. His knees gave out on him when he tried to move and he had to throw a hand out and catch himself against the wall so he wouldn't collapse. The white lights in his vision slid sideways as everything started to spin.

Jefferson staggered over to a black leather lounge seat and collapsed onto it. He put his face in his hands, trying to block out the piercing glow of the lamp over his head. He really wanted to lie down and close his eyes.

Something inside him told him that he couldn't let himself. There was something he needed to do . . . why couldn't he remember what?

"Agent Haines?" someone asked. He felt a gentle hand on his shoulder.

The touch made him jump violently. When he dropped his hands, the walls lurched.

"Oh dear." The man speaking to him sounded concerned. "I think you've hit your head. You don't look so well."

Hit his head. There was something equally terrifying and comforting about that answer. At least it explained the way Jefferson felt, like his brain had shattered into a thousand pieces. Except the idea made him feel vulnerable, too; exposed.

"We need to get you to a doctor," the man said. "I think you should come with me."

Jefferson squinted up with vague recognition into the face of a white-haired man with sharp cheekbones. His name started with an R, maybe . . . . With effort, it came to him— Reginald. One of Jefferson's witnesses.

"I know you," Jefferson said. "I wanted to question you."

"Yes, you did," Reginald said. He took Jefferson by his right elbow to help him to his feet. "I have something to show you. Evidence that you need."

"I need to call in." Jefferson pulled his phone from his pocket then watched as it dropped to the floor, bouncing on an edge against the carpet before falling flat, about a foot away from him.

"Oops. Butterfingers. Here, let me." Reginald stooped to retrieve it. But instead of giving it back, he slid it into his own pocket. "Let's get you some help first."

Jefferson felt relieved to have someone else here who could tell him what to do. Reginald kept him steady as Jefferson picked his way down a flight of stairs. The ground level was much busier than the second floor had been. He saw two people with suitcases entering through a revolving door and another luggage set beside a set of armchairs. Right, he was at the hotel.

He'd been at a party here. Where had his date gone?

"I need to find Finny," Jefferson said, twisting to look behind him.

"He's meeting us at the hospital. This way," the man told him, leading him toward that same exit.

Jefferson followed him out onto a sidewalk. When he stopped to wait for the valet, Reginald tugged his arm, guiding him around the side of the hotel.

"Wait, you said you have evidence to show me," Jefferson protested.

"We'll take my car. I'm parked on the street." Reginald pointed. "See, it's just right there. The black one."

Reginald guided Jefferson into the backseat where he had the space to lay sideways with his legs folded onto a seat. The leather was cool against his cheek, the interior dark and quiet. As they pulled away from the curb, Jefferson closed his eyes, trying to stifle the pounding at his temple. A sensation like a swirling drain pulled him steadily downward, even deeper into the darkness.

He woke with a start in a moving car. No music played, which was a relief because his head hurt like the devil. The vehicle drove maybe thirty to forty miles an hour and occasionally came to a stop, as if hitting traffic lights.

Something was wrong. Jefferson didn't know why he was here. He couldn't remember who owned this car was or why he was in it. When he tried to crane his head, to look out the windows and get a sense of his location, the glow of the city outside stabbed through his eyes. He groaned.

"Agent Haines, good, you're awake," said a voice from the front seat—the driver.

"What's happening?" Jefferson asked.

"You've hit your head," the driver explained.

In the dim light of the interior, Jefferson could barely see the man's face. A wave of fear hit him. Why didn't he recognize his surroundings?

"You look so confused." The man laughed softly. He sounded older. Kind. "Don't fret, you have a nasty headache, that's all."

A headache. This felt like the worst hangover of Jefferson's entire life. And like he was still drunk, too. The numbers on the car dashboard swam when he tried to read them.

"Where are we going?" Jefferson asked. He spoke slowly, realizing he slurred the words.

The man laughed again, not unkindly.

"Don't you remember? You asked me to drive you to the hospital."

Jefferson didn't immediately respond, so the man continued, "We'll get you taken care of. You'll have some peace and quiet soon enough."

That sounded nice. Jefferson couldn't understand why the thought made it so hard to breathe. His skin had grown so clammy that he could feel his shirt sticking to his back. He closed his eyes, trying to calm down.

He woke to the sound of a car radio. No, not a radio. A man talking. Jefferson sat in the backseat of a car and a man was speaking to him.

"I've lived in that house for thirty years," the man said. He had a nice voice; a friendly, informative voice. It reminded Jefferson of his high school geometry teacher. Mr. Johnson had told Jefferson he considered him one of his best students.

"I bought it with my wife a few years after we got married," the man continued. "She loved planting the front beds. We would go on walks every evening along the Charles River and on the way back she'd always stop and look at what was in bloom. We did that every day one summer. Until she got sick. Leukemia. After that we didn't go on very many walks anymore."

"My dad died of leukemia," Jefferson said. His throat clogged with commiseration. He'd lived through the experience of watching someone you loved waste away day after day. "I'm sorry."

The man kept talking without acknowledging Jefferson.

"She needed rest. A chance for the medicine to do its job. But did *they* care? Of course they didn't. Night after night, it was parties with them, long into the morning. Our beautiful gardens ruined, filled with trash."

Jefferson didn't know who 'they' were. He couldn't put a name to this man, even though Jefferson had the sense that he'd met him before. Why was Jefferson with him?

His inability to remember why he rode in this car was making him feel increasingly alarmed. He needed to find his phone. He patted his pockets, searching, but they were empty except for a ring of keys. The metal grew warm against his fingers as he held them in his hand.

Jefferson started, realizing he'd been staring blankly at the seat in front of him. Just a minute ago, he'd been looking for something and now he had no idea what.

"I think I might have a concussion," Jefferson realized. The driver didn't seem to hear him.

"One day I went over to talk to them," the man continued, his tone turning to acid. "I explained about my wife. I asked them to stop, go elsewhere. They didn't care. The kids just laughed at me. Like I was being ridiculous, asking them to have some common decency. And the police told me they couldn't do anything about it—that it was 'university business.'"

At once, Jefferson became certain he should not be in this car. But it continued moving, faster now than it had been before, and . . . he pawed at the surface underneath the side window. Somehow there didn't seem to be a handle. Terror crushed his chest as he frantically ran his hand along the whole interior of the door. He couldn't find a way to exit.

He found a crinkled square of paper jammed in a crevice. In the floodlight of a passing building, Jefferson barely made out the top of it. He saw doubles of some of the numbers, and those hovering figures overlapped with each other, but when he closed one eye and concentrated hard, he recognized a time, plus the words *T.D. Garden*. A receipt. Realization struck—this had come from Henry O'Brien. He slid it into his pocket for safekeeping. Caroline needed to know about this. He patted his pockets looking for his phone.

Why didn't he have his cell on him? Christ, his head hurt.

"So, I made sure they'd stop," the man said. His voice changed, went harder. "I took that smiley face they'd graffitied on the wall of our brownstone and made sure they'd never want to see it again."

"*What?*" Jefferson asked. He was surprised to hear his voice waver.

"We're here," the man said.

The car came to a stop. The engine clicked off. A seat belt clicked as it unfastened and then the driver's side door swung open.

Jefferson eased himself to sitting upright as the driver opened the door beside him. Apparently Jefferson needed to get out of the car too. When Jefferson tried to step out, the world upended. His legs buckled and he stumbled backwards into the car frame.

"My goodness," the man said. "Let me help you."

He came around the open car door and lifted one of Jefferson's arms, slinging it over his left shoulder to give Jefferson something to lean on.

"Thank you," Jefferson told him. He realized he knew this man. Jefferson had interviewed him, and the man had told that story about watching the blue heron wading through the shadows at sunset. "Reginald."

"Follow me," Reginald told him.

Reginald ended up taking most of Jefferson's weight as they walked, considering how much trouble Jefferson had convincing his feet to move forward. His heels dragged on the ground with each step.

The two of them followed a dusty path along an iron green railing and then took a sloping ramp to a dock at water level. Under a cloudy sky, the water looked inky black. To his left, Jefferson could see a small grouping of buildings, all fifteen or so stories tall, new construction. Most of the interior lights were off for the day. Offices? To his right loomed an elevated concrete railway. He didn't hear any sounds in the night, no people moving around, no cars passing by, not even the late-night call of an animal.

Reginald released him near the edge of the dock, taking a step back. The gentle rocking of the waves exacerbated the sense Jefferson had that everything around him was undulating. He wondered if he should sit down.

"What are we doing here?" Jefferson asked.

"You asked me to show you something," Reginald explained, sounding patient, like he'd had to say that several times now. "For your investigation."

"Right," Jefferson said.

Why did it feel like a heavy layer of sand covered his head? Each time Jefferson tried to reach for his thoughts, they shifted away from him.

"I love the way the Charles River looks at night," Reginald said. "So dark, like her depths are endless. She's there to take all I give her. And then she gives them back to me, made pure."

The words confused Jefferson. Wasn't that a strange thing to say? Or had Jefferson misunderstood him? He had the feeling he was missing a lot of things right now.

He looked at Reginald more closely. His pulse had skyrocketed the closer they got to the water. It felt like his veins were trying to beat their way out of his skin. The hairs on his arms stood on edge. What were they doing here, so late at night, all alone?

"I don't—" Jefferson began.

Behind him, the sound of a car door slamming startled him so much that he flinched.

"Jefferson!" someone shouted.

Jefferson turned, feeling a strange tug in his gut. Finny ran toward them, wearing a tuxedo of all things. Jefferson should've been happy to see him—it always made him happy to see Finny—but for some reason, he only felt more panicked as he watched Finny skid to a stop at the top of the ramp. Finny froze there, hair a windswept mess, face white, staring down at Jefferson.

"Jefferson, get away from him!" The tension in Finny's body set Jefferson's nerves on edge. He felt torn between wanting to assure Finny and wanting Finny to help him— explain to him what was wrong with him. More than anything, Jefferson wanted Finny to take him somewhere else where he could lie down and no one would talk to him.

"I don't know what's going on," Jefferson admitted. "My head hurts."

"This man is abducting you!" Finny cried.

"This is a misunderstanding," Reginald said, glancing earnestly at Jefferson. "I have new information that is vital to the case."

Finny shook his head, eyes glinting in the glow of a streetlight.

"Jefferson, come here," he said in a clipped voice.

Jefferson automatically took a step forward, willing to do anything to make Finny's face look less pinched.

Reginald threw out an arm as if to stop him.

"Now, now. You're hurt," Reginald said. "You stay here. I'll go and talk to him—explain what we're doing."

Nothing about this bizarre, confusing night made any sense, but Jefferson knew with a bone-deep certainty that he didn't want this man anywhere near Finny.

"No," Jefferson said, grabbing Reginald by the wrist. The abrupt motion caused a wave of dizziness that almost knocked him to his knees.

Reginald glanced at him. Something savage flashed across his face. Then, so quickly that Jefferson wondered if he'd imagined it, the congenial expression on the man's face returned.

"We'll only be a minute," Reginald told him, clearly aiming to soothe. He tried to gently shake off Jefferson's grip and Jefferson only clamped down harder.

"Don't go near him," Jefferson said, digging his fingers in.

That single goal helped him stay upright and mostly clearheaded—he needed to keep Reginald away from Finny.

"The police are almost here, Reginald," Finny said. "Don't you see their lights?"

There were blue lights, Jefferson realized, blinking in and out as they passed behind the massive columns of the elevated railway. At first, he'd thought they were spots in the corner of his vision.

"Whatever you're trying to do here, it's over," Finny insisted.

Reginald's eyes tracked the steady progress of the police cars, only a few minutes away, judging by distance. He looked at Finny, then at Jefferson.

"You're right," he said, in a tone of quiet acceptance.

Before Jefferson could take a step closer to Finny, Reginald turned and ducked, slamming his shoulder into Jefferson's gut. Instinctively, Jefferson brought his elbow down hard on the older man's back. He should have been focused on bracing his feet instead. Caught off balance, he rocked onto the backs of his heels. Momentum carried him the rest of the way until he felt himself tipping over the edge of the dock, then falling. The drop to the water only spanned about a foot, but it may as well have been a story of a building for how slowly it passed. Jefferson's back hit first, immediately followed by his head. He heard himself cry out at the shock of the impact. The water felt startlingly cold, seeping quickly into his clothes. After a sickening moment of floating, waiting, Reginald's body landed on top of him. The weight pushed him farther down, carrying his head under.

When Jefferson opened his mouth, he sucked in water, choking. He opened his eyes in surprise to pitch blackness.

He was going to drown.

At the thought, he panicked, thrashing his arms and legs, trying to cut through the water to reach the surface. Reginald loomed in his way, blocking his path. Jefferson bent his knees and kicked out, missing once before he managed to land a blow on Reginald's hip. The force of the impact bought him a precious foot of separation. Jefferson kicked again, catching Reginald on the shoulder. That propelled him even farther into the water's depths.

Without the light of the sun it was almost impossible to figure out which way to go to reach air. Jefferson whirled around, disoriented, feeling water sluicing over his skin. After a few seconds, he realized his body was trying to go one way, buoyed, so Jefferson went with that, kicking again to move. He broke the surface, sucking in a huge, gasping breath. Through the water streaming down his face, he made out the twin triangles of the Zakim Bridge—the graceful sweep of white cables on either side of concrete towers, glowing brightly against the dark, cloudy sky. Then, he slipped under again.

His limbs grew heavy, tired. His lungs burned from lack of air. Worst of all his head pounded even fiercer than it had been before.

The next time he came up, someone grabbed him, sliding an arm around his chest from behind. Jefferson threw back an elbow, catching his captor in the ribs. He heard a *whoosh* of air at the impact, right in his ear, but the firm grip didn't loosen.

"It's Finny," Finny said, sounding winded. "Hey, *hey*, it's me, Jefferson."

At the sound of his voice, Jefferson relaxed, going limp. The warmth of Finny's body along his back became welcome rather than threatening. They started to drop, and he had to will his legs to move again so he wouldn't drag them both under.

"Can you swim?" Finny asked.

"I don't know," Jefferson admitted, voice tight with pain. He spit out water.

"We'll go together," Finny said. "It's not too far."

Finny turned them mostly onto their backs. The swim challenged them both. Although the water helped them float, Jefferson had seventy pounds on Finny. Now that the adrenaline had worn off, he rapidly lost energy, limbs like cement blocks. He'd gone stiff with tension, expecting a hand from below to grab them at any moment. By the time they slowed neared the edge of the dock, Jefferson felt miserable and nauseous, his head in agony.

With the loss of forward momentum, they both went under, dropping six inches in an instant. Jefferson swallowed another mouthful of water. Finny had to kick hard to carry them back to the surface.

"Here!" a voice called.

"Tread for me just a little longer," Finny told Jefferson. "I know you can do it."

"Why are we in the water?" Jefferson asked, suddenly scared enough to stroke his arms and legs. "What's going on?"

Finny didn't answer. He let go of Jefferson only long enough to duck back underneath. There, he gripped Jefferson by the waist and pushed, raising him higher. Two sets of hands caught Jefferson by each arm and lifted him, hauling until only his knees were submerged. Then, someone else took him under his armpits, adding to the force pulling him. His thighs knocked against the edge of the dock. With one more heave, Jefferson cleared the rest of the dock. He landed with his palms flat on the wooden planks.

At the impact, Jefferson started coughing. His body convulsed as he coughed violently, expelling water from his lungs. Every time he tried to breathe, he choked, hacking up water. His throat was raw. His chest on fire. No matter how hard he tried to stop, he coughed and coughed and coughed, back heaving with it.

A hand landed on his spine, soothing him until the fit slowed. He realized who it belonged to when his vision better adjusted to the blinding lights surrounding him and he saw dark skin and caramel eyes intense with concern.

"Cee?" he finally managed, voice hoarse.

"Hey, Jay," Caroline said. "You worried us a little there."

A rush of water hit the boards behind him. A second later, Finny kneeled on his other side.

"You're okay," Finny said, although he sounded panicked. "Oh my god, you're okay."

Jefferson looked up at him, still wheezing for air. He could tell there were countless other people around them, crowding the dock, but he only had eyes for Finny. Water streamed down Finny's face, plastering his hair to his forehead.

Finny raised a hand to cup Jefferson's cheek. He looked at Jefferson like Jefferson was the best thing he'd ever seen, desperately grateful.

"Where's Reginald?" Caroline asked.

"Still in there," Finny said.

"Shit," Caroline said, starting to rise. "I've got to—can you?"

"I've got him," Finny said.

After a moment of arranging, Finny held him again, Jefferson's forehead resting against his shoulder. An object hit the water with a loud splash at the same time Finny's voice rose, calling for something. There, with the comforting line of Finny's arm across his shoulder, Jefferson could finally relax.

He woke after what felt like no time at all to the sensation of being moved. A firm grip on his shoulders tried to make him sit up.

Finny spoke in a clipped, worried tone. " . . . blow to the head. Trouble remembering things. Having a hard time staying awake."

"How long was he in the water?" a woman asked.

"Four, five minutes," Finny answered.

"Can you open your eyes for me, sir?" the woman asked, slightly louder.

When Jefferson didn't immediately respond, Finny coaxed, "Jefferson?"

Jefferson opened his eyes, wincing at the influx of light. A woman in a tan paramedic's uniform kneeled in front of him.

"Pupils are very dilated," she observed. She reached into the bag in front of her, pulling something out. "I'm going to briefly shine a light in your eye," she told Jefferson, raising what looked like a heavy pen.

A commotion on the other side of the dock interrupted her—shouting, accompanied by heavy footsteps as a group of agents crowded the edge. The backs of the onlookers blocked his view of the river.

"He's alive!" came a voice from the water. It sounded like Caroline.

More yelling sounded, followed by a noise like buckets of water were being dumped onto nearby planks.

"He needs an ambulance," the person in the water shouted.

Jefferson thought—hoped—that might be the end of his own tests and he'd be left alone to rest while someone else who needed the help more got attended to. But the woman treating him only looked away long enough to call for a colleague and then returned to what she'd been doing, using two fingers to hold his eyelids apart so she could shine a light in his eye. He swore, unsuccessfully trying to duck away.

That, and each subsequent test, only made Jefferson feel more tired. Finny took progressively more and more of his weight, holding Jefferson close while he struggled to answer a series of questions.

"I'm going to have him admitted, at least overnight," the woman eventually said. "He needs to be monitored to make sure . . ."

It didn't seem like she was talking to Jefferson, so he closed his eyes again, feeling his surroundings fade away.

CHAPTER 16

For a long time after, Jefferson drifted in and out of consciousness. Flashing lights and sirens intermittently tore him from sleep. Twice, he moved—got lifted up, then set down on something. After a while, all his pain disappeared into a strange kind of nothingness.

Eventually he awoke to calm, a pervading quiet interrupted only by a gentle whoosh of air from a nearby vent. He opened his eyes and immediately squinted against the sun streaming in through the window.

The room that gradually came into view soothed him, with pristine white walls and few decorations. He wore a lightweight blue gown and an additional blanket layered over a sheet kept him warm. Based on the few snatches he could remember of the evening before—fancy dresses; an empty hallway; the glow of a bridge; his head sliding under inky water—he figured he'd been admitted to a hospital. For some reason, the thought didn't alarm him. Maybe because the night had ended and he was clearly safe now. Or maybe some kind of drug made him more relaxed than usual? Jefferson did feel odd, a little floaty.

From his vantage point, staring straight ahead, he couldn't see anyone else in the room. He felt aware of a presence nearby, though. Slowly, he turned his head to the right. Each degree he moved took five times longer than it should have. The motion was sluggish, as if he traveled through heavy, wet sand.

The effort proved worth it when Caroline came into view, tucked into an uncomfortable-looking plastic chair. For some reason, she had on sweatpants and a T-shirt that were both several sizes too large for her. She sat typing on her phone, oblivious to the fact that he'd woken up. Her hair resisted the confines of the ponytail she'd pulled it into, the frizziest he'd ever seen it.

"What are you wearing?" Jefferson asked. The words were difficult to form. It felt like it had been years since he last spoke.

He didn't recognize his own voice, fractured and as grating as nails on a chalkboard, exactly like some of those anti-smoking ads they showed in health class in high school. Caroline jumped so badly at the sound that she dropped her phone into her lap.

"Jefferson, you're awake!" She unfolded from her chair and came to stand at the side of the bed, putting a hand on the railing. "How are you feeling?"

"Fuzzy," Jefferson croaked in that awful voice.

The corner of her mouth ticked up in what didn't entirely succeed in being a smile.

"They've got you on the good stuff," she said.

He studied her closely. She looked exhausted, with faint swelling under her eyes and the restless energy of someone functioning on too much caffeine and too little sleep.

"I only remember parts of last night," he said. "Was I . . . I was hit in the head, right?"

"Yes, and then you had the *brilliant* idea to go with Reginald to the Charles River," she said, sounding furious. "You're lucky Finny was able to follow you. You asshole."

Jefferson frowned, puzzling through that. With concentration, another piece came back to him: the straight line of Finny's back as he looked down at the dock. *Jefferson, come here.*

"I know I had my doubts about him at first," she continued. "But you picked a good one. He called 911 and then kept them apprised of Reginald's movements the whole way to the river. All from a taxi."

"Did he . . . jump in the river?" Jefferson asked.

"Yes. He helped drag you out."

"Where is he?" Jefferson asked, feeling a brief spike of alarm. "Is he okay?"

"He's fine," she said. "I'm sure you'll see him soon. He had to run back to his apartment an hour ago after spending the night here."

"Good." Jefferson relaxed. "So why do you look like you took a dunk?"

"Because I'm the one who pulled out Reginald." She didn't say it as a brag but as a statement of fact.

With more context, the bizarre getup started to make sense. She would've been soaking wet when she arrived at the hospital. Someone must have taken pity on her and given her some spare clothes. They had to be at MGH, right? It was easily the closest hospital to the area where Reginald had taken him. Did she still date that nurse?

"Was he injured?" Jefferson asked. He vaguely remembered forcefully kicking Reginald underwater.

"He's a little more energetic than you right now, but he was also held overnight," Caroline told him. "He's under guard."

"He kept talking to me last night. I couldn't completely follow it. Something about his wife? His neighbors?"

"We're still piecing his story together," Caroline said. "From what he's told Gilbert and Valdés so far, his first kill was an accident. After that, he developed a taste for it."

Thinking back through the timeline, Jefferson hazarded a guess—

"The BU student?" The first body they knew of.

"Yes. His first victim lived in a fraternity house next door to Reginald. He liked to party. After Reginald called in a series of noise complaints to no effect, he went over there in person. Said he just wanted to scare the kid a little but got carried away."

"And then Reginald always targeted fraternity members after that?" Jefferson asked.

"Right. He would lure his victims to his car with a story about needing help lifting something heavy—which they inevitably bought, thanks to his age. Once they stood inside the door, he'd inject them with Rohypnol, then trap them inside."

"I see," Jefferson said. He felt a wave of the remembered panic he'd felt running his hand over the side of Reginald's car door and never finding a handle.

Something else came back to Jefferson in a flash, distracting him.

"Can you make sure . . . there's a feather in the warehouse by the river. Behind the chairs," he explained. "That needs to be taken in for evidence. I think it will match one in his apartment."

"Will do."

A somewhat strained silence followed.

"I'm sorry," Jefferson blurted out.

She looked surprised. "For what?"

"I know I wasn't the best partner on this case."

"Oh. You weren't always," Caroline said. She heaved a breath, looking him over. "But you can have a pass this time. I'm feeling particularly grateful to see your stupid face."

"Thank you," Jefferson said, heartfelt.

"You better not ever be this distracted during a case again," she warned.

"I think this one was special," Jefferson said.

"Fuck, I hope so," she said, with a wry laugh.

✳✳✳

For the initial few days after his head injury the FBI placed him on full medical leave while he fought dizzy spells and migraine headaches. At times, Jefferson hated being left on the outskirts after solving his first major case. At others, he felt grateful for the reprieve. Like when he received a signed helmet from Valdés congratulating him on busting the investigation—and his head—wide open. Whenever he returned to the office, Jefferson would face a shit-ton of teasing for that.

Faced with overwhelming evidence, including DNA from his blood at the scene of Finny's abduction and his fingerprints on a painted mask found inside his apartment, Reginald Shapiro confessed to fifteen murders in total. Once he realized he had little hope of avoiding arrest, Reginald seemed almost happy to have the chance to speak about the murders. He detailed to Caroline and the team how his taste for avenging his wife's death had only grown with each subsequent kill.

Reginald's lawyers threatened to seek the insanity defense when the case went to trial. Although Jefferson found Reginald perfectly lucid during their interactions, the ball had left his hands now. He'd completed his duty to the victims. His first day out of the hospital, he visited Henry's parents, then Gabby Laposata, to let them know that the murderer had been arrested. The courts would decide what would be done with Reginald.

Two weeks later, Jefferson had graduated to light duty, working a few hours a day from home, then trying to avoid the bright glow of electronics as much as possible afterward to rest his eyes. He lay on his sofa with an actual hardcover book in hand—something that before this recovery process he hadn't touched since the Academy. He hoped he'd be back in the office soon. Now that he felt mostly better, being confined to his apartment so much of the day drove him increasingly stir-crazy.

At the sound of a knock at the door, he set down the book. Before he could stand, he heard a key turning in the lock. Two people held a spare key to his apartment for the span of his convalescence. Finny looked in on him often before and after work, even on the days where he didn't spend the night. And Caroline stopped by regularly to update Jefferson on their case against Reginald.

"It's me," Finny called, stepping inside. He wore his running gear. As he kicked off his shoes, he pulled a pair of headphone buds from his ears.

"Hey," Jefferson said, pushing himself upright until his back rested against the arm of the sofa. He slid his feet to the carpet.

"It's beautiful out," Finny told him, crossing the room. "You have a good run?"

"Mhmm," Finny said. He braced one hand on a sofa cushion and bent over to catch Jefferson's mouth.

It felt strange to be the one tilting his head back into a kiss. Not bad, but it offered a change of pace from usual, when Jefferson sometimes worried he would get a crick in his neck from leaning down. They kissed unhurried, open-mouthed and light, saying hello. Before the kiss could deepen, Jefferson pulled back.

"I made us dinner," he said, aiming for a casual tone.

"You did?" Finny asked, giving him a pleased smile.

Most nights so far, Finny had cooked for him. Otherwise they ordered takeout.

"Come see," Jefferson said, with a sudden flutter of nerves.

Carefully, he rose to his feet. No matter how much his cognitive functions had improved, sudden movements still weren't his friend. He led the way around his kitchen island to the corner that housed his dining table, so he heard Finny's startled intake of breath but couldn't see his expression.

He'd set two places—properly set with cloth napkins he'd had to order online and matching sets of silverware.

Although he hadn't been able to stomach putting out a vase of flowers, he'd laid a supermarket bouquet flat in the center. Between the plates three candles cheerfully glowed, lit in blatant violation of his lease. He'd even bought one of those fancy glass bottles of sparkling water they served in restaurants.

"What's this for?" Finny asked.

"Bear with me," Jefferson said, turning to face him. "I don't one-hundred-percent remember how this was supposed to go."

Back in college, when he'd originally planned this speech, he'd thought the way he felt for Finny was the most he'd ever feel for anyone. There'd been days when it seemed like Finny consumed his every waking thought; where he could barely sleep for wanting the man who shared his room. Yet that didn't remotely compare to how he felt today— having kissed Finny; having fallen asleep with Finny in his arms; having faced death with him, not once but twice.

"Finny Ashley. You're the best friend I've ever had. The best parts of every day are the times I get to see you. No matter what, you can always make me laugh. I've had a thing for you since—" Jefferson hesitated, then decided to commit, diverting from his original script. "I've been in love with you since we were eighteen. More and more every day. Will you be my boyfriend? Partner? Whatever you want to call it."

Finny's eyes looked especially bright in the glow of the overhead light. He took two steps closer, studying the table, then looked up at Jefferson through delicate golden lashes.

"This is the most romantic thing that has ever happened to me," he said, sounding awed.

Despite his nerves, Jefferson smiled. He asked, "Is that a yes?"

"*Yes*," Finny said.

Jefferson expected another kiss, but Finny threw his arms around him instead, burying his face in Jefferson's chest. Jefferson hugged him back hard, tightening his arms with enough force to briefly lift Finny off his feet. It took him a minute or so, distracted by how much he enjoyed the closeness, to realize that Finny was hiding his expression, nose cold and wet even through Jefferson's T-shirt. Under the palm he had splayed on Finny's back, Jefferson felt a distinct hitch of breath.

"What's wrong?" Jefferson asked, turning abruptly panicked.

"Sorry," Finny said, voice muffled. "I know I'm ruining the moment."

"You're not," Jefferson insisted.

"I keep thinking . . . we've lost so much time together. *Eight years.* And then you almost—" Finny broke off, seemingly unable to finish the thought.

Jefferson squeezed his arms, pressing a kiss to the soft hair at the line of Finny's temple. Then he pulled back enough that he could cup Finny's jaw, tilting it until their gazes met. Finny made a soft, startled sound. Those sepia eyes brimmed with unshed emotion. In the soft light of the room, he looked so gorgeous that it hurt to stare down at him.

"We have the rest of our lives," Jefferson told him.

ACKNOWLEDGEMENTS

Nothing But Good wouldn't be possible without the support of so many people, including:

Christine Whitlock, who made my first draft so much more polished.

Paige, who has spent endless hours sharing ideas and enthusiasm with me.

Mr. McKinley, who has supported me across all my writing deadlines.

And, Nicole Kimberling, who took a chance on me and then worked so closely with me to craft this into the novel it is today.

Thank you, sincerely.

ABOUT THE AUTHOR

Kess McKinley is a Southerner at heart living in New England. Her debut novel, *Nothing But Good* is inspired in part by a cult legend in Boston and several other northern US cities about a serial killer who leaves a smiley face drawing by his victims's bodies. She loves reading slow burn, romantic suspense, and sports romance. When she's not writing, she's probably hiking or enjoying a fine glass of wine.

Follow along with her adventures at kessmckinley.com.